RUINED WITH YOU

For all of JK's Stark World and other titles,
please visit www.jkenner.com

Praise for J. Kenner's Novels

"I have read many J. Kenner's books, but this one has to be in my top 5. It was fast paced, suspenseful and HOT." *Read.Review.Repeat Blog* (*on Shattered With You*)

"With enough emotion to rip out your heart and the right amount of sexiness and intrigue to ramp up the excitement, *Broken With You* has to be one of my favorite J. Kenner novels to date." *Harlequin Junkie Blog*

"It is not often when a book is so amazingly well-written that I find it hard to even begin to accurately describe it . . . I recommend this book to everyone who is interested in a passionate love story." *Romancebookworm's Reviews* (*on Release Me*)

"A sizzling, intoxicating, sexy read!!!! J. Kenner had me devouring *Wicked Dirty* ... With her sophisticated prose, Kenner created a love story that had the perfect blend of lust, passion, sexual tension, raw emotions and love." *Four Chicks Flipping Pages*

RUINED WITH YOU

J. KENNER

NEW YORK TIMES BESTSELLING AUTHOR

M&O

Ruined With You Copyright © 2019 by Julie Kenner

Excerpt from *Dirtiest Secret* © Copyright 2016 by Julie Kenner (used with permission from Penguin Random House/Bantam Books)

Cover design by Michele Catalano, Catalano Creative

Cover image by Annie Ray/Passion Pages

ISBN: 978-1-940673-91-2

Published by Martini & Olive Books

v-2019-9-23P

For Keeana -
thank you so much for your help and support ...
and for putting up with my crazy, partial emails!

PREFACE

I haven't gotten close to anyone for years. How can I, when every conversation is tinged with dread that someone will learn the truth? That my past will come back to haunt me, and that despite all the care I took to disappear, I'll be hauled out of the life I've built and thrust back into hell.

At first, I wore my fear like a cloak, wrapped tight around me for protection. Now it's an innate part of me, as necessary for my survival as blood and oxygen. It is constant. Familiar.

It is the core of the battlements I've constructed to keep myself hidden, and I never once believed that anyone could shatter my defenses.

Then he crashed into my world like a thunderbolt, his strong arms as soothing as his eyes are vexing. Because this is a man who sees things. But the more he breaks through the wall that surrounds me, the more I'm afraid he'll discover my secrets. And that the truth will destroy everything.

CHAPTER ONE

L iam Foster slipped on a pair of aviator glasses, shielding his eyes from the brutal Nevada sun as he stepped out of the private Stark Security jet, all the while trying to convince himself that he hadn't fucked up last week and put his client in danger.

He paused at the top of the stairs, then scanned the executive area of Las Vegas's McCarran International Airport before descending. Not that he anticipated enemy fire, but he'd spent too many years dodging bullets and bad guys to ever break the ingrained habit.

As he set foot on the tarmac, a rising wall of heat engulfed him, as if daring him to keep his suit coat on. It was late afternoon in the summer, and the place was hot as Hades. Liam had been to Vegas more times than he could count, and never under pleasant circumstances. Today wasn't any different, and he silently cursed himself as he tried to pinpoint the exact moment when he'd quit protecting Ellie Love and had instead shoved her into harm's way.

Even now, his mind echoed with the harsh words tossed at him by Xena Morgan, Love's personal assistant. He'd been at a celebration just a few hours ago, laughing and drinking with his friends over brunch, when his phone had rung. Her name had popped up, and he'd felt that familiar twisting in his gut. Longing tinged with dread. And he was such a goddamn chickenshit that he'd almost let it roll to voice mail. Almost broke his own code by dodging instead of confronting.

But he'd got his act together, and he'd hit the button to connect the call, expecting—well, he still wasn't sure what he'd expected. Not after their last hour on the patio of Ellie's house in the Hollywood Hills, her a little tipsy on wine, him a little drunk on her, and the entire city lit up below them.

He may not have known what to expect on that call, but it damn sure hadn't been the thick, controlled voice that had come across the line, telling him only that Ellie had been attacked during an early morning jog. Xena had spoken with the emotional control of a seasoned police officer, and refused to give him any other details. "*She's okay, and you can hear the whole damn story when you get here, because for some insane reason you're the only one she wants looking into this. Crazy, right? Because you're the one who said there was no legitimate threat. That she was safe."* Only a slight quiver betrayed her steady tone. *"Maybe I'm naive, but this sure as shit doesn't look like safe to me."*

"Xena..." The name had barely passed his lips when she handed the phone to her boss, and the rising pop star had said simply, "Haul your ass to Vegas, Foster. I need you on this. You're the only one I trust."

Trust.

He hadn't thought he could feel any worse after Xena's rant. But that one simple word had just about done him in.

With a sigh, he ran his hand over his shaved head. He didn't take failure lightly—he never had. Somehow, he was going to make this right. Somehow, he was going to deserve that trust.

A space gray Range Rover pulled into view beside the hanger, and Liam walked forward to meet it. The car slowed to a stop in front of him, and the driver, a poised twenty-something with a hint of a beard, started to get out. Liam held up a hand, then opened the back door himself. There were times when rank and position mattered, but this sure as hell wasn't one of them.

"The Starfire, Mr. Foster?" It was a good guess. A Stark International property, the Starfire Resort and Casino was well-equipped to provide support for any Stark Security operation taking place in the Las Vegas area.

"The Delphi, actually. And take me to the performers' entrance. I'm late for a meeting." At least as big as the Starfire, the competing Delphi Casino and Hotel also boasted the Delphi Auditorium, a venue that consistently booked the hottest acts in town.

"Right away, sir."

Liam leaned back, meeting the driver's eyes in the rearview mirror as he settled in. "What's your name?"

"Frederick."

"Summer job?"

Frederick nodded. "Yes, sir. I'm a driver at the Starfire, but I fill in at the front desk when I'm needed. I'll be a sophomore next year. UCLA."

"Did you happen to catch Ellie Love's concert last night?"

His face lit up. "Oh, yeah. It was fuc—I mean fantastic."

"No glitches? Nothing out of the ordinary?"

The kid's brow furrowed, but whether in thought or confusion, Liam wasn't sure. "Well, no. I mean, maybe something backstage, but we sure couldn't tell in the audience."

"Good to know." He'd interview everyone in Ellie's band and crew, plus the on-site employees of the Delphi Auditorium. But unless he missed his guess, the show had gone as smooth as silk, without the slightest hint of trouble. At least until this morning.

"Um—sir? Are the rumors true?"

"What rumors are those?" Liam repeated, knowing exactly what Frederick was talking about.

"My buddy—he's a bellman at the Delphi—and he told me that Ellie—well, Ms. Love—that she was attacked this morning."

"What makes you think I know anything about that?"

"Oh." He could see the kid swallow in the rearview mirror. "I guess—well, you work for Stark Security. And you're going to a meeting at the Delphi Auditorium where Ms. Love's performing tonight. So I just thought, well, you know."

"I know that you'd be an asset in my line of work," Liam said with a chuckle.

"Nah, I just read a lot of thrillers and mysteries. I'm heading for law school."

"A man with a plan. Even better."

His phone chimed with an incoming text, this one from Rye Callahan, Ellie's fiancé and manager, giving Liam the keypad code for the backstage door.

Rehearsal's running long. Feel free to watch or wait in El's dressing room. Will find you.

Liam shot back a thumbs-up, then used the rest

of the ride to scroll through his new emails. He smiled at the pictures his friend Dallas Sykes had sent of Jane, his pregnant and bedridden wife. Knowing Jane, Liam was sure she was going out of her mind, but that didn't alter the beatific look on her beautiful face. Considering everything the couple had been through, they deserved this happy ending—and new beginning.

Not for the first time, a wave of unwelcome envy hit him. Dallas and Jane were his closest friends in the world, and he didn't begrudge them one iota of happiness. He told himself he didn't want what they had, but that wasn't true. He did want it. And for a few shining months, he'd had it.

But he knew damn well he'd never have it again.

Fuck.

"Sir?"

He bit back a curse; he hadn't realized he'd spoken aloud. "Nothing," he told Frederick. "Just checking messages."

The rest of his inbox was work-related. Status updates from his team, reports he'd requested, briefings on potential clients and new matters. He shot back a half-dozen answers, including one to Ryan Hunter, the Operating Director of Stark Security and Liam's immediate supervisor, who'd requested status updates on several ongoing matters.

And then there was the message from Quince Radcliffe. Like Liam, Quince had worked for his government before signing up for Deliverance, a now-defunct vigilante group financed and run by Dallas for the purpose of finding, rescuing, and ensuring justice for kidnap victims from around the globe. Also like Liam, he'd joined the Stark Security Agency after Deliverance dissolved.

Both men had wanted to stay in the game, and they believed in the organization's mission statement. Formed after tragedy had struck the home of billionaire Damien Stark, the SSA existed to provide help where it was needed, no matter the size of the job. Moreover, because of the technical input from Stark divisions such as Stark Applied Technology, the organization was at least as well equipped as most government intelligence opera tions. Probably better.

Liam loved the work. Hell, he lived the work. And he respected the hell out of his colleagues and never withheld information about a case without a reason.

Last week, he'd had a reason.

At the request of Ellie Love, Liam had told no one at Stark Security except Ryan about the absurd outcome of the assignment. But Quince was former MI6 and the guy didn't miss a trick. *Ellie Love*, the message read. *Want to share with the class?*

Liam frowned. *Soon*, he wrote back. The rest of

the SSA team deserved to know about the bogus threat in LA last week—and about the fact that this morning's events suggested it wasn't bogus after all. Which meant that Liam had screwed up. He'd cleared the threat in LA and told the entire Ellie Love entourage that it was safe to head on to the next concert venue, and the next and the next.

The case had been open and shut—or so he'd believed. The pop star had been receiving threatening text messages and notes, causing upheaval among her crew. Vague statements about how Ms. Love would "pay," and that she needed to watch her back.

Scary, yes, but it hadn't taken long for Liam to learn that the threats had been a publicity stunt by her over-eager publicist, who'd been determined to get Love as much buzz during her tour as possible.

The publicist had confessed and resigned—fortunately before the threats were leaked on social media. After satisfying himself that the threats were a hoax, Liam had closed the case and promised the embarrassed Ms. Love that he'd file his final report only to those at the SSA who needed to know. As a result, the only people who knew about the fake threats were Ellie Love herself, her now-former publicist, her fiancé, her personal assistant, Liam, and Ryan Hunter.

Bottom line, the threats had been bullshit.

And yet Ms. Love had been attacked that very morning.

So what had he missed? What the fuck had he missed?

Or maybe it was a copycat? Someone jumping into the fray after the stage had been set?

Or even just a random mugging?

He didn't know, but he was going to figure it out. Because no matter what rationalizations and excuses got tossed around, the bottom line was that her assault this morning landed squarely in his domain. And he wasn't going to rest until he found her attacker—and proved to himself that he hadn't screwed up and inadvertently tossed Ellie Love right into her attacker's arms.

CHAPTER TWO

From his position in the wings, Liam watched as Ellie Love strutted across the stage in five-inch heels, her tiny, bronzed dynamo of a body bending and twisting to the hip-hop beat as she belted out the lyrics of the show's final song. Considering that morning's attack and the stress she'd been under since the threats started in LA, Liam had to give the rising pop icon her props. If there was anything on her mind other than preparing for tonight's show, he couldn't see it.

She was a professional, through and through. More than that, she was a star.

A narcissistic and obstinate star, but in Liam's experience, that tended to be part and parcel of the celebrity package. And the truth was, he liked her in spite of all those qualities. Or maybe because of them. The daughter of an Irish-born auto-mechanic and a third-generation Latina mother who put herself through nursing school, Ellie was a woman who worked hard, believed in her own talent, and knew what she wanted, which was why her latest album had finally shot her to the top of the charts. And why all eyes in the theater—crew, invited fans, and hotel personnel—were locked on her during the final moments of the rehearsal.

All eyes except his.

Despite admiring her talent and work ethic, Ellie wasn't the woman who kept drawing his focus. That dubious honor went to the woman directly across the stage from him. The tall, skinny white woman with the cornflower blue eyes. The sharp-tongued blonde who'd spent most of the previous week standing like a damn guard dog between him and Ellie.

As the star's personal assistant, being a wall between Ellie and the world was part of Xena's job description. Considering she was at her boss's side more than Rye, Liam knew she took her job pretty damn seriously. Seriously enough to question everything he did and every command he issued to his team and Love's staff.

On one level, she'd irritated the shit out of him. But she'd also gotten under his skin in ways he hadn't expected, and he'd been relieved to escape when the case finally wrapped. Because despite being a badass security professional who'd traveled all over the globe, spent years in military intelligence, and endured far too many heart-pounding seconds staring down the barrel of some nasty motherfucker's gun, he didn't need extra complications in his life. And though he'd never seen it coming, he learned quickly enough that Xena had the potential to be one hell of a complication, and not just because he was so inexplicably attracted to her, even though she wasn't his type at all.

Assuming that a man who rarely dated and avoided relationships could even say that he had a type. He'd started building that fence years ago, brick by solitary brick, until it was a fortress. And though he'd occasionally breach the wall when temptation or lust or whatever the hell you called it grabbed him by the balls, when he did, he went for women with curves, not Xena's straight lines and hard angles. Plus, she was blond, and blondes had never done a damn thing for him. He'd spent too many nights making inane conversation with overly bleached socialites at the endless stream of parties in the Hamptons that Dallas had dragged him to back when they were both still in their twenties and early thirties.

Hell, if he was going to have inappropriate fantasies about an off-limits woman, it should be Ellie. But no, he'd gone and fixated on a reedy blond girl with a sharp tongue and eyes that seemed to look right through him.

He told himself he didn't know why, but that wasn't entirely true. She was sharp and determined. She spoke little, but when she did it mattered. And her loyalty to Ellie shone like a beacon.

All admirable qualities, but there was more to Xena Morgan, he was sure of it. And it was that mystery that intrigued him. Something raw. Edgy. He didn't know exactly what was buried deep inside her, but he'd seen enough damaged people to know that her soul was at least as scarred as his.

But that didn't make them compatible. On the contrary, that made them combustible.

And that meant that Xena Morgan was a complication he simply didn't need. And the sooner he exorcised her from his thoughts, the better.

A burst of white light flooded the backstage area, and Liam realized with a start that rehearsal had ended. Ellie was leaning against a giant set piece, talking with one of the roadies, and there was no longer anyone standing in the wings opposite him.

Frowning, he started to step onto the stage, then hesitated, wondering if Rye would prefer he go straight to the dressing room. He turned to look for the manager, only to find Xena instead, her head slightly cocked, a knowing smirk playing at the corner of her wide, tempting mouth.

Too tempting, and he thanked his lucky stars and a deep well of self-restraint that he'd kept himself in check despite that final night at Ellie's after-party when they'd stood too close together as the alcohol flowed and the city twinkled below them.

Her hair had been loose, and her soft curls had fluttered in the midnight breeze. Today, those blond strands were pulled back into a severe pony-tail, a style that put her face on display.

It was a beautiful face, albeit in an unusual kind of way. The kind of face that probably photographed incredibly well, but in real life seemed a little too sharp, an effect that was soft-ened by a smattering of freckles across her nose and cheeks as well as by her hypnotic blue eyes.

She wore skinny jeans and a white tank top, which clearly revealed that she was about as flat as your average twelve-year-old boy. Even in the flirty black dress she'd worn at Ellie's party, she'd looked delicate. Ephemeral. As if he could break her with nothing more than a hug. He'd imagined her in his arms, their limbs entwined. His black skin in stark contrast to her pale white, so delicate she probably burned if she even thought about the sun. He wanted her under him, her fragile body crushed beneath him, her heart skittering in passion as she surrendered, trusting him not to hurt her despite his power to do exactly that.

She'd wanted him, too; he was certain of it. He'd seen it in her eyes. He'd heard it in her breath. But he'd known damn well that he'd never risk having her, not knowing where it might lead and what demons he might unleash. He'd learned that lesson the hard way, and he'd been so fucking grateful to drive away that night with only his memories of her to take with him into his bed, despite how much he craved the woman herself.

But now here he was all over again, staring temptation in the face and wondering if she knew.

In front of him, she shifted her weight, then laughed. "Cat got your tongue, Foster? Or do you just not know what to say after such a royal fuck-up?"

He sucked in a breath as a swath of anger cut through him. Apparently, she didn't know the ramblings of his mind. All she saw were his mistakes.

"Good to see you, too, Xena. Let's go see if we can get to the bottom of whatever the hell is going on."

CHAPTER THREE

They entered the dressing room to find Ellie Love seated on a padded stool, her pink-tipped hair pulled back from her face by a matching pink headband and cleansing cream smeared all over her face.

"The fans love the look," she said to their reflection in the mirror, referring to the dramatic makeup that had become her trademark, "but it's hell on my skin." She turned then, aiming her sparkling white smile at Liam. "Hey there, Foster. It's good to see you again."

"Is it?" He crossed to the table to take her outstretched hand, then leaned against the wall as she wiped the creamy residue off with a cloth.

"Hell, yes. Why wouldn't it be?"

Liam frowned, his gaze darting toward Xena,

who sat in the chair next to Ellie, her expression flat.

He cleared his throat. "Ellie, I—"

"It's Ella, remember? Ellie is for the stage. Ella is for my friends. And Ms. Love is for everybody else. You, sir, are now a friend. Isn't he?" she added, turning to face Xena.

"Keep your friends close, but your enemies closer?" Xena quipped, causing Ellie—*Ella*—to roll her eyes.

"My assistant aspires to be me. If not on the stage, then in her ability to be a bitch."

"Xena's worried about you," Liam told her, glancing sideways at Xena as the door opened and Ella's fiancé, Rye Callahan, stepped in. "She has reason to be."

"I'm worried, too," Rye said, moving to Ella and putting a hand on her shoulder.

"Exactly," Liam said, with a nod to Rye. "Gordon confessed, and I cleared the case. Next stop on the tour, you're attacked. That shouldn't sit well with anyone."

"It doesn't sit well." Ella pushed back from the dressing table and looked him straight in the eye. "But does that mean it was your fault?"

"It might. Maybe I didn't dig deep enough. Maybe there was a buried threat, and I missed it."

"Well, aren't you the dedicated martyr?"

"Ella..."

"He's right," Xena told her boss. "Gordon obviously had a bigger agenda than his asinine publicity stunt. That whole story about releasing the fake threats to the media? What if it was a blind to cover up a bigger agenda? And Mr. Foster missed it?"

Her words, so damn true, twisted inside Liam. "That's exactly what I've been trying to say," he told Ella, because he couldn't hold his head up if he didn't admit it. He took pride in his work. Hell, his work was his life, and the thought that he'd missed something so important—that his mistake left this woman open for attack—

Ella waved her hand as she stood up, clearly dismissing his runaway thoughts. "Maybe you did and maybe you didn't. I don't know. What I *do* know is that Mr. Foster did something for me in LA that very few men have managed."

"Whoa there," Rye said, feigning shock. "You're wearing my ring, baby. Do I need to be worried?"

She ran a fingertip from the V-neck of Rye's *Love Hurts* concert tee all the way down to the button fly of his jeans. "Never, *mo chroí.*" They shared a smile, and then she turned her attention back to Liam. "All kidding aside, I was a wreck in Los Angeles with those damn notes and texts. You're the one who got to the bottom with Gordon. You made me feel safe. And now I want to feel safe again."

Without thinking, he glanced toward Xena, who looked right back at him, her expression an unspoken challenge.

He shoved his hands in his pockets and nodded. "All right, then. The attack this morning was either random or it wasn't. It was either related to Gordon's bullshit scam last week, or it wasn't. So let's figure it out."

Ella's bright smile gave her makeup mirror a run for its money. "That's my guy. What do you need to know?"

"Let's start with everything," he said. "And we'll work our way up from there."

"All right then." She frowned at the small couch, currently covered in costumes. "Damn Christy," she muttered, and Liam recalled being introduced to her costume manager. "Xena, pull up some chairs. If she's got those outfits in a particular order, I'll never hear the end of it."

"We're doing this now?" Xena protested. "You have a show in under three hours, and you need to rest and then go over notes with the techs. Shouldn't we wait until morning? Or at least after the show?"

Ella's brow furrowed and her lips pursed as she settled herself on the stool again. She sighed deeply, then leaned forward as if thoughtfully considering a tricky problem. "Who works for who, again? I think one of us is confused."

Liam bit back a grin as Xena scowled, then silently turned toward a stack of folding chairs in the corner. He followed, then grabbed two.

"I can get my own," she said.

"No doubt. These are for Rye and me."

Her eyes narrowed, but she said nothing. Just continued back with the chair for herself, as Liam brought the other two, feeling unreasonably smug after his minor victory.

"Here's the situation as I see it," he said, not letting anyone else have the chance to take the lead. "You two call me and tell me I have to come, which suggests that you think I have some culpability. Neither of you gives me any details on the phone other than that Ella was out for a morning jog and was attacked. How am I doing so far?"

Ella twirled her hand. "Keep going."

"I come here ready to do whatever I can to learn who attacked you, and if necessary to make amends for my failure to properly assess the threat, despite having a full confession and a stack of corroborating evidence taller than I am. Then you announce that you don't think I'm culpable at all— something you didn't mention on the phone—while you," he added, turning from Ella to Xena, "suggest that you've never met anyone less competent."

He opened the flimsy plastic chair and sat, feeling a bit like a giant on a stool made of matchsticks as he turned to face Rye. "And to be honest, I haven't got a clue what you think."

"Well, actually—"

Liam held up his hand. "At this point, it doesn't matter." He stretched out his legs, hoping the chair wouldn't crumple and send him toppling backward. "Just tell me what happened. Not what you think, but what you know."

"Right," Ella said. "Well, I went out for a jog this morning, right after six. The hotel has a nice park area with a track, and I wanted to go while it was cool."

She paused long enough for Liam to nod, then continued. "My picture's all over this town right now—which is great because that's the point of this career—but I didn't want anyone to notice me looking all sweaty and gross. So I took one of the dancer's wigs from wardrobe—"

"Ella!" Xena's voice rose indignantly. "You didn't tell me that."

"It's not a big deal. Liam just wants the details."

"But it is a big deal."

"Why?" Ella asked, and though Liam expected the answer to fly off Xena's obviously irritated lips, instead, she just hung there, like a fly in amber with her lips parted and her brow slightly furrowed. It was only a moment—a brief, odd moment—but then her frown deepened. "Because all those wigs are styled and fitted. Christy's going to have a fit, and I'm going to be the one who gets lectured."

Ella waved the concern away. "Considering my job title, I think I can protect you. Besides, I took it from the swing closet. Just a blond wig that wasn't assigned to any dancer. Seriously, Christy won't notice or care."

Xena leaned back, her arms crossed over her chest. "If you say so."

Liam hesitated, studying Xena as he directed the next question to Ella. "You went out jogging wearing the wig and what? Shorts?"

"Right. One of my concert tees and black running shorts. And I put a ball cap over the wig—the thing didn't fit that well, so I figured the cap would keep it secure."

"A concert cap, or..."

"One of the *Love Hurts* caps. It's all I had, so I grabbed it, and then I headed out. The track is a mile, but it meanders through the park that's part of the Delphi property."

"I'm familiar with it. Where were you attacked?"

"Right past the pond. The trail goes behind some trees and there's a children's play area. It was too early for there to be any kids, and as I rounded the trees, two guys jumped me."

"What were they wearing?"

"Shorts and T-shirts. Plain black, I think. I

don't remember a logo. But one of the guys had a tattoo on his upper arm. I couldn't see all of it because of his shirt, but I think it was a snake."

"Had you seen them before?"

"No. I mean, I'm not sure. I used the fitness center entrance to get to the track. I guess they might have been using the equipment or hanging around the juice bar. There were a dozen or so folks in there."

"But you didn't notice anyone follow you outside? And there were no other joggers on the track?"

"I saw two women early on, but nobody else by the time I got to the play area. But to be honest, I had my music on and was in a groove by that time. So I can't say for sure."

Liam nodded, making a mental note to check the hotel's security tapes just in case someone fitting the description did follow Ella out the door. "Go on."

"They—they were behind me, but one of them grabbed my hair—or, rather, the wig. I heard one of them say, 'Guess you didn't see this coming,' and that's when I jerked around, and as I did, the whole wig came off, ball cap and all. Thank God I hadn't taped it on. That would have hurt like a mother."

Beside him, Xena let out a sharp "O*h!*" That was followed by, "I'm—I'm sorry. I just realized. I need to go talk to Tommy. Shit." She jumped to her feet and hurried toward the door. "It's nothing you need to worry about, but if I don't catch him before he's checked the board, it'll be—anyway, I'll meet you on stage. You're going over the new encore with the dancers once more, right?"

She was out the door before Ella even had a chance to answer.

Liam watched the door slam behind her, his thoughts spinning as he turned to Ella. "She okay?"

"Some nonsense with one of the microphones. Nothing that interrupted the show, but I'm sure she just wants to check that everything is good."

He nodded. The explanation made perfect sense, but it didn't sit right. He just couldn't put his finger on the reason why. Yet.

"We do need to hurry," Rye said. "A lot to do before a show."

"What happened after the wig came off?"

"I started to run, but I stumbled. I expected them to grab me, but they didn't. Instead, one of them cursed—I think he was from Jersey—and then they looked at each other. I still hadn't caught enough air to scream when they bolted." She shrugged. "I did, too, but in the opposite direction. Sprinted all the way back to the hotel."

"The wig?"

"I—" She frowned. "I don't know. I don't think they took it. Maybe it's still out there."

"You told hotel security?"

She shook her head. "I called you."

He ran his hand over his head. "We talked about this. You need a full-time security staff."

"Liam's right," Rye said. "Even if it's only one guy. Maybe this guy," he added, hooking his thumb toward Liam.

"Not my gig, but I can recommend good people."

"Not on the table, boys. I'm not hiring a body-guard to shadow me everyday, and the Delphi provides security during the shows. This was a fluke, right? They were thugs who were trying to mug a random woman and freaked when the wig came off."

"It's a solid theory," Liam agreed, "but I'm not assuming anything." He thought of the way Xena reacted when she heard about the wig. And he thought of how similar in color her hair was to the wig the dancers wore.

"Foster?" Ella pressed. "What are you thinking?"

He shook his head. "Just running through it all. Right now, I'm going to—"

"Hold up there, guy," Rye said. "Whatever you're doing now is fine, but Ella's got a show, and she needs to start preparing."

Born on a Nebraska farm, Rye had washed away any lingering small town innocence, replacing it with a hard-hitting business sense and a cool demeanor. With his total access to Ella, Rye had been at the top of Liam's suspect list last week. But the background check had come back clean, and when Gordon had confessed, Liam had mentally cleared the manager.

Now, though, he intended to take another look. It was probably a random attack—and if so, he could take off the damn hair shirt he'd been wearing since that morning's call—but he wasn't hanging Ella's life on *probably*.

Which meant that right now it was time for Ella to go to work, and for Liam to do the same. Starting with digging deeper into the backgrounds of both Rye Callahan and Xena Morgan.

CHAPTER FOUR

Holy crap, holy fuck, holy shit.
I pace the dark hallway in front of the empty sound booth, thankful that Tommy isn't here so that I have time to gather myself, and at the same time hoping he gets here soon so that it doesn't look like I completely fabricated an excuse to leave.

Which I did. Of course I did.

Because I couldn't stay in that room a minute longer without risking absolutely everything. I mean, I was already on edge from seeing Liam Foster, a man I hadn't expected to see again once the tour left for Vegas. A man who, for reasons I haven't been able to fathom, completely rattles me.

And then there was that wig.

My God, that fucking wig.

Why hadn't Ella mentioned that to me? I would never have agreed with her plan to get Foster back if I'd known. I would have said it was a job for hotel security. A random mugging on the property. An attack that surely had nothing to do with who she was.

Because it didn't. It had nothing to do with her at all. And everything to do with me.

Back it off, Xena. Take a deep breath and back it the fuck off.

I try to take my own advice, urging myself to calm down. Telling myself it's a coincidence. Just one of those screwed up, scary, paranoia-inducing coincidences.

After all, it's been six years. Six long, wonderful, horrible years. And even though I know they looked for me during that first year, they never even came close. And that was back when I'd been a complete wreck with no resources, no skills, no support network. Still, they couldn't find me. So why should things suddenly change now when I have a new name and a new look and whole new life to shield me?

Things wouldn't change. They *haven't* changed. There's no reason to think they've found me. No reason to think they're even still looking.

Except that's bullshit.

Of course they're still looking. I know damn well they'll never stop looking. Not men like that. Not ever.

My heart starts to pound, and my head starts to

swim. The world is doing that thing where it shifts toward red, and I feel a full-blown panic attack coming on. And right now is really *not* a good time.

I draw a deep breath and order myself to be calm. There's no reason to panic. It's not possible that they've found me. After all, I'm a behind the scenes kind of girl. I'm not a woman who stands out. They'd have to know where to look, and why the hell would they look for me in a pop star's entourage?

They wouldn't. I'm fine. I'm safe.

"Xena?"

I jump a goddamn mile, then turn to Tommy with a sharp cry of, "Jesus!"

"Hey, hey, sorry." He holds up his hands with a friendly smile. Tommy's been in the business since the dawn of time, and I know we're lucky to have him running sound for Ella. But my God, he made my heart stop.

"Didn't mean to scare you," he says, but the words are full of laughter. "Guess you were off in la-la land, huh?"

"Something like that," I admit.

He takes a step closer, and I watch his well-lined face shift into a frown. "What the hell, girl? You look like you ran a mile."

"Just a billion things to do before tonight's show." I flash one of my practiced bright smiles; I'm an expert at looking happy and content when I'm anything but. "I wanted to make sure the short in that backup mic got fixed."

He looks down his nose at me. "Good golly. I didn't even think about doing that."

I ignore the sarcasm. "I know you probably fixed it about thirty seconds after last night's show ended. But it's my job to not assume anything."

"Nice save. Now go tell Ms. Love we're ready for the sound check whenever she is."

I nod, wave, and scurry away, pulling out my mobile phone so I can text Ella and all the backup singers that Tommy's ready for them.

I'm almost to the end of what we call tech alley when I look up and see a man striding down the dim walkway. *Liam Foster.* The few shafts of light hit him only on the left, and with his gorgeous black skin only partially illuminated, broad shoulders, and tailored gray suit coat, he looks like a conqueror emerging from the shadows.

I swallow as panic once again flutters in my chest. But not because I'm afraid of what Liam might do to me. On the contrary, I'm afraid of what he *does* do to me. Because this is a man who has come close to breaking through my defenses. I let down my guard with him once—that stupid, foolish, almost-kiss at Ella's party—but that's not something I can let myself do again. Not now. Not later. Not ever.

And that makes Liam Foster a very, very

dangerous man.

I force a smile and lift my hand in a casual wave, ignoring the beads of sweat between my breasts. "Hey, Foster. You looking for Tommy? Or Grant?" I add the second name since we're right by the light booth and Grant is the show's lighting designer.

"You, actually."

"Gee. I'm flattered." I add an edge of sarcasm to my voice. "But maybe we can put a pin in it? I have a lot to do before tonight."

"You think I fucked up."

I cross my arms and tilt my head. "Thanks for the recap. Did you think I'd forgotten?"

"You think I fucked up," he repeats. "Or you did until Ella mentioned the wig."

I swallow, but say nothing.

"Come on, Xena. Why did that shake you up?"

"I really do have work." I try to push past him, but he holds out an arm, blocking my way. "Um, hello, Foster? What the fuck?"

"Please. Just ten minutes. Five." He drops his arm, and I know that if I keep walking he won't stop me.

I should keep walking. I'm stupid not to. But maybe if I say the right things he'll finally back off.

"Thank you," he says, his voice so gentle that for one foolish moment I wonder what it would be like to tell him all my secrets. That, however, is a

dangerous urge. Like those people who have to
fight a compulsion to jump from high places. I force
it down, then meet his eyes. "Fine. What was it you
wanted to know?" Like I don't remember what he
asked four seconds ago. Like his question isn't
completely freaking me out.

Can he tell?

I don't think so; I truly don't. I had years to
learn how to hide my feelings, my fears. And I got
damn good at it. Hell, I could win an Oscar if it
weren't for that whole being in the public eye thing.
Because that part really wouldn't work for me.

"The wig, Xena." He's the epitome of patience.
"When you learned that part, it freaked you out."

"Freaked me out?" Damn right it freaked me
out. "No, it didn't. I was just—hell, I'm not even
sure I can put it in words." I'm buying time as I spin
my lie. Finally, I take a deep breath, then nod.
"Okay, you know what? You're right. It did freak
me out. Because it's all so futile, you know?"

I watch his eyes move as he studies me, clearly
trying to suss me out.

"The fame thing, I mean. She's worked her ass
off for so long reaching for that prize, and it's
supposed to be great. I mean, everyone thinks so.
And everyone's rooting for her. But then it's like
running a gauntlet, because there's always some
nutcase. But that's part of the price. For fame I
mean. Right?"

He nods, but I can see he doesn't understand. Not too surprising; I'm making this up as I go.

"She tried to circumvent that. She took precautions. She wore a disguise. And she's *still* attacked. So maybe it really was random, like you said. But then that means that no one's safe, right? Or maybe they did know it was her—in which case what's the point of a disguise? You hit that magical celebrity point and you're just screwed? It's totally unfair. And no one can live their life in bubble wrap. So I guess—I guess the whole thing just made me feel terribly sad and worried for her all at the same time."

I lift my shoulders in a *so that's that* gesture, and Liam nods thoughtfully. I work hard to keep my facial expression bland. I think he bought the bullshit I've been selling. Considering I pulled it out of my ass, it sounded pretty good. But that doesn't mean it'll be good enough for the likes of Liam Foster.

"I do understand," he says, taking a single step closer to me. He's strong. I can feel it in the air, and part of me wants to beg him to hold me, just so I can soak up his strength. But I can't be that vulnerable. Not with him. Not with anybody.

"I can only imagine what a shock this morning was after the tension of last week, especially considering how close you and Ella are."

I nod. Even though he doesn't know the entire

truth, everything he just said is dead-on. Especially the part about Ella and me. She may be the most high maintenance star in the world, but as far as I'm concerned, that woman is a goddess, and last week, I told him why. Not the entire story, but most of it. And every word I said was true.

But I also left a lot of stuff unspoken.

"Thanks for that," I say.

He tips his head and smiles. A nice smile on a guy who could be scary as shit if he wanted to. I've been around men like that. More than I like to remember, actually, and every one of their slow, dangerous smiles haunts me. So much that I'd spent years seeing a counselor at one of the free clinics in Los Angeles. I'd used a fake name—well, another one—and I'd worn a wig and overly baggy clothes, because you can never be too sure. But I'd gone. And it had even helped. A little. Maybe.

Actually, it must have helped, because Liam's exactly the kind of man I used to flinch away from. Big. Powerful. Determined. And strong enough to throw me across a room if he wanted to. Or to bruise my arm simply by holding me in place.

The kind of man I normally avoid, even after all this time and all those sessions. But for some reason with Liam, I stepped closer and closer until last week when we were both ready to jump into the flames.

But I can't ever go there again.

"We—" I cut myself off with a shake of my head. "Never mind."

"What?"

"I was just—I was just thinking about Ella," I lie. "Somehow we have to convince her that she needs someone watching her back."

"Agreed," he says, and I'm about to sigh with relief when he adds, "But that's not what you were going to say."

I swallow. "Wasn't it?" I should stay quiet. I should tell him I'm late and just go. Instead, I ask, "What was I going to say?"

He doesn't hesitate, and he doesn't look away. "That it was a mistake." He looks straight at me with such intensity that I can't glance away either. "That we'd both drunk too much, and we both wanted it. But that we're both too professional to cross that line, and that neither of us has any intention of taking it any farther."

Don't we?

Except of course, we don't. Because intentions aren't desires. And while he may be wrong about being drunk, he's one hundred percent on-point about intentions.

I draw in a breath, my eyes still locked on his. "I don't even know what you're talking about."

"Yes," he says. "You do. You know exactly what I'm talking about, because you wanted it as much as I did."

I start to protest, but he continues before I can get out a sound.

"You wanted me to kiss you. Or maybe you wanted to kiss me. I don't think it matters. All that matters is that we both wanted it. Wanted each other. Wanted to get lost for just a moment in that private corner of the patio, with the stars above us and the lights below. To feel lips on lips and skin on skin. To let ourselves go, even if we never spoke of it again."

I'm breathing hard when he takes another step toward me, then lifts my chin with his fingertip. That's when I realize that I'd stopped looking at him and had shifted my focus to the floor. Now, I have no choice but to look at this man. His skin seems to absorb the dim light, making him glow from the inside even as his dark eyes invite me to spiral down with him to someplace warm and wild, and all I can think is that he's a dark angel come to torment me.

When he speaks, it's barely a whisper. "So tell me, Xena. Have I jogged your memory?"

"You've jogged something," I admit. "But we can't. We won't. It's not—it's not what I want." I silently curse, because after what he just admitted, he deserves the truth. "Okay, yeah, maybe I do want it. But I'm not going to have it."

"Do you think I don't understand that?"

"I don't know." My head feels like it's swimming, and I lower my voice, aware of the rising noise as crew and performers enter the venue for the various pre-performance checks. "I thought you understood. But then why are we talking about it? Why are you torturing us both?"

"Everyone has a code." He shrugs. "Part of mine is that I never look away from reality. And that means that I see you. I see this," he adds, gesturing between us. "I know that I want it. And I know that I'm walking away."

I draw in a breath, unsure what to say.

"Maybe I'm wrong," he says gently, "but I think that's your code, too."

"No," I say, thinking of the past that I've been running from. "Most of the time I'd rather do anything but look."

He leans forward, and I can see the question in his eyes. He's wondering what it is that I don't want to confront, and I want to kick myself for giving so much away. What the hell happened to my shields?

"I believe you," he says. "But here's why we're alike. Whatever it is that's behind you that you don't want to see? You turn to it, Xena. And you look anyway."

The words ricochet through me, full of truth and danger and fear. I swallow, waiting for the other shoe to drop. Afraid he's going to ask what monster is behind me. "I—I should go," I blurt.

"They're starting, and I need to be on stage with Ella, and—"

"I know. Go. I'll see you after the show."

"Oh, no. We're not going to—"

"At the after party," he says gently. "In Ella's suite."

"Oh. Right." I'm glad it's dark, because I'm sure I'm blushing. "I'll see you there. I'm looking forward to it," I add recklessly. And, surprisingly, I really am.

He stays where he is, and I walk past him, hurrying toward the stairs that lead down to the auditorium seats and the stage. I've gone about ten feet when I pause and turn back. He's in the same place, his back to me.

"Mr. Foster."

He turns. "Liam."

My lips twitch in what could be called a smile. "Thank you."

It's dark, but I think I see his brow furrow, the tiniest hint that I've confused him. "For what?"

"For not asking questions that I don't want to answer."

"Don't thank me for that. I have a whole list I want to ask you."

"I know," I say. "That's why I'm thanking you. Maybe you do force yourself to confront reality, but you also have restraint. And that's something I admire in a man."

CHAPTER FIVE

R *estraint.*
Liam frowned as the word rattled around in his head.

He had restraint now; she was right about that. Now, but not always. There was a time when he'd never held back. When he'd worked hard and played hard. A time when he'd let himself fall in love.

That, of course, had been his mistake.

A familiar pain cut through him as he thought about Dion's sweet smile. The way his heart had swelled when she whispered his name, and how his body had fired when she touched him. And he thought about Franklin, the fucker who had stolen that beautiful soul from him. From the whole goddamn world.

They were both gone now. Dion, murdered

because Liam had loved her. Franklin, gone because Liam had killed him.

Liam had shown no restraint on that moonless night. Not one goddamn iota of restraint, and it had felt incredible to avenge the death of the woman he loved.

But now...

Well, now he had restraint in spades, at least as far as relationships were concerned. He couldn't get involved. A fling, a night, an encounter to blow off steam— why not? But to give his heart? To hold fast to a woman's love? Considering the life he led, that was far too dangerous. She'd be a target. A weak spot. The wound into which his enemies could rub salt.

After all, a bullet to his brain would only kill him. But a bullet in the head of another woman he loved?

He'd barely survived that first time. A second time would destroy him forever.

With a frustrated sigh, he gave himself a mental shake, forcing his mind back on track. Franklin and Dion were in the past. Right then, he had only one thing to worry about, and that was determining the reason behind Ella's mugging. Who were the perps? Was it random? And if not, then who was the intended victim?

Because despite the carefully crafted story about Xena's deep concern for Ella's well-being and celebrity status, Liam didn't believe a word of it. What he didn't know was why she'd lie. Did she believe that the attackers mistook Ella for her? That seemed the most likely possibility. But that conclusion was based on the evidence before him. The wig. Xena's voice and mannerisms. The fact that the perps bolted when the wig and hat came off.

All the evidence suggested that the perps didn't realize the jogger was Ella. And the reasonable conclusion was that they'd targeted Xena. But Liam knew better than to jump to conclusions, and he couldn't discount the possibility that there was something else going on, but he was standing too close to see the bigger picture.

He sighed, shoving his hands into his pockets. The bottom line was that he didn't know. But he intended to find out.

He was still standing in the back of the auditorium by the light and sound boards. He glanced over and saw Tommy looking at him, his craggy face scrunched with concern. Not surprising. Ella's entire team was worried. Only a select few knew that Gordon had manufactured last week's intrigue. The rest believed that it was an outside hoax that Liam had forestalled before it spread out to the world.

As for Liam's own team back at Stark Security, he'd gone with the uncomfortable lie that Ellie Love was a high maintenance prima donna and that she and Rye had simply overreacted to a hoax that Liam had shut down. Considering no one at Stark Security knew anyone connected with the show, the subterfuge was simple.

He and Ryan had made peace with the lie, but it still didn't sit well, even though it was in some ways true. Ella really was high maintenance, and she could be an absolute dictator where her show was concerned—a fact that was evidenced right then, because she was on stage, leading her team in a walk-through of the show that involved both praise and a few well-placed curses.

Still, she was fair, and her people seemed to love her. She worked her ass off, and she was beyond dedicated to her team, a fact that had been borne out when she'd insisted that Gordon be protected from his own overeager tendencies.

He lifted a hand to Tommy, waving goodbye, but stopped after only one step toward the brightly marked exit.

Ella *was* loyal, there was no doubt about that. Her team mattered to her.

Xena mattered to her.

And whether Ella wanted to or not, now was the time to tell him the whole story about the woman who'd risen in the organization to become Ella's friend, confidante, and personal assistant.

He shifted directions, heading not to the door, but down to the stage. He knew he wouldn't get Ella right now, but he could leave a message for her to meet him after the concert.

He didn't see Xena, and he assumed she was probably off enjoying the light meal that he knew had been set up backstage for the performers. But Rye was talking with one of the choreographers, and he went over to him.

"I'm heading to the resort's security office to check the fitness center footage. Can you tell Ella I want to see her in her dressing room after the show?"

"Sure. No problem. Just don't take too much of her time. She'll be wired, and everyone's coming to our suite for the after party."

"I'll be quick. And Rye—I want to talk to her alone."

The other man's eyes widened. "Whoa. Am I in trouble, coach?"

Liam crossed his arms as he studied Rye. "What do you think?"

"That if you think I had something to do with what happened this morning, you are seriously off your rocker. I might beat the shit out of someone I caught messing with my girl, but I'd never lay a hand on her."

"Good to know."

"You're just messing with me, right? I'm not seriously on your radar?"

"Everyone's on my radar." He added a smile. "But you're not pinging too loudly."

"Wow. Well, good to hear it." He chuckled. "Do you know I've never even gotten a speeding ticket? The idea someone would think that I—" He cut himself off with a shake of the head. "Just a little surreal."

Liam started to step away. "You'll tell her?"

"Yeah. Um, there's one other—never mind. I'll let El know."

"What's on your mind?"

Rye shrugged, running his fingers through his tousled dark blond hair.

"It's nothing. Honestly. Just—nothing."

"Rye, your fiancée was attacked, and under the circumstances I'm better equipped to assess what is or is not nothing. So spit it out."

"It's just that I saw you talking with Xena up there, and ... hell, I hate to say anything. I might be totally off base."

"Say it anyway."

He exhaled loudly. "Fine. Okay. I did a background check on her."

"When? Today?"

"No, no. Years ago, back when Ella hired her. We'd barely started dating, but I was her manager, and something felt off."

"What did you find?"

He met Liam's eyes. "Not a goddamn thing.

Seriously. Nothing. No credit. No property. No anything. I mean, yeah. I found her in the system. We had her social security number. Susan Morgan —no idea why she started calling herself Xena. Anyway, that was it. Born in Idaho. Parents both dead—killed in a car accident. And that's it." He shrugged. "So I told Ella I was concerned. This girl had started working in Ella's house. You know, buying groceries, sorting mail. And I was afraid she was going to scam her. Get her financial info. Whatever."

"So what did Ella say?"

"She told me not to poke around anymore. That there wasn't anything to find, and that Xena'd had a hard life." He shrugged. "I assumed that was code for her being a runaway. What with her parents' accident, she probably got tossed into the system, and it was a bad situation. El's got a big heart, and I figured she wanted to help the girl out."

"But now?"

He exhaled loudly. "Listen, El thinks a lot of Xena. I do, too. She's a great employee. She loves El, I'm sure of it. But I'm worried that maybe there's stuff in her past that's more than just a messed up family life and blowing off a foster home."

Liam didn't disagree, but he kept his expression bland as he said, "Thanks for telling me."

"Sure, sure."

"I still want to see Ella. Tell her I'll come to her dressing room after the show."

"Yeah. I will. Anything you need. I just want her safe."

"That's what I'm here for."

Rye exhaled loudly. "Yeah, you are. No offense, man, but it sucks that you had to come."

Xena's sideways grin popped into Liam's head. "Maybe so, but I'm glad I did. And we will get to the bottom of this."

"Sooner the better. You going to watch the concert? We keep a few front row VIP seats open."

"No, but thanks. I'm heading over to watch security videos. With any luck, maybe I'll spot a mugger."

CHAPTER SIX

C arlos Martinez, the head of security for the Delphi Casino and Hotel, was in a meeting, so Liam ended up grabbing dinner—his first meal of the day—in one of the property's many restaurants, then meeting Martinez right about the time Ella was taking the stage.

"Good to see you again," Martinez said, looking up from where he sat in front of a security console, a spot usually reserved for one of the techs. But Liam had worked with Martinez before and wasn't surprised to see that the man was hands-on. A woman had been attacked on his watch, and he wanted to find the perp as much as Liam did.

"You're already reviewing?" Liam asked, peering over his friend's shoulder.

"You mind?"

"Hell, no. The more eyes the better."

Martinez made a scoffing noise. "If she'd reported the attack, we could have had eyes on a live stream. As it is, you know the score. There's no way we can monitor every security feed at all times."

"No one's blaming your team," Liam said. Martinez knew that, of course. But he'd still take the whole situation very, very personally. "What have you got for me?"

Martinez nodded toward the chair next to him, and Liam sat as the tech on his other side scooted down the console to make room for him. "I've cued it up to where Ms. Love leaves the fitness center to start her run." He maneuvered the controls, and that footage popped onto the screen.

"Nice equipment," Liam said. He'd been the head of security for the entire Sykes Department Store enterprise during the time he'd been moon-lighting at Deliverance. The Sykes family had spared no expense in any aspect of their business, but the security system they'd had was a toddler's video recorder compared to this.

"State of the art," Martinez said with as much pride as a new father. "And with cloud storage, we can save our footage indefinitely. We've learned that some women have to talk themselves into reporting bad behavior, and years ago, the evidence was often overwritten." He met Liam's eyes, his own hard. "You see a lot working in this town, and sometimes the hotel guests misinterpret what it means to have a good time. You know what I'm sayin'?"

"Unfortunately, yeah."

As they talked, Martinez stepped through the images. Ella walking through the fitness center. Ella pausing at the juice bar by the exterior door. Ella filling her water bottle. And then Ella exiting through the glass exterior door. And, yes, especially with the cap on, the hair really did look like Xena's.

Of course, Ella was wearing shorts and a tank, which revealed her significant curves. A feature that Xena definitely didn't share, and Liam mentally put a check mark in the *random attack* column.

On screen, Martinez jumped to the point he'd bookmarked from another feed on the jogging trail. "Unfortunately, we don't have complete coverage outside," he said, but he did have enough to confirm Ella's version of the attack.

"Any chance we can get a closer image of this arm?" Liam said, tapping the eraser end of a pencil against the screen. Martinez gave it a shot, but the image never got clearer than a blurry dark splotch.

"Tattoo?" Martinez asked.

"A snake, most likely. Ms. Love said she could

only see part of it." He leaned back in the chair, his twined fingers cupping his head. "Show the fitness center footage again. If they were watching her, chances are they were in that room, too."

"Agreed." Martinez pulled up the footage they'd already reviewed, then put the video from the room's second camera on the neighboring monitor. Both covered the open area of the fitness center, but one showed the interior door that led into the heart of the hotel. The other showed the exterior door that led to the track.

With Martinez at one control and Liam at the other, they went frame by frame through the footage, backing up to five minutes before Ella entered and continuing to five minutes after she left.

"This guy," Liam said on their third run through. He tapped the screen again, indicating a stocky man in black shorts and a black tank. He left the treadmill and went to the dispenser to fill his water bottle. Never once did he lift his head.

"Almost like he knows there are cameras," Martinez said, echoing Liam's thoughts.

"Keep watching," Liam said, and as they did, the guy turned toward the interior door, putting the side of his arm in clear view of the camera. "Bingo," Liam whispered.

"That's a snake, all right. But your boy's exiting into the hotel. And Ella's leaving right now into the great outdoors," he added, pointing to the other monitor that showed activity at the exterior door at the same time-stamp.

Another man in black followed Snake Man, his head also down. "Can you pull up a floor plan?"

"No sweat." Within seconds, Martinez replaced the exterior door cam with a floor plan that showed the layout around the fitness center.

"There," Liam said, pointing to a door a few yards down. "An exterior exit?"

"That it is. The sidewalk leads to the poolside bar. But there's no reason why someone couldn't walk on the grass and catch up with Ms. Love."

"Exactly what I was thinking. I'm also thinking these guys are professionals."

"No face shots."

"None," Liam agreed, frowning as something occurred to him. "Can you run the footage back to when they went through the door?" Like many entrances to hotel fitness centers, the center of the door had an eye-level glass pane. In this case, it was etched with an ornate D for Delphi.

"He turned, didn't he? The one following your snake man?"

Liam nodded. "The door was already swinging shut, and he was in the shadows, but yeah. He did."

"Did he look up?"

"I think so. Let's see if I'm right."

He was—but it wasn't a full victory. Most of the bastard's face was hidden behind the etched D.

"Not sure we're going to get something useful." Martinez frowned as he leaned forward, slowly enlarging the image.

"Can you make a copy for me? If anyone can pull enough information off that image to run it through facial recognition, Mario can." He thought of the young, smart-mouthed analyst who oversaw tech at Stark Security. The kid was always telling everyone he was a genius. Maybe today, he'd prove himself right.

"I'll put it on a shared server. He can pull the feed directly." He manipulated some keys, then pulled up a text message box and typed in a password and a URL. A moment later, Liam's phone pinged. "Send him there. And if he runs into any trouble, give him my phone number. You can log in, too, in case you want to review it on your phone."

"Perfect." Liam pushed his chair back and stood. "I owe you one."

"I'll remember that," Martinez promised. "Always good to bank favors."

Liam was grinning as he left the Delphi's Security Operations Center. He didn't have answers yet, but at least he could report to Ella that he was moving forward. A good thing in its own right, but also a nice buffer to the questions he intended to ask about Xena.

He glanced at his watch, surprised to realize how late it was. The concert would be almost over, and he decided to go straight to the dressing room to wait for Ella and call Mario.

"Foster, my man," Mario said as soon as he answered. "How are things in the land of sex and sin?"

"I'm more concerned about assault, actually."

"I'm listening."

"Where are you? At a computer?"

"How long have we known each other?"

Liam chuckled. "Good point. I need you to manipulate some footage for me."

"Sweet. Are we scamming someone?"

"Not like that. Hang on, let me forward you the text. You may need to use the office computers. I'm assuming we still have a few bells and whistles that you don't have at home?"

"Not many. Ryan's cool with me upgrading my home system so long as the security and firewalls stay top-notch. But not an issue, anyway. I'm at my desk right now. Doing some work for Denny."

Liam frowned. "Denny? She's taking a month off with Mason." An agent with Stark Security from its inception, Denny had spent most of her time on the job mourning the loss of her husband, who'd been gone for years after a mission gone wrong. Recently, he'd resurfaced, but without any memory of Denny, himself, or his past.

Things were solid between the two of them now—thank God—but Liam still couldn't fathom the depths of their anguish ... and the challenges they still faced.

And he certainly didn't understand what Mario had to do with any of it.

"Denny wants to make memories," he explained. "So she's sending me daily images and videos from their travels to compile into an interactive virtual album. Editable—I think she's leaving out the juicy footage—so she can add stuff later."

"Except for you, I've never met anyone better with tech skills than Denny. Why are you doing it and not her?"

"One, I think she'd rather make the memories than record them."

"Point taken."

"And two, I was working remotely from Austin when all that drama with Mason's return went down. So now I want to help."

"Good for you," Liam said, meaning it. He loved Denny like a sister, and he'd taken a liking to Jack—well, Mason—the moment he met the man. "Anyway, I need you to take a break from your vicarious vacation with them and see if you can rebuild an image. I'm texting you the access info and the timecode for the part I'm interested in."

"Hold on," Mario said, as Liam heard his phone

ping in the background. "Oh, yeah. This guy in the window." He let out a low whistle. "Tough one."

"Too tough?"

"I didn't say that. Give me a chance to work my magic. You want to put it through facial recognition, right?"

"That's the goal." Stark Security was fortunate to have many high-level connections that allowed for access to several databases not officially available to civilians. Not that Mario couldn't get through government security, but best to be aboveboard if possible.

"I'll buzz you as soon as I've got something. It won't be fast, though. Fair warning."

"Whatever you can do, as soon as you can do it," he said as the door opened and Ella stepped in. He waved in greeting as he ended the call with Mario, then smiled at her. "Thanks for letting me invade your space."

"I already told you. Anything you need. I want to know what's going on." She moved past him to sit at the dressing table. "Rye says you were going to look at the security footage. Was it from the fitness center? Did you find anything?"

"Maybe. I'll get back to you."

She squinted, looking ready to argue, but apparently decided against it. "He also said you wanted to talk to me, and it had to be tonight. Before my after-party."

"I didn't see any profit in waiting."

"I'll admit I'm intrigued. This all feels very espionage-ish. Are you going to interrogate me about my dark past?"

He chuckled, then took a seat on her sofa, no longer covered with costumes. "Unless you're better than Witness Protection at crafting a fake past, I know pretty much all I need to know about you. And while you may have pissed off a few record producers over the years, I don't think any of them would attack you."

"You're saying it was random."

He leaned back, spreading his arms along the top of the sofa. "I think we both know it wasn't."

She'd been looking straight at him, but now her eyes flickered away before returning to his face. "Do we?"

"Don't play games. We're both too old and too smart for that."

She licked her lips. "Then stop trying to trap me and just tell me."

He almost laughed. The woman definitely had his number. "It wasn't random, but it also wasn't about you. It was about Xena." He caught her eyes again, then held them. "But you already knew that, didn't you?"

She lifted her chin, then looked defiantly at Liam. "Not at first. I figured it out after her reaction about the wig. I'm assuming you did, too."

He nodded. "So let's call her in and get some answers." Finally, they were making some progress. And if Xena knew who her attackers were, maybe he could wrap this thing up by morning.

Ella wrinkled her nose. "Well, actually, that's going to be a problem. Xena's gone."

CHAPTER SEVEN

The sound of a revving engine startles me awake, and I leap out of bed, terrified that they've found me. I scramble for the gun I keep in my purse, then glance at the digital alarm clock by the bed. Two in the morning.

Shit. I'm in a tiny mountain cottage on a dead-end street with no other houses. So this really isn't good.

I remind myself that there's no way they can know I'm here. I came by the craziest route imaginable, and I'm confident that I covered my tracks. There's no car outside to suggest I'm here, and the interior of the house is completely dark except for the glowing blue light of the various pieces of electronic equipment that Ella keeps running even when the house is closed up.

Besides, it's quiet now. Probably nothing. Just a

coincidence. Someone who got lost and was turning around at the dead end. No big deal.

At least, that's what I tell myself as I tiptoe through the house in the yoga pants and tank that I'd slept in. Usually, I sleep naked, but tonight I'd been too nervous, and wanted to be ready to bolt. I check the doors and carefully peek out the windows, trying to see something other than shadows from the trees. But there's nothing. No cars, no anything.

I tell myself that's good, and go with my lost driver theory. No big deal and I should just go back to sleep.

Instead, I put on my slip-on sneakers, just in case, then start to do another circuit around Ella's private getaway. A place I know she holds dear, and that I'm so, so grateful she's entrusting to me despite everything.

I've been here twice before, both times after our working relationship turned friendly. Even a little sisterly. I'd loved the place then, with its amazing refurbished bathroom and rustic back patio.

Tonight, I love it even more. It's my hideaway, and considering what I'm hiding from, is it any wonder I'm being paranoid about street sounds?

But is it paranoia if they're really out to get you?

I scowl, and tell myself that no one but Ella knows I'm here. For that matter, only a handful of

Ella's closest staff and advisors even know the cabin exists. It's owned by a shell company in a shell company. She wanted a getaway. A real getaway. So she had someone buy it on behalf of a pretend rental company, and she keeps it empty. It's watched over by a caretaker who comes in once a month and whenever she calls to say she's coming.

It's her sanctuary. Her happy place.

I love her for letting me stay here. And all the more for swearing that she understood why I had to leave.

I wipe my eyes with the back of my hand, forcing myself not to cry. I hate that I have to run. That I have to hide. I loved my job, and I feel like I'm letting her down.

I've made the circuit twice now, and I don't see anything that suggests someone is out there. I double-check the alarm, and it's set. I disarm it and then re-arm it, just in case.

That's another reason I love Ella. She told me how to reprogram the system, and even told me not to tell her the code. That way, I'm the only one who knows it. "You'll tell me when you come back," she'd told me.

"What if I don't come back?"

"In that case, we both have bigger things to worry about than dealing with the damn alarm company."

A twig snaps at the back door, and I swallow a

yelp. This time I'm certain I'm not imagining things.

With shaking hands, I hold the gun in front of me. "Go away," I call. "I'm armed. And this is private property."

"Xena, it's Liam."

Liam? My pulse picks up tempo, but this time it's not in fear. Relief? Hope?

Or maybe something much more complicated.

I put the gun down on the table by the door. My hands are still shaking, and I'm not taking any chances.

"Xena," he presses. "Open the door."

"How did you find me?"

"You know how," he says, his voice both firm and matter of fact.

I do?

Yes, of course I do. "Ella told you." I hear the accusation in my voice. She promised to keep it a secret. From everyone.

"Ella *sent* me."

What the hell? "Well, I didn't ask her to. And I'm fine. I don't need a babysitter. And I don't—I don't want her in the middle of my problems."

"Considering she was mugged because of your problems, I'd say she already is."

Anger flares inside me, cold and biting. "I mean it. Go away."

I hear him sigh. "Xena, please. Ella's worried

about you. I'm worried about you. And I saw your face when she told me about the wig, so I'm pretty damn certain that you're worried about you, too."

I say nothing. He's right, but I'm not going to give him the satisfaction of admitting it.

"Xena, please. It's the middle of the night."

I suck in a breath, punch in the code to disarm the system, then open the door just long enough for him to swoop in. Then I set the code, wait for the green light to show the system's engaged, then turn around and study him.

He's wearing jeans, a black T-shirt, and a sport coat, and he looks just as sexy and commanding as he had in the tailored suit he had on when I saw him last.

Weirdly, that gives me confidence. I wouldn't open that door to just anyone, but a guy this pulled together? A guy that Ella trusts? Well, maybe it wouldn't be so bad having that guy watching my back.

Except, of course, that it might get him killed.

"Xena?" He reaches out and gently strokes my hair.

I flinch away, hugging myself, and he backs off immediately, then says, very gently, "Go sit down."

He nods toward the sofa in the small living room. I take the chair, curling myself up into a ball under the soft, purple blanket.

"What do you want?" he asks, and before I can

ask what he means, he's continuing. "Water? Wine? Something harder?"

"Definitely something harder," I say, running my hands over my newly cut hair. "Coffee."

His face lights up with laughter, and I like the sound of it. For such a big guy, he has a very gentle laugh.

"Coffee sounds perfect. I'll be right back."

He leaves, and for a moment I think I should play hostess and follow him. But I don't. Despite telling him to go away not five seconds ago, now I want nothing more than to rest in this overstuffed chair and let Liam take care of me.

I have to fight that urge—I know that. Who knows better than I do the dangers of trusting other people? The only way to stay alive in this world is to watch your own back and not trust other people. And the corollary—let other people into your problems, and they could end up dead. I learned both the hard way, and those are lessons not easily forgotten.

But the truth is, I bent my own rule with Ella. I trusted her the way a wounded puppy trusts a human with a kind scent. I let her tend to me and take care of me, and although I was terrified for those first few months under her roof, my mind finally came to believe what instinct already knew. That she was a good woman who'd never betray me.

I trust her. Which means I can trust Liam. Or I can try to, anyway.

"Cream?" he calls from the kitchen, where I can hear the sound of the Keurig doing its thing.

"Yes, please." I hadn't thought much about the stocked refrigerator and pantry when I first arrived, but now I realize that Ella must have called the caretaker while I was on the road, and I'm grateful for it. I can drink my coffee black, but it's so much more comforting with cream.

He comes back with two huge mugs, hands me one, then sits on the sofa opposite me.

I take a sip, relishing the warmth and the way it gives me strength. "So what now?"

"Now, we talk."

"Right. Okay." I take another sip, but I don't volunteer any more information.

"I like your hair. Had a sudden urge for a change?"

I scowl. I'm not naturally platinum, but I'd been uber-blond for the last three years, hiding myself behind a curtain of long, silvery locks. Now, my hair is chin-length and ebony, still a far cry from my naturally warm, golden tones.

I'd grabbed a bottle of dye from Hair and Makeup before I left Vegas, then used the shower facilities at a truck stop to turn myself into a brunette. As for the cut, I'd popped into a Supercuts in San Bernardino before switching taxis for my trek up the mountain.

I can't say I'm crazy about my new look, but with my naturally pale skin, it suits me, though it's a little bit overdramatic. I feel like a flapper or a silent film star. But none of that matters; it's not as if I have a photo shoot booked. My only goal is to stay alive.

"It was the hair, wasn't it?" he says. "They thought Ella was you because of the hair."

My instinct is to deny, of course. But I nod. Ella trusts him, so I'll answer truthfully. But I'm not going to volunteer information.

He leans back against the sofa cushions. His dark eyes study me, but I see compassion in them. "What happened, Susan? Who are you running from?"

I go cold at the sound of that name. "I go by Xena now. And I really don't want to talk about it."

"I know you don't. But I need information if I'm going to help you."

My body is tense, my jaw so tight my mouth aches. I draw a deep breath and force myself to relax. "I didn't ask for your help."

"Nonetheless, you have it. Tell me the truth, and I can be useful. Block me, and I might be a detriment instead of an asset. Is that a risk you want to take?"

"What I want is for you to leave."

He studies me, then stands. "Why?"

I pull the blanket tighter around me. "I don't owe you an explanation. Why do you want to stay? The world's a dangerous place. I'm sure someone else will happily pay Stark Security's hourly rate."

"One, the SSA doesn't charge by the hour. And two, no one is paying me to be here."

I blink, legitimately surprised. "Oh."

"Xena," he says gently. "Tell me your story. Let me help."

I say nothing, my mind whirring as I keep my lips tight together, afraid if I relax for even a second, then all of my secrets will spill out.

I watch as his shoulders slump, and I feel a pang in my gut. I've disappointed him.

"You were a runaway," he says, and since that's close enough to the truth, I nod. "Tell me how you came to work for Ella."

I run the question around in my head, not sure if I should open the door to this man even a crack. But I can't deny that I do need help, even if only to get away, get a new identity, and get settled. Would he do that for me? I'm not sure—how can I be sure? —but if he's really here because Ella asked him to help me, then I think maybe he will.

Even she doesn't know the real truth, but she knows the essence. She knows I was running. She knows I was hiding. She knows I was afraid for my life.

And she knows that I have to go hide again.

"Xena," he presses. "Tell me about the name. How did Xena end up being a nickname for Susan?"

"I can't tell you that without telling you more of the story."

"I don't have anywhere else to be, and I'm not particularly sleepy."

"Me either," I admit. My terror-induced adrenaline rush has faded, but I'm still wide-awake, and not just because of the coffee.

"Then we might as well stay up and talk."

I finish my coffee, then sigh. "Fine. I'm pretty sure I'm not going to get rid of you, so I might as well talk to you."

"I'll take conversation with you anyway I can get it."

I know he's just being agreeable, soothing me like a skittish colt, but I still melt a little under his words.

When I continue to stay silent, he clears his throat. "Why did you run away?"

I lick my lips, debating how much fiction to mix with my facts. "Things were bad," I say simply. "Considering how you grew up, I'm not sure you can really understand that."

I see his eyes widen and know I've surprised him. "What do you know about how I grew up?"

I shrug. "I looked you up before you came to

work for Ella in Los Angeles. I knew the SSA had a good rep, but—"

"You look out for her."

I nod.

"Now you've intrigued me. What did you find out?"

"That you grew up in a mansion in Southampton. That your mom was the housekeeper for the Sykes family, you moved there when you were a baby, and you were raised like you were part of the family. Oh, and they have more money than God."

"I haven't actually reviewed God's books lately, but that's probably a fair assessment."

"And I know that Dallas Sykes is your best friend, and that the family sent you to school with him, at least until he went overseas to boarding school. I know you served in the army and that for years you worked as the head of security for the Sykes Department Store chain."

I watch Liam's chest expand as he draws in a long breath. "So that's all?"

I grin at his flippant tone. "I couldn't find as much recent stuff," I admit. "But somehow you ended up at Stark Security."

"Not a bad bit of research."

"It wasn't too hard. You hang around with the Sykes family, and you can't really stay invisible."

"I suppose that's true."

"And while I can tell you my story, it's not like

it matters. It's not like you'll get it at all. I mean, I'm *so* not a Hamptons kind of girl."

"No, you're an Idaho transplant to LA. And your parents are dead, and until Ella you didn't have a support network. I haven't had the chance to dig in, but I'm guessing you were a runaway, probably lived on the streets for a while. Maybe even turned tricks."

My cheeks heat, because he's so far from the truth, but also so very close to it.

"Somewhere along the way, you crossed the wrong person." He tilts his head, as if examining me from another angle. "Maybe drugs, maybe money-laundering, maybe something else. I don't know. But it was big enough that they still want to make sure you stay silent, even after all these years."

He straightens, then leans forward, his elbows on his knees. "How am I doing so far?"

"Good enough to prove my point." My voice is colder than I intend it to be. Deep down, I know he really wants to help me. But despite my fantasies of having someone at my side offering aid, I know that can't happen. And he has no idea what kind of rabbit hole we'd both fall into if I let him.

"Your point?" he asks.

"You can't possibly have a clue about my life."

He studies me for a while, long enough that I

start to squirm under his attention. Finally, he says, "You know about the Sykes kidnapping?"

I nod. "Dallas Sykes and his sister were kidnapped when they were teenagers. Around fifteen, I think. They were both finally released." I don't know a lot about it, actually. My research was focused on Liam, not the Sykes family. But Dallas Sykes is a huge celebrity by virtue of his family money, his playboy heir attitude, and the parties he use to throw and attend. I've never been much on social media—and for a long time I couldn't afford a smart phone—but for a while everyone was calling him The King of Fuck, and it would have taken superpowers to avoid the gossip entirely.

"They were both my best friends growing up," Liam says. "Dallas and Jane. They're still my best friends, and I love them like family. I would do anything for them. They've endured more than any human should have to endure, and I don't begrudge them a moment of happiness."

I nod, assuming he's talking about the fact that they're now married, which is utterly bizarre to me.

"I told Jane to go to Dallas that night."

I shake my head, not following. "What night?"

"Outside of London. The night they were kidnapped. Dallas was in boarding school, and Jane wanted to talk with him. She called me before she snuck away from her family in the city, asking me if she should." He swallows. "I said yes. And that night, they were both kidnapped."

"I'm so sorry." I lick my lips. "But it's not your fault."

"No, but they were still taken. And they were tortured."

"Tortured?" I repeat.

"Horribly, brutally tortured. The worst you can imagine."

Considering my own history, I can imagine a lot. "Sexually," I whisper. A statement, not a question.

"And there I was safe and sound back in the States, completely oblivious until it was over, then completely impotent after I learned some of the truth. I wanted to make it better. But there wasn't a damn thing I could do for them."

"No." I shake my head. "No, there wouldn't be."

"I joined the Army," he says. "At the time, I didn't even know why. God knows I wasn't from a military family. My father died before I was born. A drug deal gone bad."

"I'm sorry."

"Yeah, well, I'm not. I love my mom, and from what she tells me, my father was bad news. The shooting and the pregnancy pushed her out of the city, and she managed to land a job on the Sykes estate even though she had a baby. I still don't know how, and all she says is that God was looking out for us. But not the point. I ended up in the military."

"Because you felt helpless," I say. "About Dallas and Jane. And maybe even a little about your dad."

"Maybe." He exhales. "Actually, yes."

"Did it help?"

The corner of his mouth curves up just slightly. "No."

"You thought it would."

He nods. "But I learned skills. I formed friendships. The years weren't wasted."

"Maybe not, but you're still chasing that guilt. That helplessness. It's why you work in security."

"That's definitely part of it."

"And the rest of it?" I ask.

"I really do like the work. And I'm good at it. And there are far too many people in the world who need help."

I exhale. He's right about that.

"I'm sorry," I say after a moment. "For you. For your friends." I drop my gaze. "And for being a brat who thinks she's the only one who has a hell-bitch for a guardian angel."

"But you don't," he says, and I look up into those kind, determined eyes. "Not anymore."

My heart skitters in my chest. "Liam..."

I think he's going to press me to allow him to

play bodyguard. Instead, he changes topics. "How did they find you? Do you know?"

"Ella didn't tell you?"

He shakes his head.

"Those damn super fan invitations." I can see he doesn't understand, so I continue. "Ella's known from the beginning that I was running, and when I told her I wanted to be sure and never be in a photo, she was totally cool with that. Sometimes reporters would ask, you know? Because no one knows a celebrity like their personal assistant. But she'd always tell them that I'm not a public figure and privacy is important and yada yada." I trail off with a shrug.

"But somehow a picture got out there?"

"Oh, yeah." I release a noisy sigh. "You know how we invite fans to the final full rehearsal? Well, we tell them no photography except during the rehearsal performance. Nothing on breaks or behind the scenes. But last week at the LA rehearsal, some clown took a pic when I went on stage during a break to talk to Ella about something that needed to be adjusted before the performance."

"It got posted on social media, and someone saw it."

"Right. And since the attack was in the wake of the Gordon bullshit, the connection to me wasn't even on Ella's radar."

"But it was on yours. They recognized your face despite changing your hair when you ran."

I nod. "I'm not naturally a blond." I run my fingers through my current strands. "This isn't really me, either."

"Well, so far I've liked all the versions of you." His voice is mild, but I think I see a hint of heat in his eyes.

I look away. "Yeah, well, after the attack, I knew I had to go. So I went to see her before the concert. That was when she showed me the photo on Twitter. Someone had tagged her, and it was just random that she saw it. She usually doesn't pay that much attention to her account. She has a social media team that handles that."

"So she helped you run. Sent you here."

I nod.

"And you're sure they didn't follow you?"

"Positive."

"Tell me how you got here?"

I roll my eyes, but comply. "I took a taxi—cash —to the airport in Vegas, then flew to Burbank. Then I took a taxi to LAX and used a pre-paid debit card that Ella gave me to buy a ticket on one airline to Newark and on another airline to Atlanta. Then I took a taxi to a truck stop in Riverside. That's where I changed my hair. And then another taxi to San Bernardino."

"Why not the bus?"

I shrug. "Faster."

He nods, and I continue. "I took one last taxi up here." I shrug. "If they followed me, I'd call it a miracle."

"I'm impressed."

I don't bother telling him I've had a lot of practice. "Wait," I say, suddenly alarmed. "Could they have followed you?"

"No." The word is firm. "My route was as random as yours. We're safe."

"Okay." I'm sure my relief is visible.

"Listen, Xena. You're obviously capable, but you're still alone, and we don't know for sure what you're up against. Let me help you. Think of it as an entirely altruistic act."

I shake my head. "No. I appreciate it, but no."

"Why not?"

"Because I don't want you involved. And I don't need you. Don't you get it? They don't know where I am. I'm going to stay here a couple of days to regroup, and then I'm going to disappear again. Another state. Maybe another country. I have money this time. I saved a lot from working with Ella. And she told me to take some cash from the safe in there," I add, pointing to the kitchen. "I'm going to—but only because I plan to pay it back."

He watches me even after I finish talking, studying me like I'm a problem that has to be solved.

"What?" I demand when I can't stand it anymore.

"I'm sorry, but I can't agree to that."

"I'm pretty sure I never asked you to."

"Xena, be realistic. Someone is after you. Let me help you find them. Take them out. Let me help you fix your life so that you can stop running and looking over your shoulder."

The very thought sends cold chills coursing up my spine, and I can feel my heart start to skitter with the precursor to a full-blown panic attack. I tell myself to breathe. To count to ten. And as Liam watches me, I slowly calm down.

"Xena?"

I just shake my head, not quite up to forming words yet. The reality would be horrible enough, but just the *idea* of confronting them terrifies me. I'm not going to tell Liam that. He has no idea how big the monster is. But I do. And I've seen enough scary movies to know that sometimes the only way to survive is to get the hell away from the demon.

"No," I finally say. "I'm sorry, but no."

He doesn't answer, but it doesn't matter. At the end of the day, it's my decision.

After a moment, he stands. "I'm going to raid Ella's bar. Do you want a whiskey? Or wine? I bet she has red. You need sleep, and it might help."

I shake my head. "I don't drink."

His brow furrows. "But that night on Ella's patio..."

"Ella makes sure the parties have non-alcoholic wine for me. It's easier than explaining."

I'm not sure he realizes it, but he takes a step closer to me.

"Funny." That's all he says, but his expression suggests that there's a lot more thought behind the word.

"What?"

"It's just—I thought you were a little drunk that night."

"Oh." And I must be more tired than I realize, because I can't stop what comes out of my mouth next. "You made me feel a little drunk." I meet his eyes, then look down, a tiny smile tugging at my mouth. Why I'm smiling, though, I don't know. God knows I've just revealed more to this man than I ever thought I would. And definitely more than I should.

I bite my lower lip. We'd both stayed in check that night, even though we both wanted so much more. Neither of us had said so, but it was in the air, so thick and potent it's a wonder the other guests didn't notice.

It occurs to me that I won't be seeing him again, because after tonight he'll be gone, and in a few days, I'll disappear and become someone else. But tonight...

Tonight there's no risk of exposing myself. Of getting in too deep with someone I can't have.

He clears his throat. "Right. Well, I still want that whiskey." He starts to take a step, and before I have time to think about what I'm doing, I reach for his hand.

He stops, turning to look at me, and I pull myself up. He's right there, my hand in his, his other on my back, holding me steady, though how it got there, I really don't know.

That hint of a flame I'd seen earlier in his eyes is a blaze now, and I melt under the heat of it. I want this, dammit. This night. This man. Not because I have no choice. Not because I'm trying to survive.

I want it for me. *Me.*

Because he'll be gone tomorrow, and I'll be on the run. And I want to take this moment with me. Something real and wild to fire my strength. And something warm and tender to soothe my soul.

I see hesitation in his eyes, and I can hear his unspoken words. *We shouldn't.*

"Yes," I whisper. "We should."

For a moment, the world stops turning and the only thing happening in the entire universe is the two of us looking into each other's eyes. Then he groans, and in one bold move pulls me closer and crushes his mouth against mine.

I cling to him, melting against him as I part my

lips, welcoming the delicious assault of this kiss I feel all through me, making me tingle all the way to my toes and bringing to life parts of me I thought were dead forever.

All too soon, he pulls away, his questioning eyes searching my face.

"Yes," I whisper, but my word is swallowed by the flash of light that fills the room, the heavy pounding against the wooden front door, and the sharp pain in my arm as Liam yanks me violently down to the floor.

CHAPTER EIGHT

A scream shatters the air, and in the same moment that Liam closes his hand over my mouth, I realize it's coming from me.

He's looking at me hard, and I nod, hoping he understands that I've gotten myself under control. Slowly, he takes his hand off my mouth. "It's them," I say, as if he hasn't already figured that out all on his own. "They must have followed you."

I hear the accusation in my voice, but I don't care. Damn him for coming here, and damn Ella for sending him. I love her for caring, but they're both going to get me killed.

"They didn't follow me," he says. "Believe me when I say I know how to hide my tracks, and I know how to tell when I'm being tailed."

"Well, it wasn't me." I have *no* idea why I'm

arguing about this, except that it pisses me off. I was supposed to have a chance to relax.

"I believe you," he says.

"Then how—"

"Right now, it doesn't matter."

"What was the light?"

"Headlights, I think. Maybe a high power flashlight."

"Why haven't they come in?"

"They must know about the alarm. It's wired to 911?"

I nod. The siren won't disturb neighbors since there are none, but the little police station that serves this part of the San Bernardino Mountains is only one block over. The cops could be here in no time, and they can block the only way off the street even faster than that.

With a start, I realize our intruder—intruders? —must know that.

"Wait here." He stays low as he heads back to the door. He flips the light switch to off, leaving the room illuminated only by the thin blue light of the electronics and the faint glow of moonlight coming in through the windows.

He grabs my tiny Ruger from the table, then comes back to my side. "Do you know how to use this?" he asks when he returns.

I lift a brow. "Point and pull the trigger?"

I can tell from his face that he doesn't appre-

ciate the sarcasm, so I pull back the slide to reveal
that there's a round in the chamber, then pop out
the magazine before I expel the bullet. I shove the
bullet back into the magazine, click the magazine
into place, then once again pull the slide back to
chamber the round.

"Yeah," I say. "I know how to use it."

He nods, then reaches under his jacket and
pulls out a much larger black gun. I think it's a
Glock, but wouldn't swear to it. Suddenly, I'm
feeling better about our chances.

"Do you trust me to get us out of here?"

"Yes," I say, meaning it wholeheartedly.

He glances around the room, sees the backpack I use as a purse, and asks if I have a
compact.

"Um, maybe?" I start to crawl over there but he
holds me back, then goes himself, returning with
the pack. I rummage through it, find a small gold
compact that Ella gave me one Christmas, and pass
it to him.

With the compact in his left hand and the
pistol in his right, he creeps to the window by the
front door as I hold my breath. He uses the
compact to look outside, then slowly lowers it.
Then he holds up a finger before miming a steering
wheel.

One guy and a car. Got it.

I point to the back door, and he goes there next,

repeating the process and holding up another finger. *Fuck.*

He comes back to me. "It's too dark to get a good look, but I think they're the same goons from Vegas. Does Ella use some sort of front porch camera? If so, we might have a solid image of his face now."

I shrug.

"I'll find out later," Liam says. "Right now, we need to get out of here, because sooner or later they're going to hack the alarm code or decide to say screw it and come in anyway. They're heavily armed."

I decide not to ask what that means. If they have rocket launchers or automatic weapons, I really don't want to know.

"There's a little cellar under the kitchen," I say. "But it opens up right by the back door."

"Bathroom window?"

"Oh!" How could I forget the bathroom? "Better than that. The wall looks like the side of the house, but it folds back, so that you can actually sit in the jetted tub during the snow. Or take a shower in the outdoors if you're feeling adventurous." It was the one renovation that Ella put in after buying the place, and I think it was freaking brilliant.

"Make sure you have your phone and put on your backpack. Do you need to grab anything else?"

"I'm good. I've traveled light for years."

He aims a curious look at me, but says nothing other than, "Carry the Ruger and don't accidentally shoot me."

I nod, nervous enough to not smirk at his smart aleck remark. Because unfortunately, he's right about that particular risk.

"Stay low and lead the way."

I nod, then start to scramble that way, not breathing until we're finally inside the small space. Since the entire back wall by the sunken whirlpool tub and rain-style shower opens, there is no window, just a skylight. And that means as soon as we close the door behind us, we can relax. For a second, at least.

"How does it open?" Liam asks.

I stand and step on the wide ledge that runs along the foot of the tub. "This button unlocks it. Then you fold it back and slide it into the wall."

"Noisy?"

I wince. "Not that you'd normally care about. But today…"

He nods, understanding. "Too bad there's not much wind. The sound of the leaves might camouflage it. Doesn't matter. It's our shot, and we're taking it."

I nod in agreement even though I'm nervous as shit.

"The wall opens onto the porch I noticed when

I arrived?" he asks. "With the lounge chairs and the fire pit?"

"Right. Once the wall is tucked away, the entire bathroom is an outdoor space." The toilet, thankfully, is in its own tiny room.

He looks around the space, then aims a wry grin at me. "A shame we have to bolt. This bathroom could have been an interesting part of our evening."

Despite my fear, I laugh. "Promise me we'll live to have a rain check."

But he doesn't answer, and for a moment, we simply look at each other. Then he clears his throat and points toward the tub again. "There were stairs on both sides of the patio, right? And about an eight inch drop off the long end?"

"Um, yeah," I say, impressed by his memory.

"What about the alarm. Is it silent? Or does it blare?"

"It blares."

He looks around, then frowns.

"What?"

"No keypad in here to disarm it. We could have you go back into the other room to take care of that, but I think I actually want it to blare—I assume it's loud."

"Apparently. Ella told me not to forget my code because the alarm is earsplitting."

"Okay, okay." He's talking to himself, obviously

mulling something. "This can work." He pulls some tissues from a dispenser by the sink, then steps onto the ledge and hands me one. "Rip it up and plug your ears."

"Huh?"

"Trust me," he says, and since I do, I comply without any more questions.

As soon as his own ears are plugged, he looks at my gun, then his own. I know what he's going to say even before he says it. "We can solve this problem right now. They're going to be out of commission for at least a few seconds when the alarm blares. They won't be expecting it. We can take them out before they come after us. And they *will* come after us."

Cold fear washes over me. As much as I want them dead—as much as I want this nightmare to end—it's too dangerous. For one, they surely aren't the only two after me. Like cockroaches, if I kill two, four more will replace them.

But more than that, what if I miss and my target takes Liam out? Or me? And if we do get away, then what? We're going to leave Ella to deal with my mess? Bodies in her yard that she'll have to explain?

I shake my head slowly, then tell him all of that. I expect him to argue. To go all hard ass macho on me and tell me it's time to Rambo this shit.

But he doesn't. On the contrary, he nods

slowly. "You're right." He rubs his shaved scalp, then sighs. "The fact is, we've only seen two, but there might be more. We're getting out, getting away, and regrouping. You understand?"

I nod. "But what about calling for back-up?" I don't suggest the cops. They'd investigate us as much as the bad guys, and I don't want to be under that microscope. "The SSA. You have guys, right?"

"We're a long way from LA, even by chopper. And pulling in the Sheriff's department would take too long. Unlike in the movies, getting that kind of assistance from law enforcement requires red tape. We could call 911, but I don't think that's a good idea." He meets my eyes. "Do you?"

"No." I swallow. "So how are we getting away?"

"Just stay close. I've got that covered."

I remember the engine that woke me. He must have a car parked among the trees.

"On three," he says. "It's going to be loud. Be ready."

I'm not entirely sure my rubbery legs are going to cooperate, but I nod anyway.

He counts, and on three, he presses the button and the door unlatches as the blare from the alarm starts to shake the entire house. He shoves the panel aside, grabs my hand, and races forward, jumping the short distance from the patio to the ground, then sprinting over the undergrowth into the dark, wooded area.

I stumble and fall, and Liam grabs for me. As he does, I catch sight of the guy at the back door, partially illuminated by the moonlight. Unprepared, he's on the ground, struggling to get back to his feet with his hands plastered to his ears.

It worked, I think as Liam tugs me back up and we start running again.

I expect him to take us to the street, but instead we go into the woods, following what I now realize is an overgrown path. There's a hill, and we hurry down it, and I soon realize that we're low enough now that no one in the house or around it can see us. I relax. Slightly.

I start to ask where we're going, but then I see the huge bike parked by a woodpile. He came all the way from Vegas on a bike?

He hurries me onto the motorcycle before getting on in front of me. The guy in the back has stood up now, and I can see him from the saddle. Which means he can see me.

"Hold on," Liam says, his voice tense. And before I've even locked my fingers around him, we're rocketing forward, leaves flying around us as we bounce along the path, then hit the street's asphalt. There's a black car parked in front of the house, and on the porch, a lanky guy in a ball cap turns around, his mouth open in a ridiculous maw.

I see him raise a weapon, and I tense, then scream as a shot rings out, followed by another in quick succession. I breathe deep, expecting pain, then realize that it was Liam doing the shooting. The tires, I assume, but I don't know if he hit them, because we're already careening down twisting mountain roads, and I'm terrified that we're going to wipe out and I'm going to end up dead in a fiery conflagration.

I turn around once, then twice, both times certain I'll see my attackers gaining on us. But there's nothing. No one. Just the dark road disappearing behind us.

We go for what feels like forever, turning down streets, backtracking up the mountain, then going down an alternate route. Circling and twisting until I'm both lost and dizzy and numb from the buzz of the cycle beneath me.

"Stop," I finally shout, my mouth close to the back of his ear. "Please. Please, find a place to stop."

My heart is pounding. My blood burning. I need to move. I need to—I don't even know. But being on this bike is only making it worse.

Soon, he's pulling onto a side road that dips down. I see a wooden sign with the name of a park, but I'm too frazzled to try to read it. He follows a gravel path for at least a quarter mile, then stops the bike in a patch of dirt near a battered picnic table. He gets off, then helps me off.

I tug the tissue from my ears, then bend over, my hands on my knees, and suck in air as he rubs my back and whispers soothing words. "It's okay. It's okay. You're safe. There's no way they followed us. Just breathe. We're fine."

I nod my head. He's right, but it's not enough. I stand, my pulse so loud I can barely hear my thoughts.

"Xen—"

I don't let him finish. Instead, I pull myself up on my toes and capture his mouth in a kiss, long and deep and so wonderfully delicious I feel it reverberate all the way through me.

I pull back, breathing hard, my eyes never leaving his face. His expression is tight, like a spring about to explode. But whether he's about to kiss me or push me away, I really can't tell.

"We could have died," I whisper, as I slide my hands down to cup his very fine ass. I press against him, his erection hard against me. "We could have died," I repeat. "So don't you dare say no."

CHAPTER NINE

Xena wrapped herself around him before he could even react, her mouth hot against his. He knew they shouldn't—that they'd regret it in the morning. That *she'd* regret it. But dear Christ, he wanted her. He'd wanted her from the first moment he'd seen her.

That slim body. Those innocent eyes. That kissable, fuckable mouth that even then was warm and wet against his own, her tongue teasing and tempting him, making his already heated blood burn hotter.

Good God, he should hold back. He needed to rein it in and exercise some of that control he was so famous for. But right then they were safe, and she was wild and hot in his arms, and he was breathless and hard and definitely not thinking straight.

She was right—they could have died. And now that the coast was clear, he needed this. They both did. Needed to burn this crazed lust out of their systems, to boil down the adrenaline so they could think again. To push through the fear and the pain.

All of which were just rationalizations to justify taking her right then, right there, on a damned park bench while her skin glowed in the moonlight.

He stumbled back, then collapsed onto the bench. She gasped, one hand going to the button on his jeans as she climbed onto his lap, her legs on either side of his.

He had one hand at her lower back and the other on her breast. She wasn't wearing a bra, just that sexy black tank top, and he stroked his thumb over her hard nipple as it strained against the material.

She moaned against his mouth, her tongue still warring with his as he hitched the shirt up in the back, then slid his fingers under the waistband of her yoga pants. Her body shook as she drew a shuddering breath, and he cupped one of her ass cheeks, then pulled her closer, so that her body stroked his erection.

Her low, sexy moan teased his senses, and she started to move her hips, the slow, grinding movement making him completely insane. At the same time, the fingers at his fly started tugging down his zipper, while her other hand closed over his, increasing the pressure to her breast as she arched back and ground harder against him.

As her fingers eased into his jeans, she lifted her hips up to free his cock. He shifted long enough to tug his jeans down a bit so that blood would continue to flow, then returned one hand to her breast and rolled that tight, perfect nipple between his thumb and forefinger.

Their mouths were still locked, but she pulled back, her teeth tugging at his lower lip. "We shouldn't do this," she murmured, her voice low and breathy.

"No," he agreed as her hips rose and he took advantage, finding her slick, wet core. "No, we shouldn't," he said, burying two fingers inside her. She bore down on his hand, her head tilted back as she bit her lip and moaned.

"Then let's do it fast. Before we change our minds."

Laughter bubbled up out of him, and she took her hands off him, then started to tug down her yoga pants. "Get these off me."

"Off?"

She grabbed her top and pulled it over her head, then tossed it onto the picnic table behind him.

"Christ, Xena, what are you doing?"

"What *I* want. Please, please, for the first time in forever, just let me do this."

He didn't understand what she meant, but the question evaporated quickly enough as she wriggled out of the pants, managing the whole thing more efficiently than he could have, most likely because he half-believed he was dreaming.

"Touch me," she begged, and when he hesitated, she added, "We're safe. You said so. And if you didn't believe it one hundred percent you never would have let it get this far."

She was right, and he didn't protest when she took his hand and stroked his fingers over her clit. He was so damn hard, and he cupped his hands on her ass as she grabbed his shoulders, using the leverage to lift her hips, then wriggling until she was right over his cock. She settled there, teasing him mercilessly as she looked in his eyes, taking him in bit by bit, making them both crazy, until finally he was buried inside her, and she arched back, begging him to touch her as she rode him like a wild thing.

He cupped one breast and stroked her clit, but he didn't kiss her. He wanted to watch her. The way the moonlight cast shadows on her face. The way her lips parted with passion. The tremors in the tight muscles of her abdomen. And then, when release finally came, the way her entire body trembled and shook as she cried out and pounded a fist against his shoulder.

She was the most alive thing he'd ever held in his arms, and as her core spasmed around him, he exploded inside her. His moans joined hers, their loud cries sending a flock of birds rising out of the trees, their wings black against the night sky.

She collapsed against him, breathing hard. "Thank you," she murmured. "I'm sorry. And thank you."

"Sorry?" He cupped her face and gazed into those shining blue eyes. "Baby, you don't have anything to be sorry about."

A wry smile played at her mouth. "I think I used you."

"I think I liked it." Hell yes, he'd liked it. The way she'd taken control, and the way he'd completely surrendered to the live wire in his arms. It had been beyond delicious, and utterly unexpected.

"Are you okay?"

He realized that he'd closed his eyes, his forehead pressed against hers. He pulled back so that he could see her—then kissed her gently. "I'm fine. You do some crazy things to me."

"Crazy good? Or crazy bad?"

He grinned. "Maybe a little of both," he said, and as he'd hoped, she laughed.

And then he remembered. "*Fuck.*"

Her eyes widened. "What? What's wrong?"

"No condom. I'm sorry. I didn't even think. What the hell is wrong with me?"

Her brow furrowed, and he wished he could kick himself in the balls. *Idiot.*

"But you're okay, right? You're clean?"

"Yes. God, yes. Of course." He ran his hand over his scalp, still cursing his own stupidity. "I swear."

"I believe you." She brushed her thumb over his lower lip. "You have such a fabulous mouth. You know that, right?"

He caught her hand, then kissed the pad of her thumb. "I'm glad you believe me, but it was still unprotected sex."

"It's okay. I promise. I'm clean, too. Tested and everything." Her voice sliced the air. "And if it's pregnancy you're worried about, well, that won't be a problem either."

"Xena..." He wanted to ask about the knife edge in her tone, but something stopped him. That wasn't a question for now. Not when he was still inhaling her scent and she was still naked in his lap.

She blinked at him, obviously waiting for him to continue.

"Get dressed," he said gently. "We need to find someplace safe for the night. And then tomorrow, we're heading for LA."

CHAPTER TEN

B y the time they left the park, found a crappy motel, and checked in, it was past four in the morning and they had officially crossed the line into a Very Long Day.

Even so, Liam was still wired when he slipped the key into the scuffed lock and pushed open the dingy gray door. The faint scent of mildew lingered under the stronger odor of bleach. He grimaced, but even the tacky room and the unappealing smell couldn't shake the happy out of him. Maybe it was a mistake and maybe it wasn't, but right then, Liam wouldn't have traded the last hour for anything.

The attack before, sure. That he could have lived without. But to hold Xena's naked body in his arms—to feel her shatter around him as her orgasm exploded through her—Christ, he wouldn't trade that memory or that moment for anything. And all he wished right then was that they could have gone to the fucking Ritz instead of the Inland Motor Inn, the sign for which must have been designed in the fifties. And from what he saw as he stepped into the room, neither the furniture nor the carpet had been changed since then.

He said a silent prayer that someone had washed the sheets.

"Welcome to our suite," he said, holding the door open so she could enter.

He saw her nose wrinkle, but when she looked at him, she was smiling. "It's perfect."

"Our definitions of perfect are wildly disparate. But it'll do."

"We paid cash, there's a bed, and there's a door in front of the toilet. Trust me when I say I've seen worse. Much worse."

"Then I pity you," he quipped, then immediately regretted the words. He knew she'd been a runaway. Undoubtedly she really had slept in much worse conditions than this.

"Sorry," he said, but she just laughed.

"It's okay." She took his hand and pulled him the rest of the way in so the door swung shut behind them. She stumbled a little as she headed to the queen size bed.

He lingered to flip the bolt and add the chain, then unholstered his Glock and put it on the bedside table. He placed her Ruger there, too; he'd put it in the bike's storage compartment after they'd bolted from the house, then retrieved it when they'd arrived here.

"Sleep," he ordered. "You're dead on your feet."

She was sitting on the edge of the bed, and now she yawned, as if his words had given her permission. With drooping eyes, she started to wriggle out of her yoga pants, then stopped. "Oh. Sorry. I usually don't sleep in my clothes."

He chuckled. "Fine by me, but don't expect me to keep my hands to myself."

She met his eyes, hers bloodshot with heavy lids, but the corner of her mouth curved up and she held his gaze as she pulled off the pants, then the tank. Then she held them out to him. "I was going to drop them on the floor, but..." She trailed off, her nose wrinkling with disgust as she looked down at the stained carpet.

He nodded. "Right," he said, then laid her clothes over the back of a chair. By the time he turned to face her again, she was under the covers, her eyes were closed, and her breathing was slow and even. She was either asleep or doing a damn good job of faking it.

He took off his jacket and shirt, then followed with his jeans, leaving only his boxer briefs on. He considered adding them to the chair's decoration, but there was only one bed, and it was going to be hard enough to let her sleep peacefully, even as tired as he was. Because the truth was, their wild coupling in the park had been running in a continuous loop through his mind.

He slid carefully into the bed, his eyes never leaving her. She'd been incredible. Hot. Dangerous. *Fabulous.* And, yes, he wanted more. He wanted to push her to the limit, to go wild with her. He wanted to take control and see all that heat and sensuality bound up in a beautiful package for him. To immerse her in inescapable pleasure even while he pushed himself to his own limits, crossing lines he hadn't stepped over in years.

He'd take her—them both—to the edge. And only when he was certain that she couldn't stand it any longer, would he let the full force of passion consume her, as pure, undiluted pleasure exploded inside her.

Slowly, he brushed his fingertips over her skin, so pale she looked like a doll asleep beside him. He couldn't remember the last time he'd wanted a woman so much...or met a woman who matched him so well. And he wondered if maybe—just maybe—this woman might—

He slammed a door on those thoughts as he felt the tightening in his chest. A low burn of anger and self-loathing. Fear, too, which was ironic considering everything he'd faced in his life. But it was real. And it was inescapable.

With a sigh, he rolled to his back, his head on

the pillow as he stared up at the ceiling. He was so damn tired, and he was letting his mind go into forbidden corners. He needed to stay on course. He had a job to do, after all, and sex really wasn't part of it.

His phone was on the table beside his gun, and he reached for it, needing to do one last thing before he could finally sleep. The text to Ella was short: He'd reached Xena, and Ella should call when she got the message. Considering it wasn't yet dawn, he figured he'd get at least an hour of sleep before she replied.

To his surprise, the phone buzzed immediately in his hands.

He stood up, taking the call with a soft, "Ella. I wasn't expecting to hear back so soon."

"I do yoga and meditate before dawn. It's the only time I have. I'd hoped to hear from you last night. You found the cabin okay?"

"Xena and I are safe," he said, to which she replied, "Oh, fuck."

He almost laughed. He'd known from the minute he met her that she was a sharp woman.

"What happened?"

"We had visitors. Not long after I arrived." He gave her the quick version, ending with the motel and skipping the park.

"They followed you." The accusation was clear in her voice.

"I don't think so.

"Xena, then?"

Since he didn't have an answer, he said nothing.

"But you're okay now? They didn't follow you to the motel?"

"No." That much, he was certain of.

"Okay. Good. *Shit*."

He let her get it out of her system. After a moment, he heard her take a breath. "How's my cabin?"

"I'm going to guess they searched the interior. And you need to send your caretaker—with the cops, just in case, though I doubt they're still around. The bathroom wall is wide open."

"Right. Okay." He gave her props for not asking for more details.

"Do you have front porch cams?"

"Do I—what?"

"Remote security cameras. Sometimes mounted in the doorbell?"

"Oh, yes. Both doors."

"Ella, you just made my morning." He was about to ask her to send him the access information when she texted that exact thing. "You're fabulous. I'll get this to Mario. With any luck, he can pull both faces off those feeds. The image from the fitness center doesn't seem too promising."

"How's Xena doing? Can I talk to her? She must be so scared."

"She's sleeping right now. I'd rather not wake her."

"Oh, God no. She's had a hell of an ordeal." A thickness had entered her voice, and he realized that she'd started to cry. "Do you know what she told me before she left? That she hated being a thorn in my side. That girl has worked for me for over four years now. She's become one of my closest friends. How can she not know that?"

"I think she does. I think that's why it bothers her so much that you're involved in all this."

"I don't even know what all this is. Not really. All this time ... why would her past come back to haunt her after so many years?"

"I don't know either," he said, though he had some ideas. At the core, there had to be something very, very bad. Murder, maybe. Or worse. Because otherwise, Tweedledee and Tweedledum would have stayed hidden. The only reason to come out of the woodwork was if it was very, very important to them that Xena could never, ever cause any trouble.

He glanced at the sleeping woman and sighed. He knew Xena wasn't going to want to talk about it. He also knew that she had to.

"I'm worried about you, too," he told Ella, returning his exhausted mind to the call. "They have their eye on you. And they knew about the cabin. Possibly they followed Xena, but she told me how she covered her tracks, and it was solid."

"Fuck."

"Most likely, nothing will happen. But they know she was your assistant, and once they learn how long she's been with you, they may assume you know where she is."

"Right." She exhaled loudly. "Okay, so what—"

"I'm sending someone. You're probably in the clear, but I don't want to take chances. I'll text his name and information as soon as I confirm he's available." Any of the team at the SSA could do the job, but he wanted Winston Starr. The former West Texas sheriff had an easy manner and serious skills. The best thing about him was that no one ever saw Winston coming.

As soon as he ended the call with Ella, he dialed his friend.

"Do you know what time it is?"

Liam scoffed. "I know you're up. Don't cowboys always rise before the sun?"

"I'd try to find a snappy comeback," Winston drawled, his Texas twang more pronounced than usual. "But you're not worth the effort."

"I didn't really wake you, did I?"

"Hell, no. I'm at the gym. But I haven't had my coffee yet, so I'm in a mood. What do you need?"

"How does an all expense paid trip to Vegas sound?"

"Hong Kong, DC, now Vegas." He chuckled. "When Stark and Ryan convinced me to take this job, I didn't realize I'd be getting so many frequent flier miles, too."

"Got you out of West Texas, didn't it?"

"I got myself out of West Texas, my friend. And as for Vegas, why the hell not?"

They quickly worked through the details, then added Ryan Hunter to the call. As the head of Stark Security, he needed to both be in the loop and sign off on the plan.

Ryan answered on the first ring, wide awake. "Christ," Liam said. "Do none of you sleep?"

"Didn't realize you were such a slacker, Foster."

"I need my beauty rest," Liam quipped, before explaining the situation. Ryan approved, and Winston promised to leave within the hour and text Liam as soon as he was settled with Ella.

"Until we wrap this, I'd like to keep someone on her twenty-four/seven," Liam added, knowing full well what he was asking. The SSA was still a relatively new operation, and the mission statement didn't focus on bodyguard services. Even if it did, the agency simply didn't have the manpower yet, particularly because Ryan and Stark were very selective in who they brought onto the team.

"Pull who you need from the Starfire's security team," Ryan instructed Winston. "And if we hit a snag, we'll figure it out. You coming in today?" The last question was directed at Liam.

"Yeah. We're holed up at the moment. We need to get some sleep, then we'll head back to LA. I'd like the whole team available. Say one o'clock? And I've already got a project for Mario. I'll ping him next and get him working his magic."

Once the call ended, he shot Mario the details of the assignment and the log-on for the cameras, figuring he'd call the kid when he woke up if he didn't find a reply waiting on his phone. Might as well let at least one person sleep until morning.

The kid pinged him back in less than a minute. *On it.*

Liam just shook his head, then laid back and closed his eyes, only to open them moments later when the smell of coffee roused him.

Except it wasn't mere moments later. He'd gone to sleep in the dark, and now light was streaming in through the gap in the cheap, ugly curtains. The aroma was coming from a white paper cup, being held by the beautiful—and once again clothed—woman sitting on the edge of the bed and smiling at him.

"Tell me you didn't walk down to the office."

"Crappy coffee maker. I found it under the bathroom sink."

He pushed himself up and took the cup she offered. She was right; it was crappy coffee. But it was hot and it was caffeinated, and that made it perfect. "What time is it?"

"Just past eight."

He frowned. "We should get going. All the way to LA riding tandem on the Ducati..." He shook his head. "You're going to want a few breaks."

"I'll be fine," she assured him, then looked down at her hands, which were twisting in her lap. "Listen, I'm sorry about jumping you last night."

"Are you? I'm not." The moment the words were out of his mouth he regretted them, fearing that was exactly what she didn't want to hear.

But then he saw the tension leave her shoulders, and heard her soft, breathy, "Oh, thank God," and an unexpected but not unwelcome flood of relief flowed over him, too.

He took her hand in his. "And just so you know, you're stuck with me now. It's an old security agent code. Once a woman jumps you, you're bound to protect her."

"I'm pretty sure that's not a thing."

"It's my thing." He stood up, still holding the half-finished coffee. "Susan," he said, intentionally using her given name to underscore his words, "those men are dangerous, and they're not going to stop. I'm going to help you no matter what. It will be easier if you simply tell me what's going on. The full story. But even if you don't say a word, one way or another, I'll figure it out."

He used the tip of his forefinger to tilt her chin up, then waited until she'd met his eyes. "You're more than just my mission now, and I will keep you safe."

Her lips twitched as if she was fighting a smile. "This time it's personal?"

He held her gaze. "Yes." The word was flat, even, and very true.

She looked away before she reached for his coffee and took a sip. It was an oddly intimate moment, and he couldn't deny that he liked it.

She glanced down at the cup, then handed it back to him with an embarrassed smile. She was still seated on the edge of the bed, and now she put her hands on her knees, her eyes on the floor.

"I don't want to tell you. I haven't even told Ella. Not all of it, anyway."

"Maybe it's time."

"Yeah. Maybe it is."

Her shoulders rose and fell as she drew in two deep breaths. Then she sat up straight, faced him dead on, and said, "First of all, my name isn't Susan."

CHAPTER ELEVEN

I don't want to tell him this. I don't want to think about it. I don't want to let any of it into my head.

Except it's never really left my head. I'm twenty-eight years old, and I've been carrying a nightmare around with me for eleven long years. I may have escaped the house of horror I'd been locked in for what felt like a lifetime, but I never escaped the memories.

To his credit, Liam hasn't said a word in response to my revelation that I'm not the woman he thought I was. He's giving me time, which I guess proves what a mess I am if it's that obvious I need a moment to pull my shit together and figure out how the hell I can tell him my story without making it sound like I'm looking for a career writing telenovellas.

Finally, I get into bed, my back against the wall, my knees up, and the covers over me. He hesitates, then sits at the foot of the bed, watching me warily.

"My name's Jenny. Jenny Smith. Seriously," I add, when his brow twitches. "Boring name, and it used to fit my pretty boring life."

"I find it hard to believe you were ever boring," he says, and I roll my eyes.

"I'm from Missouri. My dad had a high school education and managed a convenience store. My mom worked part-time at a day care center. I made average grades, was horribly shy, and dreamt about blossoming one day and becoming a famous actress." I let my shoulders rise and fall. "Like I said, boring."

"I don't know," Liam says. "Sounds normal. And that's not the same thing."

"Maybe, but I spent a lot of time fantasizing about escaping and being discovered. I skipped over the whole auditioning and performing part in those fantasies, of course. But that's the point of fantasies." I shake my head. "God, I was so naive."

"What changed?"

"Everything," I say, then wave away my words. "Sorry. That's actually true, but I'll talk you through it." I don't want to. I don't want to share my humiliation with him, not to mention my fear. But I know he's right. If he's going to help me, he needs to know everything. And the bottom line is that I do want his help.

If it weren't for the attack on Ella in Vegas and us in the cabin, maybe I wouldn't. Maybe I would have been happy to stick with the status quo, living in semi-hiding by riding on Ella's coattails.

I don't know. But now that things have changed, I don't want to go back. I want to get free.

But what scares me the most is that my newfound resolve isn't just because I want to escape the ever-looming threat. It's because of the man. He's given me hope. A glimpse at a real life. I don't mean with him—I won't allow myself to think that boldly—but a future. A real one in the real world, and hopefully I'll find someone to share it with.

"Did I lose you?"

His gentle words pull me back to the moment. "Yeah. Sorry. My mind started wandering."

"You were boring," he says, both prompting me and making me laugh.

"You make fun, but it's true." I draw a breath. "Anyway, when I was a junior, my mom died. Cancer. She'd been feeling bad for a while, but blew it off, thinking she was just tired. By the time she went to the doctor there wasn't anything he could do."

I close my eyes, fighting back my tears. "That was the one part of my life that wasn't boring," I whisper, then look at him. "My parents were great. They loved me and I loved them, and we all actually liked each other, too. And my mom and dad? God, they were so in love it was disgusting. Major PDA, you know. I used to think it was cringeworthy, but now…"

"Your father must have been a wreck," Liam says gently.

"Understatement." I wipe my runny nose. "That was the beginning of it all, not that me or Daddy knew it at the time. But looking back—I can't even mourn my mom's death without mourning my own life, too. Because burying her set everything in motion."

"How?"

"Daddy spiraled down. I mean, he really went off the rails. I was just starting to think about college. I would have been the first in my family to go. And then one day my dad came home and said that he'd sent in my picture to some modeling agency. He said he knew it wasn't the same as acting, but maybe it was a start."

I look at Liam, expecting him to say something, but he's silent, so I press on, wishing that he'd derailed me.

"He told me that the agency wanted to meet me in person. In New York. He seemed so excited, and I was, too. I mean, *me*. Shy Jenny Smith who was halfway invisible in school."

"It's not unreasonable," Liam says. "You're both stunning and unique, and you definitely have the build and height of a runway model."

"All of which I told myself on the days when I feared that the whole trip would be a waste of time. But they actually paid for the plane ticket. The agency, I mean. And the hotel. And when we got to the office, there were all these posters of models and framed pages from advertisements and it was all so very, very legitimate."

"Except it wasn't."

I lick my suddenly dry lips and hug my knees tighter to my chest. "No." I open my mouth to speak, and then close it again. "I'm sorry," I finally whisper. "It's just that it was—"

"Sex trafficking," he says, and my entire body sags with relief that I don't have to say it out loud or explain or any of that.

"I'm sorry to say I have some knowledge of that," he continues. "I mentioned Dallas and Jane before? Well, their kidnapping wasn't part of a sex trafficking ring, but Dallas started an organization. More of a vigilante group. Deliverance. And part of its mission was to rescue victims of kidnapping, trafficking, anything of that sort."

"You were part of that?"

"I was. I'd still be except that Deliverance doesn't exist as such anymore."

"So you ended up at the SSA?"

"That's about the extent of it. And you? How did you survive?"

I swallow, not wanting to go back to the topic, but knowing I have to. And the small diversion has calmed me down, so that it's easier to talk about.

"They told my dad I had talent and that they were certain I'd be a star. They had an apartment building for their candidates and told him that the board had decided to grant me a scholarship to train as a model—most girls had to pay they said."

"Your father believed them."

"I never blamed him for that. I thought so, too. They were very convincing. And me and my dad were pretty naive." I suck in air. "Right, well, anyway. My dad left that first night and said he'd be back. But he wasn't. And after a while—it was really subtle—they started to suggest that he'd left me there because he didn't love me and didn't want me around after Mom died. And then..."

I pause because I have to swallow, and I realize I'm crying. "They got me hooked on drugs. Pills they forced us to take to get our food. Supposedly appetite suppressants so that we could get model fit, but that was bullshit. And then suddenly my photo shoots were nudes. And my head was swimming all the time. And there were parties and these men, and they'd choose me and touch me and—well, they did things to me."

"You don't have to—"

"Yes. I do. They made me have sex to survive. I had no control over anything. My life. My clothes. Sex. Anything. They'd tie me up and let men use me. Sometimes one. Sometimes many. Sometimes for days on end. Sometime the men would be gentle, but not usually. I was a fucking sex slave, and they were in charge of everything, even down to tying my tubes—I told you I wouldn't get pregnant—and doing that laser hair removal thing on me so they didn't have to worry about getting me waxed. Fuckers."

I've been mostly talking to my knees, but now I look at his face. It's tight; I can see the anger and tension. And a single muscle in his cheek twitches. The sight warms me, because he cares. He genuinely cares, and I blink again, staving off more tears.

"Anyway," I continue. "I tried to escape. We were right in the middle of Manhattan, but I might as well have been on the moon. It was a nightmare. I was high all the time. Or drunk. And I hated it but I was so miserable and lonely that high was better than living in the real world. Especially since they kept telling me that my father left me there because he didn't want to deal with me after my mother died, and if I just made the investors happy my life would change."

"You believed them."

"Not at first. But more and more I started to

think it had to be true. And then—oh, God—after about a year they brought me into a room and my dad was there. And he saw me and started crying. He apologized for not knowing what they would do to me. He told me he'd tried and tried to get me out, but they were powerful and he kept hitting walls, and then they grabbed him. He'd been locked up in the same building as me for almost three months, and I didn't even know."

"Jenny..."

"*No*. Please. Xena. Jenny was a fool. A stupid little girl." I look at him defiantly. "I'm Xena now. I'm a goddamn warrior."

"Damn right you are." He takes my hand, then gently squeezes it. "Tell me what happened."

"They told me I was never getting out, and that neither was my father. And then—and then they shot him." I gasp as that horrible memory cuts through me. "And then they brought another girl in. I had no idea why. I was still in shock. And they told me that she wanted out, too. And they shot her as well. I just stood there, completely numb. I didn't do a damn thing."

Tears streak down my cheeks, but I don't wipe them away. "And then the head guy, he looks at me and he says, "How about you, Jenny? Do you want out, too?"

I force myself to look at Liam then, and I'm so goddamned ashamed. "I couldn't say yes. They gave me an out, but I couldn't say yes. I chose the pain and the degradation and living like that because I couldn't—"

"You chose life." His voice is gentle, and his eyes glisten. "And you were right. Because you did get away."

"I did," I agree. "I figured out ways not to take the pills. To not drink at the parties. I hadn't made enough of an effort before because I didn't care. My dad had thrown me away, after all. But when I learned the truth ... well, I didn't want to be numb anymore."

"You got clean?"

"Not completely when I was in there, but mostly. But after I got out, yeah. I got help in California. Counseling for all the—well, everything. And I started going to AA." My heart is pounding and I'm breathing hard. "I've been clean for years now—no alcohol, no drugs, because they fucking got me addicted and now I can't even enjoy a glass of wine without risking sliding back. I don't think I would—I really don't—but I'm damn sure not going to take the risk. But those assholes had no qualms about stealing every bit of control from me."

"But you did get away. How? For that matter, when?"

"A few days after I turned twenty-one."

His eyes widen. "They had you for four years?"

"Just about. Later, they moved me to a country

estate where they held these elaborate sex parties. It was all very surreal."

"How did you get away?"

"I pretended to be docile. And I pretended to be high. They pay less attention to the older girls. We're pretty beaten by then. And so one night I was supposed to entertain this old prick who wanted to walk the grounds. He—well, let's just say he was very nature-oriented. And we were deep in the woods and he had me bent over, and there was a rock, and—" I shrug.

"Christ. Good for you."

I exhale, only then realizing I was afraid he'd chastise me for banging the fucker over the head with a rock.

"I didn't kill him, but he was out cold when I ran. I took his jacket, and my dress was short. So I was mostly invisible in the dark woods. And I worked my way around the house to the side lot where the valets parked the guests' cars. I found an unlocked SUV, got into the back, and waited, terrified someone would find my guy or realize I was gone. But it worked out. The SUV's owner came out with one of the few female guests at these things, and they drove off. Neither of them looked in the back, and she spent the entire drive to Manhattan giving him blowjobs."

"You're pretty damn lucky."

"Don't I know it. It was a huge risk, and I was

sure I was done for, but I was desperate, and they didn't catch me, and I ended up in a car park in Manhattan, and suddenly I was free."

Even now, that sounds amazing to say, despite the fact that I was beyond terrified for months after that. Liam asks me how I survived, and I tell him I stole a woman's wallet—something I'm still ashamed of—and she had over five hundred in cash and an ID that was passable enough for me to use. I bought sweats and a T-shirt from a place that was open in Times Square, and hair dye from a Duane Reade. Then I got on a train and went to Pennsylvania. And from there I hitchhiked to Los Angeles.

"And Ella doesn't know any of that?"

I shake my head. "As far as she's concerned, I was a runaway turning tricks in Hollywood. And that's not really a lie, either. I did run away. And I did turn tricks."

"And you survived." He cups my face, then kisses me gently. "Baby, you are an amazing woman."

"No, I'm not. But I guess I am a survivor."

He strokes my hair, my shoulder. It feels nice, as if he's trying to reassure himself that I'm here and I'm whole. As if my story has broken him a little, too.

He asks me questions about the sex scheme. The names of the men, the location of the buildings. I tell him what I can, and he seems to absorb it all.

"But now they've found me," I say with a shrug. "I guess I always knew they would."

"It's good that they did," he says firmly. "Because now we can take them out, and you won't have to worry about them anymore."

"I'm scared." My words are a whisper, and I feel weak even saying them.

"I don't blame you," he says. "But I'm with you now. And just remember what you already told me. You, Xena, are a survivor."

CHAPTER TWELVE

A survivor.

"I am," I say. "But that doesn't mean I want to be. I thought I was past it when I was with Ella. But then one stupid picture, and every horrible thing I did to survive suddenly means nothing anymore."

"It means everything," he says. "Because you did survive. And you have those skills—that grit—to keep you going now."

I screw up my mouth and shrug. "Sometimes it all feels so futile. And random." I reach for the cup and the dregs of cold coffee, but he takes it from my hand with a shake of his head.

"Random how?" he asks, as he goes to the bathroom and fills the coffee maker.

"Do you know how I became Susie Morgan?"

He looks at me over his shoulder. "I've seen

some of the world you lived in, Xena. So yeah, I can probably guess."

"Try." I hear the challenge in my voice, because there is no way he'll guess the depths of my shame.

"She was a hooker," he says. "Parents dead. Ran away from foster care. Ended up turning tricks in the City of Angels. Not an uncommon story, really."

My mouth is dry. He's dead on point.

"How am I doing so far?"

"You cheated."

"Rye told me some—he checked you out years ago. I did a bit more on my way to the cabin. Or I had my team do it. Of course, those are the dry facts. For the rest, I'll have to be a little more creative."

"All right. Go on."

"You met her in LA, somewhere near Hollywood Boulevard. Maybe at a diner. A laundromat. She may have even been the girl who showed you the ropes. Who taught you how to survive without a pimp, because after what you went through, you wouldn't have gone that route."

"No." My voice is thin. "I definitely wouldn't."

He brings me the cup of coffee, and I blow on it before taking a tiny sip.

"I can't guess what happened, but somehow she died. And you assumed her identity, because you needed a clean slate, and you knew she would have wanted to help you."

My eyes are welling up again, but I nod. "She was a user. It was the one thing we fought about. And she got in deep with a dealer—owed him a lot of money. He decided to make an example of her."

"The cops never ID'd her?"

"As far as I know, her body was never found. I got one of those concrete garden marker kits and made one in her honor. Then I buried this goofy stuffed cat she loved and her lucky rabbit's tail." I look at him defiantly. "But I kept her life. She would have wanted me to."

"No argument from me. Did you keep turning tricks?"

I nod. "I didn't like it, but it was like being the CEO of my own business compared to the life I had before. But I also enrolled in school, because I wasn't going to turn tricks forever. I'd have to lay low no matter what job I got—I knew that. But I also knew that if I couldn't have a family, then I at least needed a job where I didn't have to sell myself."

I wait for him to ask why I had to be alone, but instead he tells me the reason.

"Because they'd never stop looking for you. Because your past—your life—could put them at risk."

"Yes," I whisper, hating that basic truth. "No

way would I—" My voice breaks, and I force myself to go on. "I saw my father murdered in front of me. And I knew they'd do the same thing to anyone else I cared about. If they found me—*when* they found me—they'd kill everyone I loved in front of me."

I take a deep breath, certain he's going to try to placate me. Tell me that I shouldn't distance myself or that love is worth the risk or some such bullshit.

He looks right at me, but I don't think he sees me at all. And he whispers, "You're right."

The words linger between us, dark and horrible. I fight the urge to ask what's in his head, because I'm certain it's more than just me and my problems. He's seen tragedy, too, and in that moment, I want to hold him. To share what little strength I have. Right then, I think he needs it.

But then he stands, his hands in his pockets, as he goes and looks out that small slit in the curtains. "So you went to school."

I hesitate, wondering if I should push, but I don't. It's not my place, and what would be the point? This man is here to protect me because Ella wants him to. And I want it, too. I want him and his friends and the fucking National Guard if he can arrange it to be on my side. I want him to find out who's after me and I want him to make them go away.

And then I want to disappear again and hope for a few calm years before someone else from my horrific past surfaces again. In my dreams, yes, I might want Liam to disappear with me. But I learned a long time ago that storybooks lie, and dreams don't really come true.

He turns to me. "Xena?"

"School. Right, yes." I clear my throat, trying to remember what I was saying. "So, yeah. I had to take the GED, but it wasn't a big deal. I started taking business classes at a community college during the day and turning tricks at night. And I kept going to my AA and NA meetings, and I kept seeing my counselor every week." I meet his eyes dead on. "You might say I had a few issues."

"I'm shocked," he says, making me laugh.

"Yeah, well, I was determined to get it behind me and make something of myself. Make my dad proud, you know?"

"I guess you did. You ended up with a great job working with Ella."

"Oh, man. That was a freaky day. It was my twenty-fourth birthday, and I'd been beat up by a John the night before, so I had this nasty bruise on my cheek."

I point, as if it's still red and swollen. Sometimes I think it should be, the fucker hit me so hard.

"I was in a pissy mood because I'd gotten a shit score on a paper I'd turned in about services for the homeless, and the professor had the audacity to say that I hadn't put in enough research and—" I make a slashing motion with my hand and rein myself in.

"Anyway," I continue, "the point is that I was a mess. But I went to the interview anyway. I figured it was good practice, but I was certain I wouldn't get the job. I'd had no idea who she was when I applied, but after I got the interview, I learned she was this rising pop singer. Nowhere close to where she is now, but she was getting radio play and, well, I figured there was no way in hell she'd hire me."

"But you went anyway."

"Like I said, practice. And, I don't know. I just felt like going."

He grins as he comes to sit on the bed again, only closer this time. "The universe was starting to shift in your favor."

"Maybe so. Anyway, I go in, and she immediately asks about my cheek. I wasn't sure what to say, so I just sort of evaded. Then she asked about school, and since I was steamed about the paper, I told her. She asked me about my research and I went off on her completely."

"She was a stand-in for your professor."

"Big time. I told her I worked on the street and knew what I was talking about, and that I interacted with the homeless daily, and that I'd been homeless for two months when I first moved there, and that if she really wanted to know, my cheek got busted when a John decided to demonstrate his right hook."

"So what happened?"

"She asked me when I could start." I laugh. "At first I thought she wanted to sleep with me—I knew from my research that she'd had girlfriends."

"But nothing there?"

I shake my head, glance at him, then look down at my knees. "Nothing. I like men, even though I haven't slept with that many who, you know, I actually wanted to be with. You're kind of a notable exception."

He reaches out, his hand resting on my covered foot. "I'm flattered."

I look up, then get a little lost in his eyes. In the strength I see there, and the compassion. I'm spilling all this shit onto him, and I don't see anything reflected back at me that makes me want to curl into myself. I'm the same person to him I was yesterday and the day before. And right then, I really want to kiss him.

"Thank you," I whisper.

"For what?"

I try to wrap my thoughts into words. "For everything I guess. For protecting me. For the way you've touched me." I glance down, no longer meeting his eyes. "For not asking me if I've been tested now that you know my history. I have, you know. Lots." I draw a breath, and look up to see his eyes on me, soft with compassion ... and something more, too. "Anyway, thanks for being a really great guy."

"My pleasure." He smiles as he says it, but his words are underscored with just a tiny bit of heat. Or maybe I'm just hopeful. Or stupid. Because I like this man more than I should. And I want him more than is safe.

He's had it rough, too, I think. More than suffering through a friend's kidnapping and surviving combat. But I don't want to ask. I'm melancholy enough simply from going over my own dark past.

"You and Ella went from employer/employee to genuine friends," he says, and I'm both grateful and frustrated that he hasn't been reading my mind. Because I'm suddenly very aware of the pressure of his hand on my foot. And the fact that he's so close to me on the bed.

I shouldn't feel this way—I know that. And yet I want. I just *want*.

I bite my lower lip, then barrel forward. "You're kind of like Ella."

"It's the hair, isn't it?"

I narrow my eyes, but otherwise ignore the quip. "I just mean that you're the kind of guy that usually scares me."

"Usually?"

I silently curse as he takes his hand off my foot,

then smile with relief as he slides a bit closer before reaching over to take my hand, making my pulse kick up its tempo. I like this feeling. This will-we or won't-we. I haven't done this much—the real thing between men and women. I'm not an expert in reading clues or flirting. When a man is forcing or paying, there's really no need for subtlety.

Most of the time I'm terrified of my own emotions. But right now, I want this. Whatever the hell *this* is.

He holds my hand lightly, his fingertips moving over my skin. "Usually," he repeats thoughtfully. "So are you saying I don't scare you?"

I swallow. "If you were paying attention last night, you should know that you don't."

"I'm glad."

I look down at our joined hands. "I'll admit to a bit of nervousness."

His eyes meet mine. "What do you have to be nervous about?"

Everything.

"The fact that you don't scare me." I hear the breathiness in my voice. "That's kind of terrifying."

He tilts his head, but doesn't say anything.

"Don't take this the wrong way, but I want more than to not be scared. I want to trust you, too."

"And you don't?" I can't read anything in his face or his tone. I don't know if I've amused him or offended him, but I rush to reassure and explain anyway.

"On some level, I do. I mean, I'm here with you and my life is in your hands. But that's not really trust."

"Isn't it?"

Once again, I try to read his face, but fail. "No," I confirm. "It's just pragmatism. I don't think I'll ever really trust anyone again. I've gone too long looking over my shoulder."

"And yet there's Ella."

I look at him, and wonder if it's hope that I'm hearing in his voice. Or if that emotion belongs entirely to me.

"Yes," I say. "There's Ella."

"But she's a woman. I'm not a woman, Xena."

"No, you definitely aren't."

"And I would never, ever hurt you."

"I believe you."

He reaches out, then strokes my cheek before sliding his fingers into my hair. "So soft," he murmurs, then brushes my lower lip with his fingertip. "So beautiful."

"Liam," I whisper.

"You don't trust me, but you want me."

"Yes," I say.

"Why?"

"Because you make me feel safe, and I don't mean from whoever is chasing me. I mean in here,"

I explain, pressing a hand to my heart. "Safe to be me and not what they wanted me to be."

His brow furrows, his expression growing dark.

"I'm sorry," I say quickly. "I don't want to burden you or make you think you're part of a therapy session. Last night was a frenzy, but right now is desire." My words are tumbling out, and I'm not even sure if I'm making sense. "I just want you, Liam. Right now, I think I need you." I lick my lips. "Don't you want me, too?"

He makes a soft scoffing noise. "How can you even ask that? Of course I want you. But I can't have you," he adds as he runs his fingers through my hair. "Not the way I want."

"Sure, you can," I say. "Of course you can."

But he just shakes his head, and it's like a fist squeezing my heart because I'm certain he's saying no. Then he whispers, "You break down all my defenses."

"That's good," I say.

He shakes his head. "No. It isn't."

I sag with disappointment, but before I can argue or ask him to explain, he cups my head, tugs me toward him, and kisses me.

I melt into it, the bed covers dropping as I shift onto my knees and scoot closer toward him.

"No," he says, then eases me back so that I'm flat on the mattress, my body dwarfed beneath his. "Like this."

I melt into the kiss, his lips on mine, his hands roaming over my tank, then easing under the hem as he gently pulls it off me. He tosses it on the chair by the window then closes his mouth on my breast, his tongue doing incredible things to my nipple.

I arch up, wanting more. Expecting the same wicked wildness from last night. A raw, primal passion that I can lose myself in.

But this touch isn't wild. It's contained—as if he's holding back. His touch feels so damn good, but I crave more, and I want to pound on him to let go. To ravage me. To *take* me. To let me feel whatever passion he feels. To be real, because I've never actually had real before.

I want all that, and yet those thoughts and demands fade against the sweetness of his touch. As his teeth lightly graze my nipple. As his hands trace down my belly, then gently tug my yoga pants off and send them flying toward my top.

"Your turn," I murmur, and he nods as I start to tug at his clothes until he's as naked as I am. "Better," I say, sliding my hand down to find his cock, only to be stymied when he gently pulls it away.

"Put your hands on my back," he says, and I do, relishing the sensations of his muscles moving beneath my touch as he kisses his way down my body, using his own hands to spread my legs even wider as the tip of his tongue finds my clit.

I moan and arch up, trying to wiggle my hips,

but he has me held firmly in place, and all I can do is surrender to the glorious sensation. I move one hand from his shoulder to his head, then press him harder against me. I'm rewarded when he shifts from the tiny, teasing movements of his tongue, to laving me completely as his fingers slide inside me, and my hips rock of their own accord in a primal effort to bring this man further and further inside me.

"Yes, yes." The word seems to fill the room, and it takes a second before I realize it's me.

He slides up me again, capturing my mouth as he enters me. It's sweet and gentle and so unexpected. So different from everything I've known. And as he moves inside me, I feel the growing pressure of a coming climax. The tingling on my inner thighs. The tightening of my belly. He murmurs gentle sounds, and I cling to them like a ladder, climbing higher and higher until I'm at the top and have no choice but to fall off and shatter into a million pieces as I break through the blanket of stars below me.

I tremble in his arms, warm and content. Last night in the park had been a wonderful, insane treasure. A celebration of being alive. A testament to my freedom, because God knows I'd never been able to take control like that before.

But this ... for the first time in my life I feel cherished. Adored. Respected.

It's not everything I need in bed—I know that. But what I crave is something I shouldn't want. Something that scares me and makes me fear that I'll never truly get past what happened to me.

I roll over and stroke his face, rough with beard stubble, then trace his lips, soft and swollen from my kisses.

"Thank you," I say, and I sigh as a tiny bit of hope creeps into me. This man is a miracle, and I've never been a woman who believes in miracles.

CHAPTER THIRTEEN

"This bathroom is freaking amazing," Xena said, her voice drifting to Liam from behind the closed door.

He grinned; that was a guest's typical reaction to his master bath, a room that always made him smile. "You've met the fish."

The door opened, and she stood there in a pair of Universal Studios Hollywood sweat pants and a souvenir Santa Monica T-shirt, her freshly washed hair hanging in damp waves around her face. "Fish?" She cocked her head and crossed her arms. "What fish?"

"Funny. I've invited a comedian into my home for a shower and some lunch. What was I thinking?" They'd arrived back in town with time to spare before the meeting at the SSA, and so Liam had brought her to Malibu for food, fresh clothes, and a change of transportation. As much as he loved his bike, he'd happily switch to a car for the rest of the day.

"If that was your idea of humor, I feel very sorry for you." She smiled, and he smiled back, unable to resist the bubble of joy that rose inside him simply from the sight of her looking so comfortable and relaxed.

"Seriously," she continued. "That aquarium is amazing. All those incredible colored fish. And all these plants, too."

"I travel too much to have a dog or a cat, but I like the feeling of having life in the house. It reminds me of home." Though the public areas of the Sykes mansion had regular deliveries of flowers and plants from a local nursery, the wing that he shared with his mother had been filled solely with the flowers and greenery that she tended. He'd missed the scent of the dirt, the coolness of the leaves, and the varied colors of the flowers during his time in the Middle East. And during his years traveling for the department store and Deliverance, he'd only managed to keep a cactus and an aloe vera plant growing in his window.

When he'd started working for the SSA and moved into the condo, he'd made sure that the massive remodel included sufficient windows to provide light for the interior plants. And he'd put enough greenery on the balcony to rival a rain forest.

"Have you named them?"

"The plants?"

"Now you're just messing with me. The fish. Because in case you hadn't noticed, they take up an entire wall in that bathroom."

"Yeah. I'm aware."

"And the shower is glass."

"I'm also clued in to that." He had to fight a smile.

"I just feel that since every one of those fish was checking me out, we're kind of intimate now. I should probably know their names."

"I'll get right on that. In the meantime," he said, moving to stand in front of her and sliding an arm around her waist, "let's just call them what they are —some very lucky fish."

"That's true," she said. "After all, you shower in there almost every day."

"Sometimes twice a day. It's my favorite room. That and the patio," he added, hooking his thumb over his shoulder to indicate the glass doors that led to the balcony—and the stunning view of the Pacific.

"Oh, really?" Her voice rose with a tease. "Not the bedroom?"

"To be honest, the bedroom's not used for much more than sleeping and reading and blowing off steam."

"Blowing off steam?" Her brows rose with interest. "That sounds like a euphemism for what we did this morning. And last night."

He wanted to say no. To tell her that she was so much more than one of his rare hook-ups. But he honestly didn't know what she was. All he knew for sure was that he wanted to touch her again.

And that she couldn't be his.

So what he said instead was, "As euphemisms go, that's probably fair. But not frequent."

"A selective man." The lightness in her voice sounded a bit forced, and her throat moved as she swallowed. "I'm flattered."

"Listen, Xena—" He cut himself off. What the hell was he supposed to say? That there wasn't anything between them? She knew that. That he wanted her in his bed again? She knew that, too. That a fuck didn't mean a future? Once again, she knew that as well. Moreover, she was already well settled on the no-relationship train.

"What?"

He rubbed his temples. "That euphemism is exactly what it sounds like. I don't do relationships, and there is no woman in my life. But every once in a while, I want what I want."

Her mouth twisted. "You don't have to be coy with me, you know. I mean, hey, I could probably find you an expert call girl at a really reasonable rate."

"Christ, Xena, I—"

"Sorry. I'm sorry." She ran her fingers through her hair. "I'm tired and I'm hungry and even though we aren't a thing, it still feels really fucked up for you to be telling me that you don't do relationships and don't have a girlfriend. I mean, why lie?"

"What are you talking about?"

She pointed to the pants, then the shirt. "These just happened to be in a drawer? A drawer completely filled with girl-stuff, including a vibrator?"

"A vibrator?" He had to fight a laugh. "Everything in that drawer belongs to Denny." And it would take all his willpower not to give her shit about the vibrator.

"That means nothing to me. You know that, right?"

"She's a friend, and she's with the SSA," he began. "She takes care of my fish and plants when I'm out of town. She stays in the downstairs guest room, but I gave her a drawer up here so she could use the fish shower." He went on to tell her about Denny's husband, Mason, and how he'd come back after being lost to her for so long. "I'm guessing the toy was a pre-Mason thing. Either that or she left it in the drawer to embarrass me if I ever poked around in her stuff."

That, he thought, would be just like Denny. It also fouled up his plans to give her grief.

Well, hell.

"So there's nothing between you two?"

"Pretty sure I just made that clear. I told you. I don't do relationships. And I don't do friends with benefits, either."

"Out of curiosity, what am I?" She leaned against the dresser, studying him openly. "Or are we done, um, blowing off steam?"

"You're a damsel in distress," he said, making her laugh.

"Yeah, I'm *so* the damsel. But the distress part is pretty accurate."

"Exactly. And in the kind of a stressful situation that you're in—that we're both in—blowing off a little steam could be good for both of us."

"Agreed. It's—what's that word?—pragmatic. Or maybe cathartic."

"Could be both."

"We just totally justified fucking again, didn't we?"

"I think we did."

She grinned at him. "Do you know what I want right this very second?"

He lifted his brows and made an attempt to leer at her. "Lunch?"

"God, yes," she said, and he realized that he was having more fun with this woman than he'd had in a very long time.

"How does lasagna sound?"

"Fabulous, considering I haven't had anything since that Snickers we got from the motel vending machine. But I don't think we have time to go out. Do we?"

"Who said anything about going out? Come on." He ushered her out of the bedroom and down the stairs to the kitchen. "I made it the night before I flew to Vegas. It's still fine," he said, pulling a casserole dish of lasagna out of the fridge and sliding two generous pieces onto microwavable plates.

She looked from the lasagna to him and back again. "Seriously?"

"What? I promise it's still good." He popped the first plate into the microwave. "Lasagna will last four, five days as leftovers."

"No, no. I'm sure it's fine," she said. "I'm just impressed." She shrugged. "Of course, I'm a natural in the kitchen, too."

"Yeah?"

"Oh, sure. Pasta, even. My ramen could totally give that piddly-ass lasagna a run for its money."

"And you said you didn't get to do the college thing."

She smirked, then sat on the bar-height stool on the other side of the kitchen island. "Serious question for you."

"Uh-oh."

"Why don't you do relationships?"

He hesitated, then turned to the microwave when it dinged. "Let's just say that you and I are more alike than either of us probably imagined."

His back was to her when he spoke, and when he turned to pass her the plate and a fork, he could see the questions forming on her face and was grateful when she didn't ask him to explain.

He heated up his own serving, and they both dug into the food, her at the bar and him still in the kitchen, eating at the counter. He was going back for a second piece when she mentioned that she'd talked to Ella.

"She called while I was in the bathroom. They can't trace me through my phone, can they?"

"No," he said automatically, then added, "probably not. We'll replace it at the office, just in case." He had no idea how well funded the men after her were, but considering their years of persistence, he assumed there was a large cash pool financing the enterprise. And while the odds were slim, there was at least a theoretical possibility that they could track her when she used her phone. And as far as

Liam was concerned, "slim" wasn't good odds at all.

"Okay," she said, and he was grateful she didn't argue. Then again, unlike most clients he'd been tasked with protecting, for Xena the endgame was real, not hypothetical. She knew they would kill her because she'd witnessed them do that very thing to her father. Most people didn't really believe it, even when they were running for their lives.

"—so thank you."

Shit. He grimaced. "Sorry. My mind wandered. What did I do to deserve your thanks?"

"Ella said you sent a guy. Winston? Thanks for watching her back."

"That's what I'm here for. I hope he's bored out of his mind and has nothing to do, but I want him there since they may believe that she knows where you are. And they may try to convince her to tell them."

"She doesn't know. I didn't tell her."

"Good." He took a sip of sparkling water. "Winston texted me, too. Told me that Ella's thrilled he's there, but Rye seems a little on edge."

She took another bite, then swallowed. "I suppose that makes sense. He probably thought with me gone, all would be well." She shrugged. "He's a good manager, and he really does love her, but he's a little overprotective. And I think my sordid past always disturbed him."

"I'm sorry about that. You've been doing a great job for Ella for years. Any hesitations he had should have been alleviated by now."

"And yet, bad guys." She shrugged. "So maybe he was right."

He wanted to argue—to tell her she didn't deserve Rye's hesitation or condemnation or whatever the hell it was—but she'd already moved on and was thanking him for the food. "It was delicious," she said. "You really made it from scratch?"

"I'm a man of many talents."

"You're an interesting guy, Liam."

"Am I?"

"All these plants thriving. A refrigerator with real food."

"Truly, I am amazing."

She smirked. "You've fed me, clothed me. Fucked me."

"Not exactly a hardship."

"You've taken care of me in every way possible." She smiled, a little shyly. "I really do appreciate it. I know it's a job, and I should be scared out of my mind right now, but I'm not." She indicated the room, the food. "You've made me feel normal. Special, even. So thank you."

"You're welcome, but with talk like that, you're going to completely destroy my reputation as a badass, you know that right?"

"I could be persuaded to keep your secret."

He took both their dishes and slid them into the sink, then leaned back against the refrigerator, facing her. "Could you? And what's your price?"

"We still have some time," she said with a grin. "I thought we could blow off some steam."

CHAPTER FOURTEEN

"So, forgive the fan girl thing, but I really do love Ellie Love's music."

"She's amazing," I agree, unable to take my eyes off of the stunning woman standing in front of me. She's tall and ridiculously beautiful, with coal black hair streaked with pink and purple, and a tiny diamond stud in her nose that catches the sunlight streaming in through the windows in the open area of the Stark Security offices.

But what really draws my focus is the incredible bird tattoo that starts at her shoulder blade and trails down her arm. She's wearing a sleeveless silk top and skinny jeans, and the colorful plumage was the first thing I noticed when Liam ushered me into the room.

"What's it like working for her?"

"Ellie's great," I say honestly, trying to

remember this woman's name. "Really. I don't have anything bad to say. Except when she's being a bitch, and then I say it to her face. But honestly, she's hardly ever a bitch."

"You really like her."

"I really do."

"Glad to hear it. Hanging around with Jackson and Damien, I've met a few celebrities. Most are nice, but some are fucking nuts."

"True that." I frown, mentally untangling her words. Damien Stark I've heard of, obviously. A billionaire businessman who used to be a pro tennis player, he's in the news a lot. Plus, his name's on the door, and Liam told me that Stark founded the SSA after his daughter was kidnapped. "Who's Jackson?"

"Stark's half-brother. Jackson Steele. You know his work," she adds. "You're staying with Liam, right? He did the remodel. And this building, too. This whole complex, actually."

"Oh! I have heard of him." The Domino is a high-end business complex in the part of Santa Monica now known as Silicon Beach because it has so many tech companies. There was some controversy about the complex and it was all over the news during construction.

"He's great. And his wife Sylvia and I have been besties since the beginning of time."

I nod, knowing that I won't manage to keep any

of this straight. "So what do you do here? It's Cassie, right?" I ask, pleased with myself for finally remembering.

"Cassidy, actually. Cassidy Cunningham. But everyone calls me Cass. And I don't do a thing except occasionally pop by to steal Denny for lunch."

I look around the room, which is ridiculous since I have no idea what Denny looks like. "I thought she was on vacation. Liam told me a horrible story about her husband and amnesia." He's in Ryan Hunter's office, and he'd left me here with Cass, who's doing a great job of entertaining me, but I'm definitely a bit overwhelmed.

"Happy ending, though," she says, still on Mason and Denny. "And yeah, she's lazing on a beach somewhere. No, today I'm here with Eliza and Emma. We're doing happy hour before girls' night, and I figured I'd come get them."

"Which ones are they?"

"Um, there's Eliza," she says, pointing to a woman with chestnut hair talking with a good-looking guy with a lean face and slightly tousled hair. "Eliza!" she calls. "You ready?"

Eliza gives her a thumbs-up, then kisses the guy. A polite enough kiss for the semi-public setting, but I can still feel the heat beneath it from here.

"And that is Quince," Cass says. "They're a thing."

I laugh. "Figured that out on my own."

"Have fun, love," Quince calls as Eliza approaches us. His voice is deep and rich and deliciously British. "And don't get wankered."

She flashes a flirty smile back over her shoulder to him. "But you like it when I do," she replies with a wink, and I'm absolutely certain I'm missing something.

When she turns back around, she smiles at me and holds out a hand. "Hey, you're Liam's, right?"

"Uh." I take her hand. "Liam's what?"

Her eyes crinkle. "His assignment. Or have I been misinformed?"

"Oh. Right. Yeah. He's doing a stellar job of keeping me alive."

Her head tilts as if she's studying me, and I wonder if I've made some horrible faux pas. Like no gallows humor in the office. But soon enough, her mouth twitches with amusement. "I'm sure he'll stick close," she says, and I actually start to blush. Which is something I haven't done in years.

"Seriously, he's great at what he does. Whatever's going on, he's got your back."

"I know. Do you work with him?"

"Work? Oh, no. I don't work here. I'm an actress. Currently out of work, but I have an audition for a small part in Francesca Muratti's next film," she adds, mentioning an A-list star I've heard of. "So I'm hoping to be gainfully employed again, soon."

"Oh." I frown between her and Cass, neither of whom are actually employed by this place.

Eliza laughs. "I'm only here right now because I'm Quince's girlfriend. God, I love saying that." She shifts her attention to Cass. "We're taking an Uber, right? Because there are three of us, and I'm not riding on the back of either one of your bikes."

Cass rolls her eyes, but Eliza lifts her phone. "Em! I'm calling an Uber now. Come on!"

I turn, and see that she's signaling to a stunning redhead standing with Liam in the doorway of Ryan Hunter's office. Mr. Hunter is there, too—dark hair, blue eyes, and looking at least as good in a suit as Liam does. When he wears one. Right now he's in jeans, which I appreciate since my attire consists of sweats and a tee.

There's another guy with them, too, and since he's holding an open laptop, I'm guessing he's Mario, the tech genius who is trying to get clear facial images of my tormentors.

Liam catches my eye and holds up a finger, indicating he'll be right over, but Emma comes right away. "Sorry, sorry," she says, then, "Oh, hey. You must be Xena."

"That's me," I say, before Eliza and Cass tell me that it was nice to meet me. Emma tells them she'll be along, and I notice the way Cass reaches for her hand, her fingers lightly skimming Emma's before Cass and Eliza head out.

"Nice to meet you," Emma says, as I wonder if she and Cass are an item. "Sorry about all the shit you're dealing with."

"Thanks. Are you one of the agents here?"

"No, I don't work here," she says, and I'm starting to feel like I'm in a sitcom.

She must notice my expression, because she laughs. "I'm a PI. But I have an offer on the table, and since the SSA frequently works in teams of two, Ryan wanted to talk to me and Liam together."

"I thought Denny worked with Liam."

"Not usually. I think they're just really good friends. Denny and Quince team up a lot, but I guess she'll be with Mason now. At least until the baby benches her for a while. And there's Winston and Leah," she continues, making my head spin. "Between you and me, they need more women here. I know they're actively looking. And I also know they're incredibly selective. I'm flattered, but I also love my job and calling my own shots, and—and all of this is probably very boring to you. Short answer. I don't work here. Yet. Maybe never. I'm still debating."

"Well, good luck deciding."

"Thanks. And it really is great to meet you. I'm

sorry it's under such horrible circumstances, but you are in exceptionally good hands."

"Yeah," I say, glancing across the room to find Liam. "I am."

"The cameras at her doors are pieces of shit," Mario says. "You should tell her to replace them, stat," he adds, pointing at me.

"On it," I say, while Liam shoots me a *what can you do* look.

"Fortunately," Mario continues, "I have mad skills. A few more passes with my extremely propri- etary, no where else to be found, one hundred percent a Sanchez specialty, facial re-generation software, and I should have an image that's clean enough to get us some solid results once we feed it into the facial recognition databases."

"How long until we get a hit from that?" I ask.

Mario shrugs. "That depends on how chari- table the system is feeling that day and how lucky you are."

"With my luck, we'll get results sometime around the next millennium."

"With your luck," Liam says firmly, squeezing my hand under the table, "we'll get them tomorrow."

I raise a brow, because clearly he's delusional.

"I'm with Liam," Quince says. "After everything you've been through, you're not only still standing, but you've got a great job with an incredibly generous woman." Because Liam told me I had to, everyone in this room now knows all the details about my truly fucked up life. I know it's necessary, but it doesn't sit well with me.

"Not to mention me watching your back," Liam says, adding a teasing smile.

I shoot him a sideways smirk. "A job I can't go back to and a woman I put in the line of fire."

"Yes," Liam repeats. "But me—and this whole team—watching your back."

"Liam—"

"No," he says, without a hint of humor in his voice. "I mean it. You've survived a hell of a life, Xena. And you have good people helping you now. Ella. Us. Maybe your luck was shit for a while, but it's changing. Help change it more by helping us."

I sag a little, because he's right. "I know. I'm sorry." I look at all of them around the table in turn. Ryan—who told me not to call him Mr. Hunter, Quince, Mario, Trevor, Leah, and, of course, Liam. I know there are a few other new recruits who are on what Ryan calls probationary duties, but this is the team that's helping me—plus Winston. With Liam taking point, of course.

"Thank you," I say. "It really does feel like my luck is changing."

"The short term goal," Liam says to the group, "is to keep Xena safe and catch our two stalkers. Use them to lead us to whoever is pulling their strings. And the longer-term goal is to take down the entire organization, assuming it still exists. Obviously, we're going to need support from law enforcement to make that happen, but they should be happy to let us take point early on. Ryan's going to talk with Colonel Seagrave at the SOC to see about getting us additional intelligence support, and he's already put a call in to Agent McKee. McKee's with the FBI," he adds to me, "and the SOC is a deep-cover, government intelligence organization. We've worked with both those agencies before."

"Wait, wait." My head is literally spinning. "You're talking an investigation that could take years."

"Possibly," Ryan says. "But if we take them down, it's worth it."

"I can't—" I cut myself off, feeling stupid. I was about to say I can't put my life on hold for years, but my life has already been on hold. Hell, I never got the chance to start my life. And I never will unless I can get this albatross off my back.

I could run, of course. I could leave Liam's house in the middle of the night and just bolt. Leave the country, manufacture a new identity. A week ago, that's probably what I would have done.

But being with Liam—talking with him, touching him—has made me crave a real life all the more. He's opened a door for me, and I think—no, I *know* —that I want to walk through it.

I draw a deep breath and nod. "This is all really overwhelming," I say. "But okay. I just—" I look at Liam, feeling suddenly desperate.

"It's okay," he says. "What?"

"Well, I can't just hang out here forever. And I can't go back to Ella, can I? I mean, that would put her in danger, right? But I have to eat and live somewhere and all that good stuff. And, well, what am I going to do for a job?"

"I think we can work that out," Ryan says. "We're ridiculously low on administrative help at the moment."

"Really?" I look between him and Liam. "I can work here while you guys are doing whatever it is you're doing?"

"According to Ella, you're hardworking, detail-oriented, and efficient. I think we could use that."

I frown, considering his words. "You already thought about this, didn't you?"

"I asked Ryan to call Ella when we were in his office," Liam says.

"Oh." I'm ridiculously pleased that he was so thoughtful. "Thank you."

We share a smile, until I break our connection and look down at my hands.

"First thing," Ryan says, "is to get as much information from you as we can. Locations. Names. I know it's been years, but any details that you can remember."

Across the table, Mario's phone makes a *ka-ching* noise, like a slot machine paying off. He jumps to his feet, mumbles, "Mainframe," and scurries away.

"Cross your fingers that's something on the facial recognition software," Trevor says dryly. "And not a new profile hit on this week's coolest dating site."

Leah nudges him and mutters, "Stop." Mario, I'm assuming, doesn't date much.

Leah's about my height, with a mass of tight curls. I think her hair is naturally brown, but golden highlights frame her face. She has a strong jaw balanced by oval-shaped black glasses. She's not pretty so much as cute. And from the few minutes I've spent talking to her, I can tell she's super sharp.

According to Liam, she and Trevor and Denny all did security-related work under Ryan at Stark International before Stark Security was formed. And before that, Trevor and Leah worked with him at his own security company, one that Damien Stark bought out years and years ago.

There's an easiness between Trevor and Leah, so it's not hard to believe they've been in the trenches together. And the way they joke around with each other, I thought at first they were dating.

"Trev's gay, so that's a no," Liam told me after we'd arrived at the office but before he went into the meeting. "But his husband walked out a couple of years ago, and they've been rooming together since. So they're definitely close."

"What about Leah? Is she gay, too?"

"I don't think so. Denny mentioned a guy she used to date. Honestly, I don't know. She plays her life pretty close to the vest, and I'm not much for prying."

Now, Ryan pulls the conversation back by focusing on me. "Names?" he repeats. "Details?"

"Right. I don't know many. The customers always used code names."

"That's okay. We're not interested in the clients as much as the players. The big guns and the cogs. Anyone at all."

"I didn't overhear a lot. But the man who—who shot my father. I made it a point to learn his name. It's Noyce. Edward Noyce."

"Excellent," Quince says, then taps something into his phone. "If Mario's at the mainframe, he can start a search. Anyone else?" he asks me.

"I was high all the time. A lot of what's in my head is fuzzy. Surreal. But there was one time I remember, or I think I do. The memory may not even be real."

"Tell us what's in your head," Liam says, putting his hand on mine. "And we'll sort it out from there."

"Right. Sure. Okay." I draw a deep breath, not wanting to fall back into those memories, but knowing that I have to. "There was this one time when everyone in the building was freaking out. Like the world was going to end if everything wasn't perfect. The guy was coming from some-where in Europe, and he was the big money man. I don't know why I know that, but I think I'm right. Everyone was talking like he was the absolute shit, you know?"

"And you heard his name?" Trevor asks.

"I think so. It was odd. Foreign. So I might be misremembering. But I think they called him Corbu."

Liam's eyes widen, and Quince lets out a low whistle.

"What?" I ask, looking around the table.

"You didn't misremember," Liam says. "And you may have just made this whole case ten times easier."

CHAPTER FIFTEEN

Corbu.

Liam caught Quince's eye, and saw the other man frown. Quince and Eliza had been reunited recently when the SSA had worked with an EU task force in an effort to bring down the infamous kingpin of an international sex trafficking organization. Specifically, the SSA had been tasked with obtaining information about Corbu's operations from a local scumbag, Scott Lassiter. A man that Eliza had also been pursuing, for decidedly different reasons.

"I don't understand," Xena said when Ryan excused himself to go to his office. "What did I say?"

"The magic word," Quince told her. "Corbu's in custody. And that means we have a solid shot at getting some answers."

"Seriously?" This time the question was a whisper, and her hand grasped Liam's, squeezing tight. He squeezed back, relishing the easy familiarity between them.

"Seriously," Liam assured her, then gave her the quick and dirty rundown of the operation.

"So, he's not just sitting in prison somewhere? He's been giving this task force information about all the various cells?"

"The SSA hasn't played a part since his capture," Liam told her. "But my understanding is that he's cooperating. And his various captains around the globe are singing with more force than The Three Tenors."

He had to smile. Sometimes, the system really did work. And this just might be one of those times. And maybe, just maybe, Xena really was about to get lucky.

A door slammed on the far side of the open area, and Mario hurried in, waving a printout. "Am I a genius or what? Why yes, Mario, you are the man. Truly."

By the coffee station, Leah snorted. "I don't know about the man, but you're definitely something."

Mario held his arms out at his sides. "Come on, Leah. You know you want it."

"And yet my feet remain firmly planted."

"Children," Quince chided.

Xena leaned toward Liam. "Are they...?"

"I have no idea." He'd given up on trying to decipher Leah and Mario. Half the time he thought they were flirting. The rest of the time he didn't think about it at all. Bottom line, they'd either end up in bed or at battle stations. So long as they kept doing stellar work, he figured either result was okay.

"Why are you the man?" Xena called out, to which Mario responded with a quick bow. "Because it's in my blood, thank you. Props to the lady who's paying attention."

Liam eyed the techie and cleared his throat.

"Faces," Mario said, dropping the printouts on the desk. "And yes, they're both plugged into the database. So burn some sage, say a prayer, wear your lucky underwear. And maybe we'll get a hit soon."

"I always wear my lucky underwear," Quince said dryly. He glanced at the sheets, then slid them across the table to Xena. "Familiar?"

Liam leaned closer, looking at the images with Xena, impressed with the rendering that Mario was able to coax out of the pixels. Other than from the night at the cabin, he didn't recognize them, though there was no reason he should. But he watched Xena's face, hoping for a sign.

He got none.

"Sorry. If I knew them before, I don't now."

"It's okay," Liam assured her. "You got away years ago, and these guys are foot soldiers. Soldiers change. But they'll lead us back to whoever is pulling their strings, and I have a feeling you'll know who that is."

She hugged herself. "I want to, because I know it'll help. But at the same time, I wish none of it was left in my head."

He put his hand on her back, stroking lightly, wishing that he could do more. But he could, of course. He could do his job. He could find the man who'd sent the goons, and he could take the fucker down. And, dammit, he would.

A moment later, Ryan's office door burst open, and he crossed the room in long strides, his expression unreadable.

"Bad news?" Liam asked.

"Good, actually. Or potentially good. I just got off the phone with Enrique Castille." He turned to Xena. "He's the head of the European Union task force that brought down Corbu."

"And?" Quince pressed.

"They've been busy. Corbu's been singing. Apparently his son was kidnapped by a competitor, and he wants the task force's help getting him back. And taking down his enemy."

Leah leaned forward, her chin resting on her hand. "Which benefits us how?"

"Because every captain has been rounded up.

Including Alberto Miro, the asshole who operated the New York cell. His entire organization got caught in the net."

Xena looked between Ryan and Liam, her head moving side to side as if she wasn't quite following. Liam couldn't fault her for that; he wasn't sure where Ryan was going with this either.

"But if the whole organization was caught, who's after me?"

A hard smile crossed Ryan's face. "I said they were all caught in the net. One wiggled free."

"Noyce," Xena breathed, reaching over to take Liam's hand.

"Bingo. He had a shark of an attorney and an alibi for every offense they tried to throw at him, not to mention a history with Miro that his attorney played up."

"He killed my father, and he's walking free?"

Ryan sat on the edge of the conference table beside her. "Apparently his story is that he came to one party without realizing that the girls weren't there consensually. When he learned, he was disgusted and left."

"That's bullshit."

"I know. The task force knows. What they need is proof, and Miro didn't have it to give."

"But there is proof," Liam said, his hand tightening around Xena's. "Xena witnessed him killing her father."

She swallowed audibly. "That's why he wants to kill me."

"And it's why we're going to nail his ass," Liam said, hating the fact that she was in the crosshairs, but so damned relieved that they now knew why. More importantly they knew who.

They had a target now, and Liam wouldn't rest until the fucker was in custody or dead.

———————————

CHAPTER SIXTEEN

"I think it's time for you to take a little trip," Ryan says to me. "On paper, anyway."

I look at Liam, alarmed. "What? What does that even mean?"

"It means it's time for Leah to be on point," Liam says. "Unless Ryan has something else in mind."

"Nope, you read me perfectly."

"Ditch and switch?" Leah grins as she winks at me. "I'm game."

"What's that?"

"We want to distract anyone who might have traced you back to LA," Leah says.

"But we were careful," I insist. "There's no way they could have followed us from the cabin."

Ryan slides back into his chair at the head of the table. "Not disagreeing, but even without Liam in the picture, it makes sense you'd come here. You live here, right?"

"Yeah. I rent the garage apartment at Ella's place."

"So if you left the concert because of the attack, the odds are you'd go home. That's what they'd likely assume, anyway, and we're going to let that play out."

"But I'm not there." I shoot a frantic look at Liam. "I don't want to go back there. If they're watching it—"

"You won't," Liam says calmly. "You're staying with me."

"Tonight," Ryan amends, "she's staying with Emma."

"But—"

He holds up a hand, silencing Liam. "Let me finish."

I glance at Liam, who's looking warily at his boss and friend. But he's letting Ryan continue without argument. For now, anyway.

"Go on," I say.

"I want you to call Ellie. From your phone," he adds, sliding my phone across the table to me. The SSA already gave me another use while this nightmare is in play, and now I don't even want to touch my old one, in case Noyce and his men really have been tracking me with it. "Not from here. And don't turn it back on yet. Liam can take you to the beach later before he drops you at Emma's. Find a dive where you might have grabbed something to eat, understand?"

I look at Liam and nod.

"Then call Ellie. Thank her for the cabin and tell her what happened—don't mention that you know who's behind it. But tell her that you need to get out of LA since they'll be looking for you there. Tell her you're—"

"Going to Paris?" *With Liam*, I silently add.

I'm being silly, of course. I don't even have a passport, although I bet the SSA could manufacture one for me if need be...

"Seattle," he says.

"Oh. It's not Paris, but that's cool. I've never been there."

"And you aren't going now." Once again, Ryan is making my head spin. "Tell her you know where you're going to hole up, and you'll call her when you get there. Meanwhile, Liam, you call Ellie, too, and tell her to mention the call and Xena's plans to someone on her staff she'd normally confide in. But to do it near some other crew members. Where she can be overheard."

"Why?" I ask.

"You told me that no one followed you to Ella's cabin," Liam says. "That means someone told them you were there. Which means if they aren't monitoring your phone, hopefully the information that you've left LA will get to them through their mole."

I frown. "There aren't that many people who know about the cabin. Rye, but he'd never hurt Ella, and hurting me would hurt her. Ella's attorney and accountant know, but they're both as sweet as can be. And her producer at the label, but he wasn't there. That's it. That's everybody who knows about it."

"You think," Liam adds, and I don't have a response to that.

"Okay, fine. But why am I going to Seattle? And why are we sending them after me?"

"You're not," Leah says. "That's the point of the ditch and switch. I become you."

I shake my head. "No. No way."

Leah waves a hand. "Oh, please. This is what I do."

"Go around the country pretending to be an ex-prostitute who some dangerous sex traffickers are after? What?" I add, in response to Liam's dark look. "That's what I am."

"No. That's what you were forced to do to survive. And you dug yourself out. You're still digging, and we're here to help you. Let us help you."

"At the risk of her getting whacked?"

"I'll be fine," Leah assures me. "I'll go to Seattle and send her a text from there. From your

RUINED WITH YOU   169

phone, of course. Then Ella spreads the word on her end."

"Let's record Xena saying she's there with static," Mario suggests. "You can call Ellie and play it, but on the recording she can say she's going to text because the connection is so bad."

Leah nods. "Excellent. That way we'll get them whether they're monitoring phone, text, or Ellie's conversations."

"And then?" I ask Leah.

"And then I buy a return ticket in my own name. I come home, and Xena Morgan stays behind in Seattle."

I glance around the table at all of them. "This will work?"

"It will," Liam says firmly. "All we're doing is buying time and safety."

"What have you got for me?" Quince asks.

"I was hoping you'd go overseas and meet with Enrique in person. The task force does good work, but I want your eyes on their information, and he's willing to let you interrogate some of the men they already have in custody."

"My favorite European pastime—interrogating deviant wankers."

"And if anyone can get more details from a prisoner, it's you," Ryan adds.

"A dubious honor," Quince says. "But true."

I glance at Liam, who nods. I lean back, a little

stunned that the seemingly gentle Brit is some sort of master interrogator. Then again, this whole operation stuns me.

"I'll head over tomorrow and take Eliza with me. I've been promising her a trip to London and Paris."

"Nothing like espionage to spice up a girl's vacation," Leah says.

"I bet they'll spice it up other ways, too," Trevor puts in.

Quince grins. "You know what they say about all work and no play."

Leah rolls her eyes. "When do you want me to head out?"

"Tomorrow morning," Ryan says.

"Oh, good. I was afraid you'd say tonight, and I don't want to miss girls' night."

Ryan nods. "Which is why you're not leaving until tomorrow. You're all meeting at Emma's house, right?"

"Yeah, why?"

"Because I want Xena there, too."

"Whoa," Liam says. "She's with me, and while I wouldn't feel emasculated joining girls' night, I don't think the women want me there."

"Which is why it's good that it's at Emma's house. Do you really doubt she'd be safe?"

"Um, hello?" Leah says.

"You're skills are amazing," Ryan says.

"Emma's are better. And her house is a fucking fortress."

"Emma?" I ask, wondering what kind of badassery the woman has at her disposal. "She told me she's a PI."

"She's a hell of a lot more than a PI," Liam says, and my imagination churns. "Who else will be there?"

Leah counts the guests off on her fingers. "Me, Emma, Eliza, Cass, Jamie. Maybe Sylvia. With Denny and Nikki out of town, I think that's it."

"I keep telling them to invite me," Trevor says, winking at me. "But so far, no luck."

"Jamie and Eliza will be there," Mario points out to Liam, and I remember someone telling me that Ryan's wife is named Jamie. And I know that Eliza and Quince are together. "If Ryan and Quince aren't shutting this thing down, I think you can assume your girl is safe."

I wait for Liam to deny that I'm 'his girl,' but all he does is nod. "Fine. If they think Xena's in LA, they'll either look for her at her own apartment or mine. It makes sense that she'd be with me since I was with her at the cabin."

"Exactly," Ryan says.

"What's girls' night?" I ask.

"We drink. Talk. Usually watch a movie. Most nights we break up around midnight. But I'm thinking tonight needs to be a slumber party."

"Right," I say, wondering not only what I'm supposed to wear to sleep in, but how the hell I'm supposed to act. I've hung out with Ella before, but I've never done sleepovers. Or girls' nights. Or anything like that. Not ever. Not even in high school.

I reach over and take Liam's hand, squeezing hard. Because right now, the prospect of spending casual time with a group of women scares me even more than Edward Noyce and his well-armed cretins.

It takes about forty-seven seconds for my nervousness to fade after Emma welcomes me into her cute little house in Venice Beach. A home which, according to Liam, is a hell of a lot more than the adorable bungalow it appears to be.

"I've done a lot of work," Emma says vaguely when I ask her as much. And although I really want to pry for details, I have a feeling that it's an *I could tell you, but then I'd have to kill you* situation.

I'm the last to arrive, now decked out in a pair of Denny's jeans and my newly washed tank top, and armed with a promise from Liam that we can hit a department store tomorrow. I'd asked to swing by my apartment to get my own clothes, but I hadn't been surprised when he'd quickly shut that suggestion down.

I don't know if Liam told someone that I don't drink, but I'm thrilled to see that in addition to several bottles of wine and an impressive selection of hard liquor, the kitchen island that is currently serving as drinks-central also has a variety of sodas and flavored sparkling waters. I help myself to a raspberry flavored water and follow Emma into the living area. Cass comes over to give me a hug, telling me she's thrilled I'm joining the fun, and I notice that she switches places when she sits back down, leaving a pretty woman with pixie-styled brown hair to go sit by Emma.

Eliza and Leah both wave in greeting, and the pretty woman comes over, introducing herself as Sylvia. "I started coming to these things because of her," she says, pointing to Cass. "It's a nice break from the kids. I love them, but sometimes, you just need adult women."

"I can imagine," I say, although in truth I think I would love to be at home with kids of my own. Such a normal thing, and for so long it was a fantasy I didn't even let myself think about, because it was just too damn painful.

I keep my polite smile on, though, because I don't want to bring the mood down by even hinting that I'm thinking about my past, and if Sylvia notices my moment of melancholy, she's kind enough not to mention it.

"You must be Xena," an absolutely gorgeous raven-haired woman comes from the kitchen, a glass of wine in her hands. "I'm Jamie, Ryan's wife. Sylvia and I go back a few years. Anyway, it's great you could make it. We haven't been doing this for that long, honestly. So you're getting in on the ground floor."

"Cool," I say as I settle in next to Leah, who has scooted over to make a space for me. I mean it, too, only to remember after I've spoken that I may not be hanging around this crowd for long. According to Liam, now that the playing field has narrowed to Noyce, he expects we'll be able to wrap this up and ensure my safety within a pretty reasonable time frame.

I'll still live in LA, of course, and not that far from here in the grand scheme of things, but I doubt that I'd be coming to girls' night. Not without that connection to Liam.

A fresh wave of melancholy washes over me and I have to force a smile as Eliza starts to tell everyone about how she and Quince are heading to Europe tomorrow. "He'll be working during the day, but I'm already planning what museums I want to see. And, of course, we'll have the nights," she adds, batting her eyes and humming innocently as the others laugh.

"I bet he proposes over there," Leah says.

"Oh, I don't think so," Eliza says. "It hasn't been that long."

"You're insane," Emma counters, then glances at the rest of the room. "Raise your hand if you think my sister is insane."

Everyone except me raises their hand. "I don't think I'm qualified," I say, when Emma raises a brow.

"Fair enough. But you," she says to Eliza, "are nuts if you think it hasn't been that long. It's been years. And you know damn well you two are perfect for each other."

"Yes, but that doesn't mean he's going to—"

"He will," Leah says firmly.

"Fine," Eliza says. "But I'll just have to tell him I need time to ponder. Wouldn't want him to think I'm madly in love with him or anything."

They all laugh, and I'm too curious not to ask. "How long have you been together?"

Eliza makes a face. "That is a more complicated question than you know."

"They were all cozy and then motherfucking fate stepped in and pushed them apart," Emma says. "Hell of a journey back together. Like an epic poem by Homer or something."

"Yes," Eliza says dryly. "My relationship with Quince is exactly like *The Odyssey*. You are so weird."

"Am I weird?" Emma asks, directing the question to Cass.

"Very."

"She's right," Eliza says. "Which is probably why I love you so much. And why are we talking about me, anyway?"

"Exactly," Leah says. "We should be talking about men."

"Ahem," Cass says, and everyone laughs again.

"Is Trevor off limits?" Leah asks. "Because I really want to know what we're going to do about him. I mean, he's a terrific roommate, but that boy has been single for far too long."

"Has he brought anybody home?" Eliza asks.

"Nope." Leah raises a shoulder. "He's stayed out all night a couple of times, but when I ask him about it, he just says he stayed with a friend instead of grabbing an Uber. I'm sad for him. He and Jasper were really good together."

"His ex," Jamie says helpfully to me, though I've figured that out on my own.

The evening continues that way for another half hour or so, with the group commenting on the lives and relationships of their friends, including asking Jamie when she and Ryan are going to start a family—"Um, so not ready!"—and someone asking when Nikki and Damien will be back in the country.

Nobody knows—apparently the whole family

and their nanny are in Europe, combining a tour of Stark properties and businesses with a family vacation.

"Family vacations and work are not supposed to be on tonight's list of acceptable conversational topics," Sylvia says. "Not when I have kids at home and work spread all over the dining room table."

"Then let's talk sex," Jamie says. "Or bad television. Or sex." She turns to me. "Are you and Liam ... you know?"

Across the room, Sylvia gasps. "Jamie!" She turns to me. "You'll have to forgive her. She has no filters at all."

"Oh, I have filters," Jamie says. "I just usually keep them turned off. More fun that way."

"Um," I say, because I'm really not sure what I should say. I mean, Liam was protecting me. Could he get in trouble if his coworkers learn the truth?

"Well?" Jamie prods, and I wonder if I could conjure a slight case of Ebola and run to the bathroom.

I take the more sane approach and pretend to be clueless. "What makes you think that?"

"Something Leah said earlier. And I saw him walk you in. There was a vibe."

"A vibe?"

"There was definitely a vibe," Eliza says, and Emma and Cass both nod.

"I don't know about that," I say. And then,

because I can't help myself, I ask, "Did you pick up a vibe from me or from him?"

Jamie and Sylvia share a grin, my cheeks flame, and everyone starts laughing.

"Busted," Jamie says, and even though she's right, all I can do is laugh. I've never done this with other women before. Just hung out and talked and kidded each other and had fun. It's nice. And a little dangerous, too, because I know I could really get used to this.

Eliza brings me a fresh water. "Vibe or not, if there is something between you and Liam, I'm glad. He and Quince have been friends for ages, and I know Quince has been hoping he'd get involved with someone again."

"Again?"

She nods, then sits down next to me. "Apparently it was a long time ago. He was involved and I guess it ended badly. Quince doesn't even know the details. It was before—never mind."

"Deliverance?" I ask quietly.

"You know about that? Interesting…"

I don't bother to clarify that he told me in the context of my history and sex trafficking. Instead, I just ask her what happened.

"That's the thing," she says. "I don't know. Neither does Quince. All he knows is that Liam got burned somehow. And that he doesn't do relationships."

"He's not doing one with me, either," I tell her. "In fact, we even talked about the fact that he doesn't."

"And yet there's a vibe," she says, then clinks her glass with mine.

I consider protesting again, but don't. After all, this night is about gossip and girlfriends and having fun. And as far as I'm concerned, fantasizing about Liam is a very fun pastime.

Eventually, the conversation turns more rowdy and someone brings out Cards Against Humanity, which has us roaring. And though I'm not sure how it happens, that game leads into lazing on the floor, sofa, and chairs as we watch *Guardians of the Galaxy*, which I've never seen before, and soon I'm laughing so hard I'm crying.

Not because it's that emotional—although considering how silly it is, it does pack an emotional punch—but because this whole night has been so amazing.

And when I eventually do fall asleep on the pullout couch in Emma's loft, with Leah sleeping on a blowup bed beside me, I can't help but think that I could definitely get used to this.

CHAPTER SEVENTEEN

For the next few days, I live at Liam's side.

I go with him to work, where I scan, file, organize, summarize, and generally make myself useful in this incredibly busy office that definitely does not have enough support staff. It's interesting work, and I enjoy it. Not only because I feel like I'm contributing and not simply sitting back while others protect me, but because I'm working again, and the work is important.

While I'm working, of course Liam is, too. For the last two days, he's been primarily on the phone with Winston or working with Mario on the computer, trying to chase down leads to Noyce's whereabouts.

Unfortunately, there's been little progress on that front, but Liam assures me this is part of the process, and that eventually, I'll be free of the sword hanging over my head.

I believe him, and I'm so grateful for everything he and the SSA have done. But every time he assures me that this will all be over soon, my throat thickens and my chest feels tight. Because once I'm free of that sword, doesn't that mean I'll be freed from Liam's shadow, too?

I should want that. I should want to see my own apartment again. Work my old job. Hang out with Ella.

I should want to be able to move through the world without looking over my shoulder.

And I do. I want it painfully. Desperately.

But I also want Liam.

I'm certain he has no idea of this new direction in my thoughts, and I feel a little guilty about that. But I'm keeping my secret for now.

As far as Liam knows, nothing has changed. I've told him that I don't get involved, and I told him my reasons. If he was paying attention, he knows that I've never wanted to pull someone else into a life with a woman wearing a target on her back.

But Liam is the one working to erase that target. And once he does...

Well, once that target is gone, I guess he can do the math. If he wants to.

And that's the thing that's gnawing at my gut—I don't think he'll want to. He's told me he doesn't do relationships, either, and if what Eliza's told me is true, his words have been borne out in practice. He hasn't been in a relationship since before he and Quince became friends, and from what I can tell, they were both neck deep in Deliverance a long time ago.

"You've been quiet tonight," Liam says as he squeezes his Range Rover into his garage.

"Tired," I say, which isn't actually a lie. "I moved about eight billion boxes from the basement storage area up to Conference Room A so I can start scanning them into the system."

"Eight billion?"

"Slight exaggeration," I say. "And I might have had help. But it was still tiring. First physically, then mentally. Scanning is not the most exhilarating task in the world. But it does give you time to think."

"Oh?" He kills the engine and looks at me. "What were you thinking about?"

"You," I say truthfully.

"What a coincidence. I spent a lot of time thinking about you today, too."

"I should hope so, considering my ass is your primary investigation at the moment." I frown. "That came out wrong."

"I think it came out exactly right. I definitely need to investigate your ass more thoroughly."

Heat and desire lace his voice, firing my senses and making my skin tingle with a now-familiar need. A craving for him. For this man. For his touch. His scent. His lips. Over the last few nights, I've explored every delicious inch of him, and all I have to do is close my eyes to remember the way he feels inside me.

The memory is sweet, but I'd much rather have the reality, and as soon as we're inside the house, I push him against the wall and close my mouth over his.

"No dinner?" he murmurs when we come up for air.

"Your choice," I answer, then run the tip of my tongue along the curve of his ear. "Leftover meatloaf. Takeout. Or me."

"Well, when you put it that way..."

I squeal as he grabs me by the waist, hauls me over his shoulder, then smacks me lightly on the ass before carrying me upstairs and tossing me into the middle of the unmade bed.

I scoot backwards, laughing, as he gets on the mattress, then crawls toward me on all fours, a dangerous, possessive look in his eyes. "There's nowhere to go," he says as my back presses against the vertical iron bars of the headboard. "And now I'm going to have my feast."

On the last word, he takes hold of my ankles and slides me down the bed. I'm still in the heels and the shift-style dress I'd worn to the office, and the dress doesn't slide with me, leaving my lacy panties exposed as the dress bunches around my waist.

I'm breathing hard as our eyes meet, and I reach up, purposefully grabbing the bars. His gaze is hard and demanding, and I think about that playful smack to my rear. The truth is, I want another. I want to feel his palm against my skin. I want him to take off his belt and use it to lace my wrists to these bars.

Too many times I was helpless with a man I loathed. I want to cleanse that from my past and have my submission be a gift to Liam, not something stolen from me. I want to be claimed. Overwhelmed. But I can't get the words out.

I know that with Liam I should be able to speak freely, but for so many years I wasn't allowed to want anything. And now—now I'm afraid he'll think it's strange, even though I know that spanking and light bondage are about as low on the kink scale as it's possible to get.

I can't bring myself to take the risk. I can't seem to find the words to ask. All I can do is meet his eyes, hoping he can see the desire—the need—in mine.

His lips tease my inner thighs as his finger slips

inside my panties, lightly teasing my clit. My pussy clenches with need, and I arch up, silently begging for more until he takes the hint and thrusts two fingers deep inside me. I grind against him, wanting more—everything—then gasp as his mouth continues to roam, finally reaching the lace edge of my panties.

He tugs them aside with a finger, then laves my clit with his tongue while those other two fingers move rhythmically inside me. I buck in response, wanting more. More intensity. More wildness. More Liam.

"Please," I beg. "Liam, please."

"Tell me," he murmurs, his breath on my pussy teasing me as much as the stubble of his beard brushing my tender flesh. "Tell me what you want."

My lips part, and in my mind I spell it out for him. *Tie me up. Bind me. Spank me. Claim me. Take me.*

But it is only the last part that leaves my lips. "Take me," I murmur. "Take me, please."

"Xena, baby. Christ, you drive me crazy." He slides his way up my body, my dress a tangled mess between us. His cock teases my core, and as he pushes my knees up and thrusts slowly into me, his mouth claims mine, his tongue mimicking the movement of his cock until he is filling me completely.

I clutch his back, my fingernails most likely

drawing blood, but I don't care. How quickly I've gone from needy to desperate. To wanting what he is giving. To craving nothing but the pure pleasure of this man.

He's on top of me, his huge, muscular body blanketing mine as he thrusts into me, over and over, deeper and harder. I cry out, craving release, craving more as I pull him toward me, wishing we could crawl inside each other so that we would explode together in perfect unison.

And then, oh God, and then the world seems to turn inside out and my body arches up as everything inside me catches fire, and all I can do is burn until I'm nothing but ashes in his arms.

"Was that good?" he asks, holding me close.

"Not even remotely," I say, then feel his laugher reverberate through me. I'm still spinning, still glowing, and the siren's call of sleep is luring me under.

But even as I succumb to pleasure and exhaustion in his arms, I can't escape the tiny pinpricks of regret. Because as much as he took me high, he didn't quite take me *there*.

I want him to claim me.

I want to be *his*.

On so many levels, I want to be his.

But I'm afraid that won't ever be my reality.

I'm a girl who's spent her entire life being

disappointed. Who's always gotten the exact opposite of what she wants.

Now I want Liam.

And I'm terrified that history will repeat itself, and in the end, I'm going to lose him forever.

CHAPTER EIGHTEEN

I wake up alone, but there's a freshly cut rose waiting for me on the bedside table, which makes me smile. There's also a note, and when I read it, my smile grows broader.

Bakery. Back soon. L

In the car yesterday, I'd mentioned to him that I love blueberry muffins with crumbles on top, and he'd immediately shifted course for Upper Crust, a Malibu bakery that he swore had the best muffins in the world. A converted house, it sits on a rocky outcropping and from the drive-through lane, I could see tables out back on a patio overlooking the sea.

Unfortunately, they'd been out of blueberry muffins, so we'd made do with a fresh loaf of bread and some chocolate chip cookies. I'd expected that to be the end of it, and the knowledge that he's making an early morning jaunt for me makes me smile and stretch and hug my pillow, feeling ridiculously special.

I decide to go ahead and shower, as I imagine we'll be heading to the office after we eat, even though it's Saturday. I take longer than I need to, distracted by the multiple jets and the rain-style showerhead—not to mention a few minutes chatting with the fish, some of whom I'm sure are checking me out.

And, yes, part of the reason I linger is the hope that Liam will join me, since I don't imagine he's taken a shower yet. But by the time I'm shampooed, shaved, and scrubbed, he still hasn't slid into this steamy corner of heaven with me. Frowning, I give up, turn off the water, and reach outside the door to retrieve a fluffy towel from the warming rack.

I wrap it around me, then poke my head out of the bathroom door. "Liam?"

I wait, but there's no answer, and I frown as I quickly comb my hair, then do my makeup.

He still hasn't returned by the time I finish, and I'm genuinely starting to worry. I'm actually heading to the bedside table to grab my new phone and call him when it rings, startling me enough that I jump.

His name pops up on the screen, and I sigh with relief, then snap out, "Where on earth are you!" before he can even say a word. "Sorry," I continue, immediately contrite. "It's just that I—"

"It's my fault. I should have called earlier, but you were asleep when I left, and I didn't want to wake you. But it looks like I'll be at least another fifteen minutes, so I wanted to call and let you know I hadn't run off with a gang of pirates."

"Good to know," I say. "But I do think you'd be sexy with a cutlass and an eye patch."

"I'll keep that in mind."

"What's the hold up? Nothing bad happened, did it? No one was following you, or—"

"No, no. Nothing like that."

I exhale with relief. "Did they have to go out and actually pick blueberries?"

He chuckles. "Not that, either, and the bag on the seat beside me is wildly tempting. I'm waiting to enjoy them with you, but I'm man enough to admit that I almost caved once or twice. As for the delay, I'm stuck behind a fender bender, and there's no alternate route. They'll have it cleared soon, I think."

"You weren't in it?"

"Safe and sound but I should have taken the bike. I'd be home with you by now."

"As long as you're in one piece." I say, as I look around the room for my shopping bag from yesterday. "And thank you for going out for me. Sorry it's turned into an ordeal."

"Well, I think you're worth it. But you can thank me however you like when I get back."

The thought sends my imagination flying, and I only snap back to reality when he tells me that he can see the tow truck ahead. "So it won't be long now. I'll see you in—"

"Hang on a sec. Do you know what happened to my shopping bag yesterday?" I'd grabbed a cute pair of white capris and an off-the-shoulder blouse that I planned to wear today. Not to mention a new pair of flats.

"Closet," he says. "Sorry, I wasn't thinking. I tossed it in there with my bag."

"No problem, and thanks. I'll be dressed by the time you get back, so we can have our muffins and head out anytime."

"More's the pity."

"Well, I'm naked right now," I tease, dropping the towel so that I'm not a liar. "You're the one who left me all alone with a bed and a jetted shower."

"Clearly, I'm a fool. See you soon."

I'm still smiling after our mutual goodbyes, and I head to the closet for my bag. There are several in there, and as I grab mine from the floor, I somehow upset the bag behind it, which is sitting on an Army style footlocker. The bag falls to the floor, and I mutter a curse, pulling my own bag out of the closet as I squat to clean up my mess.

It's only when I start to set the fallen bag

upright that I get a glimpse of what's in there—and then do a double-take when I see a pair of metal handcuffs.

At first, I think it's something to do with his work. After all, the man chases bad guys. But there's also a coil of silky black rope, another set of cuffs— these lined with fur, and a pair of nipple clamps.

Oh, my, yes.

And even though I know I shouldn't keep snooping in the bag, nothing is going to stop me now. And I become more and more aroused with each new discovery. Vibrators. Massage oil. A silky blindfold. And a sleek leather paddle. These are the accoutrements of the fantasy I want to play out with Liam. The desire I couldn't manage to speak because I didn't know how he would react.

Now, though...

Now I imagine him using everything in that bag with me. *On me.*

And as I hear the garage door start to churn, I tell myself it's time to summon the courage to tell him exactly what I want.

———

"Glad you're there safe and sound," Liam says as he enters the foyer from the garage. He sees me, then holds up his phone, pulling out his earbuds as he switches it to speaker. "What do you think of Seattle?"

"Seems pretty nice," I hear Leah say. "At least what I've seen from the taxi and out my hotel window. Not that I'm going to slide into tourist mode or anything."

"Anything of substance to report?"

"Actually, yes," she says, and I immediately look to Liam, who raises his eyebrows in a show of both interest and surprise. "I got a call," she says, as if that's supposed to mean something.

Considering the pleased way that Liam says, "Oh, did you?" with a tone of rising interest, I'm assuming that it *does* mean something. I'm just not sure what, and I decide to bite the bullet and display my ignorance.

"Okay, clue me in and explain what you're talking about."

"Someone was checking me—or you—out," she says. "About an hour after I got to the room, I got a call. Some guy with a smarmy voice saying he was with the hotel and was sending up a bottle of wine to me in room 1220 to welcome me to the city. I told him I really appreciated it, but that since I didn't drink he didn't need to make the effort. But that I would love a strawberry waffle in the morning. He told me that could be arranged, and there you go."

I look at Liam and shake my head, not under-standing.

"The caller wasn't from the hotel," he says.

"Oh." I'm not sure how he knows that, but I guess that's part of his job. Anyway, Leah confirms what he's said.

"I called down to the front desk and said I'd changed my mind and wanted my complimentary wine after all. The woman assured me that wasn't something they did."

"So they know you're—or rather, *I'm*—there and they have the room number. Good God, Leah, that doesn't sound—"

"Relax. I'm already gone. I left some clothes strewn around the room and my suitcase open, put the Do Not Disturb sign on, then went down the stairs to the basement and out the employee entrance. Someone will probably deliver a waffle and a bullet tomorrow morning, but I'll be long gone."

"You've arranged for eyes on the hall and a team to take down our man?"

"Not my first time at this rodeo," she says. "Yes. Ryan pulled in a team made up of some security personnel from Stark International Seattle and several men from a civilian SWAT-style team based here that he's worked with before. I'm at Stark Applied Technology right now. We're using one of the conference rooms as base camp."

"You're not heading back to LA?" I ask.

"Not after getting such a solid lead right away. I'll ride this out. And yes, I'll watch my back. Thanks for reminding me."

Liam grins. "Watch your back," he says, and I can practically hear Leah roll her eyes.

They end the call, and Liam looks at me, his smile wide and bright. "Another step closer. This is even better than we'd hoped."

I nod. All we'd expected was to lead them away from LA. Now it looks like we may have actually set a workable trap.

"I have more good news, too," he says, holding up the bag of muffins. "And not just these tasty treats. While I was stuck in traffic, Winston called. He's back in LA, along with Ella and Rye."

"Really?" I follow him to the kitchen.

"I guess they're staying at her place before they head up to San Francisco for another show."

"Of course. Right." I wasn't even thinking. Everyone else would already be on their way to the next gig, but Ella and Rye had intended to take a few days in the cabin. Considering recent events, it makes sense that they're enjoying alone time at Ella's Hollywood Hills house instead. Which also happens to be where my apartment is.

"Could we go see them today? And I can grab some more clothes while we're there."

"Why?" he asks, as he pours us both a cup of

coffee. He looks me up and down, his eyes dancing with amusement. "You're not even wearing the clothes you have here."

"True," I say. Despite telling him I needed the bag of clothes, after my discovery, I'd decided to stay in the fluffy robe he'd put out for me this morning. "But eventually, I will have to put on real clothes. Society expects it."

"Damn society," he mutters, shaking his head and making me laugh.

I expect him to say no to the jaunt since they— the infamous *they*—might still be watching the house and my apartment. But to my surprise he agrees, although more for him than for me, as he makes it clear that he wants to talk with Winston some more. He also tells me that Ella or Rye will need to go in and get my stuff—ideally while having a conversation about how they're going to mail my clothing to Seattle for me—and that when we arrive, we're driving into the garage and entering that way once the massive door has closed and hidden us from view.

"In other words, no convertible today."

"No convertible," he confirms, then calls Winston to find out what time will work.

We end up with a plan to meet them at eleven, which leaves enough time to chat and catch up before they have to leave for a meeting with one of Ella's producers.

"Terrific," I say, but I can't help but feel a bit sad. It's been a long time since I've been left out of one of Ella's business meetings. I push it aside, though, then run through a mental map for getting from Liam's condo in Malibu to Ella's house in the Hollywood Hills. I glance at the clock, do some mental math, and decide we have enough time.

"What?" Liam is studying my face, the gleam in his narrowed eyes suggesting he knows exactly what I'm thinking.

"I realize you went to a lot of trouble to get those blueberries," I say, "but I was wondering if we could eat in the car."

His brows rise. "Crumbs in the Beemer? I don't know."

"You have a BMW, too?"

He shrugs. "I like vehicles."

"I guess so."

"You want to tell me for what good reason should I sacrifice my recently detailed car?"

"Oh, no big deal," I say airily. "Just something else I wanted to do before we left … and I don't think there's time to do both."

"Is that so?"

"Not if we do the first one right."

He takes a step toward me, the humor in his eyes now replaced by a heat that pools in my belly and seeps down between my legs. "Now you've intrigued me," he says. "What do you have in mind?"

I untie the robe, open it, then let it slide down my arms and onto the floor. "Take a guess."

He drops to his knees, his hands cupping my ass and his tongue sliding over my pussy.

I groan, my legs going so weak I probably would have crumpled to the floor if his hands weren't supporting me. "Oh my God, you are a *very* good guesser."

"Just one of my many talents," he says as he rises again, then picks me up so that my breasts are pressed against his chest, my arms are around his neck, and my legs are hooked tight around his waist. He carries me that way to the bed, then tumbles us both onto the mattress.

I meet his eyes and tremble from the desire I see there. I could stay like this for hours, just getting lost in the way he looks at me. Like I'm special. Like I'm the only thing in the world that matters to him.

It's intoxicating. A sensation that is matched only by his actual touch. Which, right now, I desperately crave.

"Finger me," I whisper, and am rewarded with a cocky grin and his fingers dipping slowly inside me.

"A woman who knows what she wants. I like that."

"Funny," I say. "I feel the same way. Tell me what you want. Anything at all."

"I have what I want," he says, his thumb rubbing distracting circles on my clit. "I have you at my mercy."

"I could be more at your mercy," I whisper, my hips moving in response to the incredible way he's firing my senses. "You can do whatever you want with me."

"What I want is to make love to you all morning, but apparently we have an appointment."

And apparently, I'm going to have to be more direct.

I untuck his T-shirt, then unbutton his jeans. I get my hands under the material so I can cup his wonderfully firm ass and pull him close to me as I make my confession. "So, I, um, found my clothes in your closet like you said."

"And yet you're not wearing them."

"Well, we can't move too fast on these things," I quip, earning a laugh. I barrel on. "The thing is, I accidentally spilled another bag. I didn't mean to snoop, but I found—"

"Oh, *fuck.*"

He rolls off me, then props himself up on an arm, facing me, his hand gently stroking my cheek. "I'm sorry," he says.

"Sorry?" I try to process his words, and the only thing I can come up with is that he's had sex with other women. Not exactly a revelation. "It's not like I thought I was the first woman in your bed. I know you blow off steam, remember?"

"Yes, and sometimes I like..." He hesitates, then sits up, two fingers squeezing the bridge of his nose. He looks utterly wrecked, and I have no idea why.

Finally, he speaks, his voice low and even. "I should have put that stuff away. I wasn't thinking. But please know that I understand what you've been through." His voice is calm. The way he might speak to a frantic child. Or a skittish cat. "And I would never, ever ask you to do that."

I stay still, stunned and unsure how to react. How to explain that he has this completely wrong despite his heart being so firmly planted in exactly the right place. "Liam, I—"

He takes my hand and presses it to his heart. "Xena, baby, I will take care of you, and I want you in my bed. And just because I sometimes need—no, that has nothing to do with you. So long as you're with me, you're in a safe place. I want you to understand that. I would never do anything to trigger those memories, and I am so, so sorry you stumbled across that."

I've clearly thrown him for a loop, and I honestly don't know if I should try to explain or if I should just let this play out and try again later. Considering we need to go soon, later is probably the better option, because I have a feeling that telling this man that even with my history, I want him to cuff me to the bed is going to be a very dicey conversation.

But I do want it. More than that, I need it.

But I need him more.

I swallow, then lick my lips. "It's okay," I say. "Really. I was, um, just embarrassed that I'd run across something so personal. But I'm not upset. Not at all. Truly."

He searches my face, then nods, apparently satisfied. "I want you to trust me," he says.

"I do, I promise." And that's the God's honest truth. I just don't know how to tell him the rest of it.

CHAPTER NINETEEN

L iam had no idea what the hell he'd been thinking leaving that damn sack of toys in the closet. Except of course that he hadn't been thinking, primarily because he'd forgotten all about the bag and the items inside it.

It had been months since he'd been with a woman that way. Hell, it had been months since he'd been with a woman other than Xena. He'd told her the truth when he'd said that he blew off steam from time to time, but the truth was that since he had no interest in starting a relationship with any of the women who'd shared his bed, he'd become less and less interested in having them in his bed at all.

He'd chalked it up to getting older and having less patience for the tedious repetition that accompanied hook-ups or even casual dating. But that wasn't the real reason. Mostly, he was just over it.

Or he'd thought he was. Because the woman now sitting beside him making small moans of satisfaction as she ate a blueberry muffin—moans that had him wanting to pull the BMW over and make her *really* moan—had snuck up on him and changed the way he looked at everything.

With Xena, he wasn't over it at all. With her, he felt alive again in ways he hadn't felt since Dion. Ways he thought he'd wanted to leave behind forever. But now ... well, now he cherished the way she made him smile and laugh. The way she looked at him with unfettered desire.

She'd opened herself to him about a time in her life that had been beyond horrific. She'd trusted him.

And he'd gone and blown it because he'd cleaned out the drawer of his bedside table a few months ago and never properly put the damn stuff away.

He wanted to fucking kick himself.

"Are you sure you don't want a muffin?" she said. "You look like you could use one."

He drew a calming breath, not wanting to add to the stress he was certain he'd caused her—despite her polite protests to the contrary. "What does someone who could use a muffin look like?"

"Duh," she said. "You."

They'd reached a three-way intersection of the canyon roads leading up to Ella's house, and he looked at her as he waited for an oncoming car to pass, shaking his head in mock exasperation. "Bad joke."

"Oh, no. It was a great joke. You must be misinformed."

"Possibly," he said. "But—" He cut himself off, frowning at the black SUV reflected in the review mirror. Common enough in LA. But had he seen that particular one before, just a few streets back?

"What is it?"

"I'm not sure. Probably a coincidence. But we're taking a different route." He'd intended to go straight, but now he took a sharp right, which had him climbing an unfamiliar street.

He followed the twists and curves until he was certain they weren't being followed, then he slowed while the Waze App recalibrated and found the quickest route.

He checked repeatedly during the remainder of the drive, but the SUV never appeared behind them again.

"Probably just my paranoia," he said to Winston later, after they were safely in Ella's house. "I didn't even suspect a tail until we were a few miles from Ella's."

"And your windows are tinted," Winston said. "So no chance one of Noyce's random flunkies saw you two and decided to follow."

He said the last with a grin, and Liam

responded with a self-deprecating shake of his head. "Yes, I'm sure Noyce has lined the streets with minions in cars just waiting for me to pass."

"Anything's possible," Winston said with equal humor.

"It's her." Liam sighed. "Xena. That woman has me twisted up, and I can't stand the thought of something happening to her because I fucked up."

"You won't fuck up," Winston said. Tall and lanky, with an easy manner and soul-searching eyes, Winston Starr looked the part of the real-life role he used to play. When they'd first met, Liam had been unsure about the value that a former West Texas sheriff could bring to an internationally elite team. But he'd learned soon enough that there was more to Winston than met the eye, and they'd become good friends. One day, he intended to learn about the demons in Winston's past. Until then, he was content to admire the man's work ethic and skills.

They were in the kitchen, and Liam took one of the bottled waters that Ella had left on the counter for him and Winston before she, Rye, and Xena had gone off to the media room to chat. Liam knew they would have preferred to sit on the patio overlooking hills—that same patio where he'd stood with Xena the night he'd been so damn tempted to kiss her. But he was taking no chances with Xena's life. Outside, she was a sitting duck for any of Noyce's assholes with a high-powered rifle. At the very least, anyone with eyes on Ella's house would know that Xena wasn't in Seattle.

It was for that reason that he'd approved the media room rather than the sunny living area. No windows.

And why he'd had Rye and Ella both walk over to the cottage and bring back a bag of clothes for Xena, all the while chatting about how they should see about renting the studio since Xena was moving out of state.

He was just about to tell Winston they should head into the other room and join the others when a text came in from Mario: *Call Me.*

He showed it to Winston, whose brows rose. "Think he got a hit?"

"I think we should find out," Liam said, then started to dial, only to pause as Ella and Rye came into the room, arm in arm.

"Are you two in here eating all my food or discussing all my bad habits?" Ella asked, grinning at them both.

"You have bad habits?" Liam asked, deadpan.

She winked. "Of course. Or don't you follow me on social media?"

He chuckled, and she waved her hand, as if dismissing the banter. "We just came to get popcorn and the two of you," she told them as Rye ducked into the pantry, then emerged with two large, red bags of pre-popped corn, the pantry door still open behind him. "We've already got drinks in the media room fridge. You ready?"

"Just need to return Mario's call," Liam said.

"Does he have news on those two guys?" Rye asked.

"Probably only checking in," Liam said, not wanting to get the manager's hopes up.

"Well, don't be long," Ella said. "We want to start."

"What are we watching?" Liam asked.

"Me, of course. Concert footage. For your entertainment and my edification. If I don't watch every show, how will I know where I can improve?"

She didn't wait for an answer, but turned on her heel and headed back, with Rye right behind her.

"Be there in a minute," Winston called, shooting Liam an amused look.

"We should get her on board at the SSA," he said while he put his phone on speaker and waited for Mario to answer. "That woman knows how to lead a team."

"Got a hit!" Mario shouted out the news without preamble, making Liam flinch, as he hadn't even realized the line had connected.

"Which one?" Liam asked.

"Square jaw. His name's Patrick Weil. Grew up in Jersey, but he lives in Manhattan. One of

Seagrave's contacts in the Defense Department called in some favors and got us confirmation."

"Have we got eyes on him?"

"On the address, yes," Mario said. "But not on the man. Confirmation of his location in the city was made twelve minutes ago. An ATM that time-stamped him at that location ninety minutes ago. I sent a team, but he was long gone."

"And his home address?"

"Got a team watching the place," Mario assured him. "Right now, no one's home."

Liam took a long swallow of water, thinking. "Odds are he's still in town, but we can't ignore the possibility that he deliberately used a Manhattan ATM to place him in the city. If he hopped on a bus or a train, he could be long gone by now."

"No argument from me," Mario said. "But this is the best we've got."

"And it's good work," Liam agreed. "I just want this wrapped up. For Xena's sake."

"I get you. And I'll call you if anything happens at his apartment."

"Good. And get in touch with Dallas Sykes, or ask Ryan to. If you need extra manpower, he'll be able to get it to you. And tell Dallas that Xena and I will see him soon."

"You're heading to New York?"

"You know me, Mario. I always go where the

action is." He grinned as he ended the call, then met Winston's eyes. "A little progress, at least."

"Always a good thing," Winston said in that slow, easy drawl. "And about time. I haven't learned a thing with Ella and Rye, either here or earlier in Vegas. Well, that's not actually true," he amended. "I learned pretty much everything there is to know about working a concert, but I didn't see a single thing that was suspicious."

"Did you interview the staff?"

"Do I look like I'm new to this game? I did interviews until I thought my ears would fall off. Swept for bugs, the whole nine yards."

"What about doing an electronics sweep here?" Liam asked. He knew it was possible that someone had gotten into the Hollywood Hills house while Ella and Rye were in Vegas and set up electronic surveillance, either audio or video.

Winston shook his head. "Did that, found nothing. But nice of you to double check me."

Liam shot him an apologetic smile.

"Don't worry about me, I don't get my nose out of joint. I know you're trying to cover all bases."

"Mostly I'm just hoping that we'll stumble over something we forgot. Something we missed. I don't know. Maybe I was too quick to assume Gordon's asinine publicity stunt was isolated. Maybe it's actually at the heart of this whole thing."

"So we get eyes on him again. Set up another interview."

Liam nodded. "I will. Although it just doesn't ring for me. But we'll check it anyway." He rubbed his hand over his scalp, then took a long frustrated breath.

"We'll figure it out," Winston assured him. "God knows, I'm invested now too. I'm camping out here with Ella and Rye while they're in town, and then I'm going to head up with them to San Francisco when they finish the tour."

"Are you sure?" Liam asked. "That might be a good time to hand them off to a full service body guard company."

"I'll do that after San Francisco if we don't have this in the bag. But like I said, I want to stick with it. I like them both, and, well..."

"What?" Liam asked, as Winston trailed off.

"Its nothing having to do with your perp. Just those two. My God, he is head over heels for that woman. Reminds me of me back in the day. God, my Linda. I would've done anything for that woman..."

He trailed off again, this time with a melancholy smile lighting his face.

Liam wanted to ask, but he couldn't quite find the words. He knew there'd been a reason that Winston had left West Texas, and he thought that he was seeing a hint of it now. But that wasn't the only thing that had him holding his tongue. Beneath Winston's pain, there was an undercurrent of something so damn familiar. A kinship between Liam and Winston. And even Rye. A kinship born of loyalty to a woman.

Because with each passing day, Liam felt more and more the same. And as far as Xena was concerned, there was nothing he wouldn't do to keep her safe.

"Do you miss it?" Liam glanced over at the woman beside him. They were back in his SUV, driving down the famous stretch of Mulholland Drive that ran along the top of the foothills, separating the west side from the San Fernando Valley.

"Do I miss what?" Xena asked.

"I was watching your face during the concert video," Liam said.

"Don't tell Ella. She'll never let you hear the end of it."

"You can help keep my secrets," Liam said.

She turned in her seat, looking at him, a small shy smile on her lips. "I'll always do that," she said. "You know that, right?"

He did, actually. It was so strange the way that they fit together. The way that she'd simply slid into his life, and fit so perfectly, as if he was one part of a jagged piece of broken pottery and she was the missing piece, and now their rough edges combined to make something perfect and beautiful.

He half laughed, amused by his own flowery thinking.

"What?"

He hesitated, wanting to tell her the direction of his thoughts. Wanting to talk with her and lay out how she made him feel wonderful and confused all at the same time.

Hell, maybe now was the time for that conversation. The famous road was romantic as hell, even in the middle of the afternoon. And he'd enjoy sharing the view with her. "Why don't I find a turn-around and pull over?" he said.

"Why, Mr. Foster. Are you suggesting that we go parking?"

"Maybe I am," he said. "Of course it is the middle of the afternoon."

"I don't have a problem with that if you don't."

He grinned. "Nope. No problem with that at all." He looked around, trying to get his bearings, and was pretty sure there was a turnaround less than a mile away, just past a particularly twisty and narrow section of the road.

They were on a curve at the moment, and when he hit a straightaway, he noticed the vehicle behind them. There had been minimal traffic during the drive so far, and most of the cars had turned off when they hit Laurel Canyon or Beverly Glen, to go down the hill to the west side or into the valley.

As far as he could tell, this one had come up fast behind him out of nowhere. And, he noticed, it was another black SUV, just like the one he'd clocked before they reached Ella's.

He scowled at his rear-view mirror, and released a silent curse. Beside him, Xena shifted. "What is it?" He could hear the nervousness in her voice.

"Hopefully nothing. I just noticed the car behind us." She twisted in her seat, looking through the back window of the BMW. "Is that the same car that was behind us on our way to Ella's?"

Liam grimaced. "Could be. Neither has a front license plate, but that's not terribly unusual. And from what I can see it's the same model."

"Shit."

"That pretty much sums up my sentiments."

"Can they see us in here?"

"No. The windows are tinted. We can see out easily, but they can't see in."

"Should we let them pass? It might just be a coincidence."

He'd been thinking something along those same lines, but on the narrow road, he didn't want to take a chance if the person behind them was up to no good. And considering the way the last few days

had been going—not to mention Xena's entire life—
the odds were good that the driver behind them did
not have their best intentions at heart.

Making a decision, he turned to her. "Are you
strapped in?"

Xena nodded. "Yes, but—"

"Hold that thought," Liam said as he hit the
accelerator hard. "And call 911. Just in case I'm
right."

The Beemer jumped forward, and he swerved
to the left, away from the drop-off that loomed just
beyond Xena's side of the car. He could hear her
tight gasp beside him, but couldn't take his attention off the road to look at her.

The SUV was closer now, and it made a sharp
jut to the right as it accelerated, hitting the driver's
side of the BMW near the back tire and shifting the
car's ass toward the drop-off.

"Oh my God oh my God oh my God oh my God."
Her phone had tumbled to the floorboard, but he could
see that she'd made the call, and the phone was automatically sharing its location with emergency services.

He wanted to tell her it would be okay, but he
didn't know that it would be. Although he damn
sure intended to do everything in his power to
make it so. And part of that attempt, unfortunately,
meant that she was just going to have to hold on
tight and hope that he knew what he was doing,

because there was no time for consoling or conversation.

The car shimmied, and Liam realized they'd blown a tire. The SUV had reversed, and was gunning its engine for another slam, and this one would surely send them tumbling over the hill.

There was a guardrail a few feet ahead, and that was what Liam needed. And as the SUV jolted forward, he hit the accelerator, praying that he could cover enough distance before impact. He managed to get close enough that, when the next blow came, the nose of the car rammed the guardrail, stopping them from going over.

But the SUV wasn't giving up, and the driver pounded them again, this time hitting the rear of the Beemer with enough force that the guardrail actually gave way.

Xena's scream filled the car as the sedan started to slide, then jolted to a stop, and Liam realized that part of the now-jutting guardrail had caught the frame.

The SUV wasn't so lucky. The damaged rail had stopped the BMW, but the SUV had hit at an angle and glanced off the rear of his car. The driver had underestimated how much the rear of the car would sway with only the front smashed into the guardrail. It overshot with too much force, and in a cacophony of twisting metal and breaking glass, went tumbling over the drop off to crash into a heap among the trees below.

"Don't move," Liam said to Xena, who was frozen beside him breathing hard.

Around them, sirens blared as emergency vehicles approached.

And it was only when the team had secured the car and safely extracted Xena, that Liam realized he could once again breathe.

CHAPTER TWENTY

W e're at the site for what feels like forever
before the police finally release us and
have a patrolman drive us home. But even safe in
the backseat of the cop car, my blood is still
pounding as I live those last, horrible moments over
and over and over.

The driver was the second Vegas attacker,
Mouse Face. His real name was Laurence Tesh
according to the license they pulled off his body,
which may or may not be bullshit. He's one of the
men who attacked Ella in Vegas. And he was one of
Noyce's men. We've been assuming as much, but
today Mario confirmed it.

So that means this horrible dead man who tried
to kill us is tied to my past. And that both Liam and
I are in danger because of a life I never wanted but
can't escape, no matter how hard I try.

That's reality, and it sucks. I want to rail against it. To scream and rant, and then cling tight to something or someone until they set it right.

Automatically, I turn and look at Liam. I'm already holding his hand—we haven't separated since the emergency crew helped us out of the BMW after they stabilized it. For a moment, I just stare, memorizing his features, amazed by how wholly and completely he has become that person in such a short amount of time. The man I want holding me. The person I want comforting me. The lover with whom I want to share my secrets, my hopes, my dreams.

I try to tell myself that it's infatuation or some type of hero awe since he's stepped in to protect me. But I know that isn't true. I've known it, I think, since that first party at Ella's house, the one where we'd both wanted to kiss, but fought the urge.

Today was horrible, but it was also confirmation of just how much this man has come to mean to me. Because as terrified as I was in that car, I was more terrified of losing him.

I suck in a deep breath as tears well in my eyes. Beside me, Liam releases my hand long enough to put his arm around me and pull me closer. And when I rest my head on his shoulder, I almost burst into tears. I'm raw, and I don't know what to do with all these emotions that are going around and around inside me.

I need release—I need *him*.

And right then, what I want more than anything is to be back at his place.

"Xena." His voice is tight, but also gentle. "Are you okay?"

I nod. "That was just—that was just scary." I meet his eyes. "I've seen scary. I've tasted terrified. But the only thing that's messed me up more than tonight was my dad." *Because I lost my dad. And I almost lost you.*

I snuggle closer against him, his body tight and tense, and I know that he is fighting his own battle, too. I've learned how he thinks, and I'm certain that he's feeling guilty. Because even though his specific mission is to keep me safe—and despite spending almost every waking moment with me—he still almost lost me.

Oh, God. He almost lost me. And I almost lost him.

I can't wrap my head around the magnitude of that, and as the cop escorts us to Liam's door, all I can think is that I want him. I want his touch, his mouth, his body. I want all of him, because he's mine—and because he will make me forget.

Best of all, I know he wants it, too, and I'm not surprised when—the moment the door shuts behind us—Liam has me up against the wall, his mouth claiming mine. It's fierce and passionate and

I surrender to him, letting myself fall under the spell of his lips, his hands, his touch.

Our kiss is fierce. Fabulous. Teeth clashing, tongues warring, as if this were the ultimate act of connection. As if by kissing me, he is claiming me as his own, marking me as his forever.

And, oh God, I want him to do exactly that. I groan, then suck in air as his hands close over my breasts, teasing my nipples through the thin material of my unpadded bra, then using one hand to unbutton the four tiny buttons that had been holding my blouse closed. He pulls my shirt open, then unfastens the front clasp of my bra to unbind my breasts before his mouth closes over one, his teeth grazing my nipple.

I squirm, unable to stay still from the force of the sensations rising though me, and I move my hands from his shoulders down to his ass, trying to urge him closer.

"No," he says, lifting his head to look at me. I see strength in his eyes along with need and determination. Mostly, though, I see him looking at me. "Arms up," he says, taking me by the wrists and thrusting my hands above my head.

He holds me there, one large hand tight around my overlapping wrists as his other hand explores me. "Close your eyes," he orders, and when I do, his finger strokes me, lightly stroking my cheek before moving lower, taking his time to caress me gently, to tease my nipple, to completely fire my senses, so that by the time he has reached the elastic waistband of the simple skirt I wore today, all I want is for him to rip it off me.

He doesn't. Instead, he hitches it up around my waist, then cups his hand over my pussy, thrusting three fingers inside me so that he has a tight, intimate grip on me. His mouth is on my breast and his other hand is above me, holding my arms firmly above my head.

I struggle, wanting to feel just how completely he has captured me, and as I do, his grip tightens, his mouth moving up to crush mine, his tongue taking me in a wild, erotic demand.

When he breaks the kiss, I am weak, my knees wobbly and my body so overheated, I'm sure that I will melt. "More," I beg.

He steps back, releasing me. "To the bedroom, baby. I promise you more."

I take his hand and slip it back under my skirt, my eyes locked on his. "More," I repeat, and only see confusion in his eyes. "I want you to bring out your bag of toys."

He steps back, releasing me, his head shaking slowly. It's as if I tossed a bucket of cold water all over us, and I desperately hope that I haven't fucked everything up.

"You don't know what you're asking," he says.

"The hell I don't." Anger sparks in me—how

dare he presume to know what I need. "You want it —do not even try to say you don't. So why the hell can't you believe that I want it, too?"

"You're sore," he says. "The wreck."

"Yeah, I am," I admit. "But I'd like to be sore from you." I put my hands on his shoulders, moving my body closer. I'm a little afraid that I'm crossing a line, but I'm past the point of caring. "Cuff my wrists," I whisper. "Spank my ass. Give me a bruise that I *want*. Make me stiff in a good way. Dammit, Liam, you want it, too, and for the same reasons."

He tilts his head, his nostrils flaring as if he's fighting some primal urge. *Good*, I think, and press on. "Do you think I don't get it? Do you think I don't understand why you shy away from relationships? Something happened," I say, and see the slice of pain cross his face and disappear, so quick I can almost convince myself that I imagined it.

"The world got out of control and you want to grab it back."

"And you?" His question is hard, almost an accusation. "You were controlled. Forced. Your choices taken away. For years, you were fucking used by those monsters. And now you want me to cuff you?"

"*Yes*." I want to scream the word, as if volume will convince him. "Yes. Cuff me. Blindfold me. Bind my legs. Spank or paddle me." I draw a deep breath, forcing myself to slow my words down. "Whatever you want, Liam. Because I want it, too."

He shakes his head, and I go to him. I press against him, knowing I'm probably pushing too hard, but I no longer care. I'm either going to win or lose, but we're going to finish this.

"I want it," I say gently, "but only from you. Don't you get that? They *took*, dammit. I want to give. You're a strong man, Liam. A powerful one. The kind of man who can make things happen, and I'd be a fool not to know that you're the kind of man who likes to be in control, in and outside of the bedroom."

"I don't need that," he says. "Not like this."

"Of course, you don't. Need isn't the same as desire. And you would never take something you want if you thought it would hurt me." I take his hands. "But please, please understand that your chivalry is misplaced. I want it too. Hell, I crave it."

"Xena, you—"

"Yes, dammit, listen. You want control? Control me. Not because you're forcing me, but because I want to finally, *finally* give someone control rather than having it be ripped from me."

For a moment, he only watches me, and I'm afraid he either doesn't understand or doesn't believe.

Then he meets my eyes and says, "Bedroom."

There's power in that word. Power and

demand, and I feel the force of those two simple syllables all through my body.

My knees are weak as I comply, then sit on the foot of the bed. He follows, pausing to lean against the doorframe as his eyes skim over me, his slow, steady gaze making my body tremble with anticipation.

"Take off your clothes," he says. "Then sit back down, legs spread."

My heart pounds in my chest as I comply, already imagining him looking at me, his eyes full of heat, and when I am naked and on the bed, my legs spread so far my inner thighs ache, I'm rewarded by his low groan of satisfaction as well as the way his hand cups his obviously stiff cock.

He moves to the closet, then pulls out the bag. He makes a point of meeting my gaze, then spills out all the toys onto the carpet. I feel my body respond, my nipples going tight as I imagine what he'll do with each toy. What he'll do to me.

"It excites you," he says, and while I hear heat in his voice, I think there is also relief, as if he is only now certain that I'd meant what I said in the hallway.

"Yes, sir," I say, allowing myself the slightest of smiles as I emphasize the last word.

His smile comes easily, and my own wave of relief washes over me as I realize that, yes, we're both finally on the same page.

"What's your safe word," he asks, picking up a blindfold and coming toward me.

I shake my head. "I don't want one."

He lifts a brow. "I don't think—"

"I don't want one," I repeat. "I don't want limits with you. I trust you not to go too far."

For a moment, I think he's going to argue, but then he bends forward and kisses me softly before settling the blindfold on my eyes and tying it just enough so that not even light seeps in under the edges.

I wait for him to ask if it's okay and am thrilled when he doesn't. I want him to claim. To take. I want it because I've given it, and now it's his turn to enjoy what I'm finally—freely—sharing.

"On your knees, baby," he says, his hand at my elbow helping me onto the floor.

I kneel there, listening to him move around the room, then suck in breath as he tugs my arms behind my back, binding my wrists with the padded cuffs before turning his attention to my nipples, his fingers teasing them each in turn as I whimper.

"I'm not asking if you want this," he says. "I'm trusting that you do. And," he adds, "I'm trusting that you'll tell me if I'm wrong."

I nod, biting my lower lip in anticipation of what I'm sure is coming. Sure enough, moments later, I feel the pressure on my nipples, one after the other. There's pain at first, but then it fades to a nice, deep intensity that seems to stretch like a thread all the way down to my sex.

"Nice," he murmurs, and although I know it's silly, I feel a ridiculous jolt of pride.

I can't see, but I know that he's right in front of me. I can feel his presence, larger than life and wonderfully commanding. And then, as if in confirmation, I hear his hands on his jeans and then the metallic scrape of his zipper followed by the rustle of material.

I make a small, needy noise as heat coils in my belly. I'm wet—I can't touch myself but I can feel the slickness on my inner thighs, and when the tip of his cock brushes my lips, I squeeze my legs together, fighting the urge to come right then as I open my mouth and take him in.

With my hands bound behind my back, I have neither balance nor control. Instead, Liam holds my head, fucking me—*controlling* me—as I submit, reveling in the fact that I am giving this to him. Willingly. Openly. And, more, that he is taking it.

I feel the subtle shifts in his body and am certain that he is close. I expect him to explode in me, but he surprises me, pulling out of my mouth, then taking my arm to tug me to my feet. He turns me around, then pushes me forward until my legs are pressed against the bed. He bends me forward so that my torso is on the mattress and my ass is in the air.

I close my eyes, enjoying the sensation of the bedcover on my clamped nipples. Of the cool air against my heated skin. And of his fingers trailing lightly over my back, then down the crack of my rear until he slips his fingers inside me, his body bending over mine so that the cotton of his shirt brushes my back and his cock rubs my ass as he whispers, "You're incredibly wet." He thrusts his fingers in deeper, then withdraws them, trailing a fingertip lightly over my perineum as I bite my lower lip, lost in a needy, sensual haze. "I like it. Do you?"

"God, yes," I murmur, and he laughs.

"I can tell. Spread your legs, baby."

I do, and he eases off me, lightly smacking my ass with the palm of his hand. I make a low noise in my throat, but press my lips closed. I want more, but I don't want to beg. On the contrary, I want to let him lead this, taking me wherever and however he wants to go.

Thankfully, I soon learn that he wants to go exactly where I do, and he gives my ass another smack, this one harder and followed by his own low moan before he rubs his palm over my skin to soothe me, then slides his hand between my legs to tease my clit.

I wiggle, wanting so much more, and he satisfies

me with another spank, then murmurs something about the sweet pink stain marking my pretty pale ass, and how he can't decide if he should keep it pink or go for deep red.

I bite my lip, my breasts aching against the mattress and my sex throbbing with need as he spanks me twice more, then says, "Fuck red. I can't take it anymore."

And then—oh, God, yes—his cock is right there, one hand on my hip and the other sliding between the bed and my body to find my clit as he thrusts into me, fucking me so hard the bed slams against the wall and I think that it's very good that he doesn't share a wall with his neighbor. But that's all I think before passion takes over and I'm incapable of thought. Of anything other than pleasure and sensation and the satisfaction of a spiraling intensity that zooms out to every cell in my body, heating me to boiling as he takes me harder and harder until—finally—I spin up and out, everything inside me ripping apart from my physical body to go whirling off into space, where I finally explode in a fountain of pure pleasure as hot and powerful as a super nova.

I'm breathing hard when I crash back down to earth, and I barely even notice when he gently uncuffs me. He gets onto the bed beside me, and I realize that somehow he'd moved me fully onto the mattress.

"That was insane," I murmur, easing against him. "That was freaking fabulous."

I feel his gentle laughter reverberate through me, and snuggle closer, my hand flat against his chest so that I can feel his heartbeat. For a moment, I simply lie there listening to the sound of our breathing and our hearts beating in the same rhythm. I want to sleep but I'm not tired. I want to know more, I want to know everything. And although I know that Liam does not want to tell me, I push myself up on my elbow and ask very simply, "Will you tell me about her?"

"Who?"

"The woman you loved. The woman who's the reason that you don't do relationships. Did she break your heart?"

For a moment I think he's going to ignore my question and silence hangs heavy between us. When he finally speaks, his voice is so low that I can barely hear him. "No," he says, rolling onto his side. "She's dead. She's dead because of me."

CHAPTER TWENTY-ONE

I let his words hang there for at least a minute, then I roll onto my side, spooning against his back. "Tell me the story," I say.

"It's not something I talk about."

"All the more reason. Don't tell it because I'm asking you too. Tell me because you owe it to her to talk about it."

He's quiet, and I press my hand on his bicep, feeling his strength, and I can't help but be struck by the irony that a man this strong can be felled by the weight of horrible memories. But why not? Don't I know better than anyone how the past can affect you?

"It was a long time ago," he says as he turns to face me, his head on the pillow only inches from mine. "But sometimes it feels like yesterday."

A small smile touches his mouth, and it warms

me. I'm glad that at least part of this memory brings him a little bit of joy.

"She worked at the makeup department in the Sykes Department Store in London. These were in my early days out of the Army, and I was working a covert job in military intelligence. I had the Sykes job as a cover, though the work was real enough."

I nod, wondering if he understands how much he's sharing with me. How much he's opening up, even though he says he doesn't want to. But I don't say anything. I don't want him to stop talking.

He rolls onto his back, as if he's talking to the ceiling. "Dion was a sweet girl," he says. "Smart, funny, great with the customers. Everybody loved her. She lit up a room when she walked in, and I never heard her say a harsh word to anybody. The moment I met her, I knew I wanted to be around her. Everyone did. She had that kind of personality. I think you would've liked her."

"I bet I would have. What happened?"

"Tragedy. That's always the way it is with these stories, isn't it? There's always tragedy and pain and heartbreak and horror, and it's all a goddamn mess." He pushes himself up so that he's sitting against the headboard. I shift as well, sitting up with my legs crossed, and pulling the blanket up around me so that I'm covered as I face him. "Are you sure you want to hear this?" he asks.

"You know I do."

He nods. "We started going out, first as friends, and then it got serious. I loved her. It boils down to that. We moved in together, bought furniture, and every day she made me smile." He waits as if expecting me to ask a question, but I hold my tongue. This is his story to tell now.

"While that simple, sweet life was going on in our small flat in London, on my off days, I was doing intelligence work, tracking down a man named Anatole Franklin. Definitely not a nice man. He would probably remind you a lot of Noyce."

I shudder simply from the mention of Noyce's name.

"I was getting close to Franklin, and somehow he found out. I don't know how. To this day I have no idea what set him off or how he found out about Dion, but he waited for her outside of the department store, followed her home, and shot her on our front porch stoop." His voice is flat, as if he's giving a police report, and I realize that he's fighting to control the anger and pain.

"Everyone who came by the building saw her splayed out on the stairs as emergency services tried to revive her. They couldn't. She was dead before I got there. I didn't even have a chance to say goodbye."

"Oh God, Liam. I'm so sorry. How did they know it was him?"

"It was a message to me. I knew it was him even before confirmation. But I guess he was afraid that I might miss the point. He made sure he was seen, and there were plenty of witnesses. Three different people identified him from mug shots. But I knew where to find the son of a bitch. He hadn't counted on that."

"What do you mean?"

"I don't think that Franklin realized how close we were on his trail. We knew where he was holed up, we knew what his next move was going to be. He'd been a high placed US official based in the embassy in London, which he'd used as a doorway to other countries we weren't so friendly with. He'd been trading government secrets and he was willing to kill to protect his ass."

"You killed him."

"I did. The government wanted him—badly. They wanted what was in his head. But goddamn it, I didn't care. I was wild with rage, crazed. I forced open his door, raised my weapon, and shot him in the head." He turns now to meet my eyes. "And I don't regret it."

I lick my lips. "What happened?"

"Well, as I'm here, I obviously didn't end up in prison, military or otherwise. He was selling very serious state secrets, after all. And although the government wasn't impressed with my decision to take him out before they were ready, they ended up

simply   discharging   me.   Thankfully   not
dishonorably."

"You were lucky," I say, and he nods.

"My superiors spoke up for me. They knew
well enough what I'd been through. And that
nothing they could do to me would be worse than
what Franklin had already done."

For a moment, I'm quiet. Then I move to sit
next to him, leaning against him, wanting to feel his
warmth against my body. I take his hand and hold
it, our fingers twined. "You know it wasn't your
fault, right? You didn't kill her."

"If I hadn't loved her, she would still be alive.
He killed her because she was important to me."

If I hadn't loved her...

That's what he's thinking of course, that's why
he can't be in a relationship. It's the fear that
anyone he gets close to will be taken from him. I
understand it. My whole life was taken from me
and God knows I'm scared of getting involved too.
But I'm hoping that the man sitting next to me will
be able to exorcise my demons and clear a path for
me to have a normal life and normal relationships.

I don't know if I can be of any help to him,
though. All I can do is try to let him see that he has
strength enough within himself already to survive
whatever life throws at him.

"If I hadn't loved her," he repeats. Then he

turns to me, his eyes dark. So dark that they almost scare me. "Please," he says, his voice tight with emotion. "Please don't ask me to love you."

I stay silent, fighting tears. But the truth is, I know that he already does.

CHAPTER TWENTY-TWO

H e knew she didn't truly understand. They were both alike in that they were avoiding relationships, but she was avoiding them because she was the one at risk. He cut himself off because being close to him put others at risk. His job was his life, and his life was dangerous.

"I know what you're thinking," she said.

"Do you?"

"You're thinking that you're a magnet. Not just that you attract women with your amazing charm and incredible looks, but that you're a magnet for pain and for suffering. After what happened to Dion, who could blame you?"

He said nothing. He had already said every-thing he wanted to say.

"But the truth is, there are a lot of things in this

world that are scarier than being in the cross hairs because I'm your girlfriend."

His body tightened at her use of the word girlfriend. But that wasn't someplace they could go.

"Scarier things," he said, trying to lighten the mood. "Like what?"

"Like being without you, dummy." She smiled, as if to underscore that she was teasing. But then she bit her lower lip, drew in a breath, and said, "I'm falling in love with you, you know."

Such simple, common words. Words he hadn't heard for a long time, and that he'd told himself he would never want to hear again.

And he didn't. He shouldn't.

Because those were dangerous words. Those were words that could get a woman killed. And yet at the same time, those gentle, wonderful words lit her from within, making her more beautiful than she already was.

"It's too soon for words like that," he said, wanting to dull the moment. To take away some of its shine. To make it not be something wonderful and precious that he wanted to hold close to his heart.

If she was offended or hurt by his seemingly casual brush-off, there was no sign. She just shook her head gently and said, "No, it's not. It's never too soon for truth. But if you need time to say it back, I understand. In the meantime, I want you to know that I do love you. And nothing you can say or do will flip off that switch inside me."

He searched her face, looking for any hesitation. But all he saw was love. And damned if he didn't have a clue what to do with it.

She yawned, then flashed an apologetic smile as she slid under the covers and curled up against him. "You made a horrible day wonderful," she said. "Now I just want to sleep and pretend like the time between leaving Ella's and walking through this condo's door never happened."

He couldn't argue with that. After almost being killed, there was nothing else he'd needed except her. And they'd made love wildly and with so much feeling, that he felt as if some core part of him had changed forever. But not changed enough to confess something as dangerous as love.

Hell, even knowing the way that she felt about him seemed dangerous. As if she was courting trouble. As if she'd opened a magic box and let all the evil spirits free.

At the same time he couldn't deny the unexpected, amazing truth. Her confession of love had filled him with a sense of warmth unlike anything he had felt in years. It was uplifting and incredible. It was everything he wanted and everything he needed, and it was everything he wanted to run from.

Except that he didn't want to run. Not really.

He fit so well with this woman that it felt like a miracle. And the irony of it was that she couldn't be his miracle. Not now; not ever. Because while he might have a reputation as a badass, the one thing he knew would destroy him was losing her.

He could have lost her tonight, and she wasn't even his yet. Not really. And knowing that she might have gone over in the car, that she might have died, that she might have been lost to him forever...

Well, that was something that ate at his soul.

He would protect her. That was the mission. That was what he'd been hired to do.

He would fall in love with her because he couldn't help it.

But in the end, he would leave her, because he had to.

Because the bottom line was that he would do whatever it took to protect the woman he loved. And that included doing something that hurt her.

Beside him, her breathing had slowed. She'd fallen asleep, and he knew that he should do the same. It had been one hell of a long day. Wonderful in many respects, trying in so many others. And now he just wanted to slide underneath the covers and let sleep settle over him.

But just as that sweet curtain was about to fall, his own thoughts came back to him—*He would do anything for her. Anything to protect her.*

He bolted out of bed, grabbed his phone, and

hurried into the other room so he wouldn't wake her. He dialed, then waited impatiently before Winston picked up the phone.

"I heard about the accident," the Texan said. "You okay? I was going to call earlier but I figured you needed the rest."

"We're both a bit shook up, but no permanent damage. What were you going to call about?"

"The coincidence, my friend. Don't tell me you haven't been thinking about it, too."

"Xena and I being followed so soon after we left Ella's house? And our New York suspect avoiding his very own Manhattan apartment?"

"You read my mind." Liam could hear Winston sigh on the other end of the phone line. "I keep running new checks on this house, thinking maybe I missed a bug, maybe the phone is tapped, but nothing pops."

"I think we need to take a closer look at Rye," Liam said.

"I don't argue with your line of thinking, but I don't see him as our perp. He's too invested in Ella. Either that or he's the world's greatest actor. And I've checked his phone. Calls, text messages, even Facebook posts. So how's he communicating?"

"I don't know. But he's our guy. I'm sure of it. But I'll say his motives are pure."

"What the hell do you mean by that?" Winston asked.

"He's protecting Ella. You said it yourself, he would do anything for her."

"And somewhere along the way, they threatened to hurt her if he didn't help them. You think he's been helping them since the cabin." It wasn't a question, Winston knew exactly what Liam was thinking. "You think he knows where Noyce is."

"I don't think it matters if he knows where Noyce is. All that matters is that he can get Square Jaw to where I'll be. Once I have Square Jaw, I'm sure I can convince him to contact Noyce for me."

Winston snorts. "I'm sure you can. So where are you heading."

"I'm heading to New York, and I want you to make sure Rye knows that. He'll get information to our good friend."

"And if he doesn't?"

"Then we have to decide if we misjudged our buddy Rye. But you and I both know we haven't."

"That's a complicated sting you're constructing. You run it by Ryan? And how do you plan to handle it?"

"I will. And I'm pulling in someone with skills to help me."

"Dallas Sykes," Winston said.

"He'll work with me on this. And I also think that Noyce will come after us himself."

"You mean if Xena is the bait, don't you? Are you willing to take that risk?"

"I'll talk to her about it, of course. But if we don't take the risk, she'll never have a normal life. And I want to end this. I want to see her safe."

And, he thought to himself, he would do whatever it took to make sure that she was.

CHAPTER TWENTY-THREE

I step from the portable staircase into the open door of a private jet. A woman with short golden hair stands there in a white blouse and freshly pressed slacks holding a highball glass with what I think is bourbon and a flute with something that looks sparkly and cool with a piece of fruit in the bottom.

"Good morning, Ms. Morgan. I'm Talia, and I'll be taking care of you and Mr. Foster on the flight. Can I offer you a glass of sparkling water with a hint of raspberry? Or perhaps lime?"

I glance back at Liam, amazed that with everything else he had to arrange to make this trip happen so quickly that he'd thought to tell the staff I wouldn't want alcohol. "Thank you," I say. "I'd love to try it with raspberry."

"My pleasure," she says, handing me the flute.

"Sit anywhere, and I'll bring some fruit and cheese after takeoff."

"Right. Thank you." I'm certain I seem overwhelmed by my surroundings, but that's only because I'm overwhelmed by my surroundings.

I step further into the cabin, and then simply pause as I take everything in. As Liam talks to Talia behind me, I take the time to look around the jet. I have no idea what type it is. As far as I know, it is simply a vehicle that flies through the sky and is fancy as hell.

The cylindrical interior is the epitome of comfort, and the furnishings are such to put an airline's first class to shame. Not that I've ever flown first class, but I do watch movies, and so I've seen a lot of airplane interiors. This interior looks like a contemporary furniture showroom with rich wood and soft, supple leather.

In the front there are several individual chairs arranged opposite a tan sofa of the same leather, making the area look like a cozy living room. At the back of the plane I see four chairs grouped together around a table, and I assume that's used as an inflight work area. I choose the sofa, hoping that Liam takes the seat beside me.

The windows behind me are small, which seems a shame, but I assume that has something to do with air pressure. I'm not afraid of heights, and I wish that one entire wall could be glass so that I could see the world disappearing beneath us.

I turn and look toward the front. Liam is still talking, standing with Talia and a man in uniform who I assume is the pilot. I notice an open folding door that probably serves as a barrier between the crew and us. Since it's open now, I can see what I'm pretty sure is the kitchen area—called the galley, I think—and beyond that I see the cockpit, where another man in uniform is adjusting knobs on a complicated console.

I catch Liam's eye, and he smiles, then hands a clipboard and pen back to Talia, who trades him for the highball glass.

A moment later, he's beside me. "Share your sofa?"

"Not with just anyone," I say, then make a show of looking him up and down. "But you'll do."

He grins, settles in next to me, and takes a sip of his bourbon before taking my hand. I sigh. The circumstances aren't ideal—we're off to trap a bad guy—but other than that, I could get used to this.

"I never thought to ask," he says. "Have you been on a private jet before?"

Considering he knows my history, I understand that he's really asking if I was one of the girls selected to go out into the world and party. Girls taken in private jets to private islands. Girls who wore fancy clothes and tiny bikinis, assuming they were lucky.

Girls who often never came back, and while those of us left behind liked to pretend that they were being treated like princesses on tropical islands, we knew it was more likely that they were dead. Or worse.

"They only kept me in New York," I say. "Actually, this is only my second time on a plane at all. Ellie doesn't like to fly, and with the band and the equipment it's easier to go by bus. Now that she's getting huge, though, I think she's going to have to start going the private jet route. Too much time wasted on the road."

"Your second time," Liam says thoughtfully. "You told me Corbu's fake modeling agency paid for your plane ticket, so I'm guessing that was the second time. When was the first?"

"My mom and dad took me to Disneyland when I was five. I know we flew, but I don't remember that part at all. Or Disneyland, really."

"Not at all? That's terribly sad."

"Well, I remember the colors, and I remember princess dresses. They must have made a big impression, because for years I imagined myself in a princess dress." My imagination suddenly conjures me in just such a dress with Liam beside me in black tie and tails.

I look up, feeling a bit ridiculous, and see him smiling enigmatically back at me. I mentally cringe, wondering if he actually read my strange thoughts.

I don't have time to worry about it, though, because a moment later, the captain's voice comes over the intercom, telling us to be sure that we're buckled up for takeoff. Talia sits in the galley in what Liam tells me is called a jump seat.

Soon we're moving, and it feels almost like being in a car until we get to the runway and start to pick up speed. We move faster and faster, and I'm starting to think that nothing is going to happen at all, when I suddenly feel the angle of the plane shift slightly. There's a sensation of something building and building, and then, finally, a sudden, cathartic release.

I look down and realize that I've been squeezing Liam's hand so hard my knuckles are white. He looks at me, his expression both gentle and concerned. "Are you okay?"

I nod and release his hand. "I don't know why I grabbed on so tight. I'm not scared at all. I promise. That was magnificent."

"A little like sex?"

I glance down, weirdly shy, but I agree, and I'm sure he knows it.

A moment later he tilts my chin up and kisses me gently. "Thank you for doing this."

"You don't have to thank me. It's my ass on the line, remember?"

"I know, but we're moving faster than we

expected, in a direction that we're not entirely sure about."

"I know." Since Winston and Liam suspect that Rye has been feeding information to Noyce through Mouse Face and Square Jaw, they decided to set up a sting to grab Square Jaw who, hopefully, can lead us to Noyce. Although, as Trevor mentioned in our pre-departure meeting, it's likely that Noyce has left the country altogether, and the best we'll be able to do is interrogate him—and hopefully use him to track his boss. That wouldn't be the ideal outcome, but I know it's likely. It means I'm a target for longer, of course, but at least I'll still have Liam beside me.

The plan is for Winston to tell Ella that I've gone to New York. He'll say that I'm staying with Liam in his Manhattan apartment while he uses some of his old resources to hopefully track down more information on Noyce. The hope is that Rye will get the impression that I'll be spending a lot of time alone in Liam's apartment while he's off doing his thing.

Of course, that won't be true. But if the bait works to lure in Square Jaw, aka Patrick Weil, or Noyce, then maybe—just maybe—I'll be able to live a life where I'm not constantly looking over my shoulder.

"And you're sure you're comfortable doing this?" Liam asks me.

I laugh. "Of course, I am. Besides, it's too late now. We're already airborne."

"Well, I could always divert to Paris."

"Sadly, I didn't think to bring my nonexistent passport," I quip. I squeeze his hand. "Seriously, I'm fine, and we need to do this. We need to get it over with. *I* need it to be over."

All of that is true, of course. But my biggest fear is that once this threat is out of my life, Liam will be, too. But I don't have a choice. I have to get free; I have to break these chains so that I can have a life.

He studies me, then finally seems convinced that I mean what I say.

"All right, then. Give me a few minutes to check a couple of things, and then we'll figure out a way to occupy the rest of the trip."

I grin at the thought of what we might figure out, then lean back, thinking about what is in store for us next. The ultimate destination is his apartment, but we're heading first to Long Island to stay overnight with his friend Dallas Sykes in Southampton, along with his very pregnant and bedridden wife Jane, a part of the equation that Rye isn't privy to.

The practical purpose of the detour is to pull in Dallas's help with both information and building a team. But since Liam grew up with both of them, and they are both his best friends, he says he wants me to meet them, along with his mother.

I'm flattered and a little heart-fluttery, but I'm trying not to read too much into that, because what I want it to mean is that Liam wants to stay with me even once I'm clear of the threat. But that's not something I can assume—I know his fears, his worries. And I know that I can't convince him not to be afraid. I can only hope he convinces himself.

Since that isn't something I want to think about, I distract myself by flipping through an entertainment magazine until Liam closes his laptop and turns to me.

"All done?" I ask.

"All done," he says, then gets up, says something to Talia, and closes the door between us and the galley.

I raise a brow when he turns back to me. "So, you said you had ideas for occupying the rest of the flight," I prompt.

"I'm full of ideas. We could talk, read, watch a movie ... or I could turn on the Do Not Disturb light and induct you into the mile high club. Your call."

"I love a guy who supports new experiences," I say, relishing the tingly sense of anticipation spreading through me.

"I'm very glad to hear it." He pushes the button for privacy and returns to the sofa. And as the plane continues to climb, I surrender to what I hope is not one of the very last times I will be with this man.

⸻

There's a car waiting for us when we land at a private airport somewhere on Long Island. A limo, actually, and Liam tells me that Dallas sent it for us. The driver, a man about Liam's age with bright red hair and a goatee, greets Liam as Mr. Foster and me as Ms. Morgan. He opens the rear door for us with a flourish, his arm indicating that we should get in.

Liam nods at me to go first, then hesitates before joining me. "Good to see you, Roger. But what the hell is up with all the pomp and circumstance?"

I lean forward to see better, and watch as the man's firm shoulders go slack and his expressionless face breaks out into a grin. "Damn, buddy, but I'm glad you're back. I wasn't sure what the protocol was with our guest."

Liam bends over and meets my eyes. "Xena, this is Roger. Roger, Xena. She's... " He hesitates for a moment, then says, "She's with me."

Roger bobs his head, the ginger strands catching the sunlight. "Nice to meet you. Shouldn't take too long to get you to the house. Traffic's light."

He shuts the door, and Liam and I are alone in

the back of the limousine. The privacy barrier is up, and I expect that Roger will open it since he and Liam are clearly friends, but he gives us our privacy, and I turn to Liam and ask who the guy is.

"He's exactly who he seems to be," Liam says. "He's one of Dallas's drivers. He also used to do odd jobs for Deliverance. He's a good guy, and he and his family have been working for the Sykes family since we were in elementary school. So I know him well."

We pass quaint shopping areas with coffee shops dotting the sidewalks, and everything has that shiny, polished sheen that comes from money. From there we move into more residential areas, and as we get further and further in, the houses become more and more impressive.

As we drive, Liam points out a few landmarks—restaurants, clubs, the houses of people he knows as well as people he doesn't, but who have a reputation.

The entire area seems to bleed money, and each home feels more and more lush until finally we turn onto a private drive leading up to a stunning multistory mansion that even compared to what I've seen driving through the ritzier areas of LA looks like a residence for a foreign prince.

"This is where you grew up?" I can't help but gawk at this incredible place that rises in front of me like a castle in the middle of a street full of castles. "This is beyond amazing."

"It is," he says. "Not that I realized it when I was a kid. My mother never made a big deal about it. Not about the fact that the house was over-and-above, not about the fact that the Sykes family has more money than the gross national product of many small countries, not about any of it. And certainly not about the fact that we weren't in that income bracket ourselves. She was the help, and I was her son, and that was why we were there."

"She sounds like a great mom. Down to earth."

His eyes warm. "She is. And she never encouraged or discouraged my friendship with Dallas. As far as she was concerned, she was an employee, but I was a guest. And the family saw it that way, too."

The house is even more impressive as we get closer, and I can tell it's larger than I originally thought. "She was *the* housekeeper? That place is huge."

"The head of a team," he clarifies. "Nowadays, she's the only one who lives on site, though. Her and Archie."

"Archie?"

"Butler," he says. "In name, anyway. He was also part of the support for Deliverance. I wish you could meet him, but he took his annual vacation early so he'd be home for Jane's due date."

"What about your mom? Did she know, too? I thought Deliverance was a secret."

"She knows now. She didn't always." He sighs as the car comes to a stop in the drive. "Anyway, this is it. This is my childhood home."

"It's amazing."

"I know it is." I can hear the emotion in his voice, but can't quite place it. A bit of melancholy mixed with pride, maybe. "It's a special place," he says. "But it wasn't until I was older and on my own that I realized what a gift it was to be part of the family."

CHAPTER TWENTY-FOUR

"Wow," I say as we step through the massive double doors that lead into a stunning entryway full of natural light.

"Impressive, isn't it?" Liam says.

I'm about to agree, when I hear a rich, cultured voice say, "My father intended this room to welcome, impress, and intimidate his guests." The words seem to hover in the air, as if drifting down from the heavens. "Somewhat contradictory goals, I'll admit. But I think he accomplished it. Then again, Eli Sykes is a man who tends to do whatever he sets his mind to."

The voice is coming from the man standing at the top of the ornate wooden stairs. He's tall and lean, and his broad shoulders strain against the simple gray T-shirt he's wearing. His hair is dark brown with hints of blond, as if it's been sun-kissed, and even from this distance I can see his vivid green eyes.

Dallas Sykes. I've seen his photograph on social media and in tabloids for years, but they don't do justice to the man.

"And you aren't?" Liam asks as Dallas strides down the stairs with the easy gait of a man who is completely at home in his surroundings. Makes sense, I suppose. This is his home, after all.

"I never said I wasn't," Dallas counters. "Then again, I usually go after what I want with less subtlety. Father builds mansions. I take a less metaphorical approach to what I want to accomplish. Right now," he adds with a flash of his famous smile, "I want to meet Xena."

"Oh," I say, a little shaken to be on this man's radar. "Hi." I take his outstretched hand, finding his handshake as firm as one would expect from a man so self-possessed.

"Liam's told me a lot about you."

"Oh," I say again, wondering where my vocabulary skittered off to. I glance at Liam, who just smiles and shrugs.

"Good things," Liam assures me, with a smile that has just enough heat to make me blush, because I'm certain that Dallas has picked up on that, too.

"Listen, Jane is dying to meet you, but she just woke up and asked if we could give her half an hour or so to shake off the sleep. No caffeine on bed rest," he adds with a grim smile to me. "There are a lot of reasons I'll be happy when the baby arrives. Not long now."

"Don't get too eager. She'll probably stay off a while longer if she's breastfeeding."

He nods slightly. "I've thought about that, but I think the trade-off is worth it. A father," he says with so much awe in his voice it almost melts my heart. "Can you believe it?" he asks Liam.

"Hell, no," Liam says, his expression deadpan except for his eyes, which totally give him away. A smile bursts onto his face, as if he just can't hold it in any longer. "Damn, buddy, part of me can't believe you're going to be a father, and the other part can't believe you two waited this long."

"You better believe it," he says. "You're going to be the godfather."

"Damn right I am."

"Are you having a boy or a girl?" I ask.

"That's a question for our doctor," Dallas says. "Although she won't tell you. Strict orders that no one knows until the birth. And that includes me and Jane."

"That's fabulous," I say. "I love that you're doing that."

"Thanks," he says, sounding sincere. "I'll put you in a room with our parents. They think we're insane." He glances at his watch. "I told Jane I'd bring her some herbal tea. Liam, you know where we are. Show Xena around, introduce her to your mom before Helen heads back to the cottage, and by that time Jane should be human again."

Liam nods. "You know I'm going to tell her you said that, right?"

Dallas looks at me. "He always liked her best."

"She's cuter than you are."

"Can't argue with that. Xena," he adds to me, "it's a pleasure. We'll talk more soon."

"Thanks," I say. "It's terrific to meet you."

He heads off, and Liam takes my hand, leading me past the staircase toward the rear of the house. I'm no stranger to luxury—the complex I lived in until I managed to escape was a gilded cage, and the mansions that we were sometimes transported to for parties and events were always ornate, even high-class, if something used for such a perverted purpose can be considered high-class.

This place, however, is different. It's clear that everything is high quality and undoubtedly expensive. It's beautiful and luxurious, but it's also comfortable. It's a home, I realize, and that makes it all the more special.

I tell as much to Liam, trying to put my thoughts into words and afraid that I'm failing miserably. But he gets it. Maybe I'm doing a better job expressing myself, I think—or maybe he just gets *me*.

Either way, he lifts our joined hands and brushes a kiss over my knuckles, the gesture so offhand that I'm not even sure he realizes that he's doing it.

We meander down long hallways, and I rubberneck, taking in everything as we walk. "What's that?" I ask, noticing clear glass discs mounted just under the ceiling at almost every corner.

"Security system," he says. "The house is equipped with a silent alarm. The discs are unobtrusive, but when the alarm is tripped, the glass flashes blood red. It turns solid red once the system contacts 911, which it does if no one disarms it within ninety seconds."

"That's fast. How far do you have to sprint to disarm it?"

"Not far. We all have the system controls on our phones. Dallas has it on his watch, too."

"So if I run in and out of the house, Dallas's arm is going to buzz? Sounds like a sadistic form of entertainment."

"You're a strange woman."

"A little," I admit.

"And yes," he says, "unless the system's been disarmed for that particular door. The windows are always armed for breakage, and the perimeter of the yard has sensors that turn on video monitoring systems. There's more—with a family this wealthy, there's always more—but the bottom line is that they're safe here. And," he adds as he holds my gaze, "you're safe here, too. I promise."

"I never doubted it," I say honestly. "I was just curious."

"What else are you curious about?"

"Where you're taking me, for one thing. We've been walking for miles." That's only a slight exaggeration. We've traversed so many hallways I regret not wearing sneakers.

"Almost there," he says as we turn yet another corner and end up in what appears to be a different wing of the house. It's as well appointed, but seems less lived-in. My perception surprises me, and I realize that even though the main part of the house is stunning and expensive and a bit like walking through a museum, it also feels real and homey. This section feels a bit like a hotel. Nice enough, but transient.

I don't think too much about it until he says, "This is it."

I frown. "What?"

"This is where I grew up."

"Really?" I don't mean to sound surprised or, worse, insensitive, but he must hear something in my voice, because he laughs.

"Trust me, it wasn't like this back then. Dallas gave Mom one of the cottages on the property and she moved out of the main house about the time I went into the service. The cottage is nice, don't get me wrong, but this place is home. Although it felt more homey before it was converted to a guest wing."

He gestures to the tiled expanse of hallway. "I rode my bike along here. Jane and Dallas and I built incredible forts down here. And this," he adds, opening the door to a medium-sized room dominated by a four-poster bed, "used to be mine." He shrugs. "Of course, the furniture's changed quite a bit. Originally, I had a bed shaped as a sports car. My mom's Christmas splurge when I turned eight. Later I got a bunk bed, although the only ones who ever slept over were Dallas or Jane. And the walls were covered with movie posters and bookshelves."

I try to imagine his childhood room, and it slowly comes to life. "What did you look like back then? In elementary school? High school?"

"Elementary school? I was scrawny. Seriously, a skinny thing like you could take me." He grins to show he's kidding.

I roll my eyes. "Let me guess, you were picked on and decided to start working out, and that's how you became this incredible specimen of maleness." I move my hand up and down, indicating his entire body, which as far as I'm concerned is about as perfect as they come.

"Not exactly," he says, and his voice is so heavy that I realize I've struck a nerve.

"I'm sorry. I didn't mean—"

"It was the kidnapping."

I frown, momentarily confused, and then it hits me. "Dallas and Jane," I say. "You felt helpless."

He nods. "And scared. If I'd been there, I would have been no help at all, and probably taken, too. Or killed. So I made myself strong."

I look at him for a moment, my heart breaking for the little boy he used to be. I think of everything he endured, and I think about the choices he made to protect himself and his friends. And I think about what he's now doing to protect me.

"No," I say. "You were already strong. You just worked out so that your muscles could catch up to the man you already were."

I hear his soft inhalation of breath and see a muscle move in his cheek. He swallows, then takes a step toward me. Slowly, he bends to kiss me, as sweet and gentle as butterfly wings. "And that's why I adore you. After everything you've been through, you still see the world with such sweet optimism."

"I see the truth," I say simply. But as I speak, my heart is dancing. Maybe he hasn't said he loves me, but his words come awfully close.

———

"There you are!" Liam's mother stands in the middle of the aromatic kitchen beside a huge work island, her arms held out to welcome Liam's hug. I smile at the way he dwarfs his mother, at least two heads shorter than him, then automatically straighten my posture when she releases him and turns to me. "You must be Xena."

She's got the brightest smile I've ever seen, wide and warm and genuine, and I smile back automatically, then let her pull me into an embrace without even thinking about it, something I rarely do.

She steps back to break the hug but keeps her hands on my upper arms, as if holding me out for inspection. Which, I realize, is exactly what she's doing when she says, "Let's have a look at you."

Since fair is fair, I take the opportunity to study her more closely. She looks to be in her early sixties, with skin slightly darker than Liam's and eyes that are just as expressive. She wears her hair cut short to her scalp, and it's dappled with silver-gray that makes me unexpectedly melancholy when I realize that neither of my parents will ever age in my memory. They will always be young, but in those circumstances, youth isn't a blessing at all.

She wears a pale blue work dress and a white apron, and she's dressed so much like Alice from *The Brady Bunch* that I really do almost cry. Because that was the show that Ella sat me down to watch after I told her my Susan Morgan runaway story. She decided that I hadn't had a normal childhood and that the remedy was a hefty dose of seventies television.

I'm not sure it helped, but it definitely didn't hurt.

Liam had actually told me about the uniform ahead of time. "Dallas and Jane have told her to wear whatever she wants," he'd said. "And Mom says she's doing exactly that. A little old-fashioned, my mother."

So I'd been prepared for the uniform, color and all. Just not for the effect it would have on me.

"You are just as pretty as Liam said you were," Mrs. Foster says, and I glance at Liam, my brows raised.

He lifts his hands in surrender. "Hey, I'm an honest man. I call them as I see them."

"Well, thank you, then," I tell him. "And you, too, Mrs. Foster."

"You call me Helen, sweetie. And you two are just in time. I made a batch of cookies and was about to take some to Jane, but I'll make a tray with enough for the four of you, and you can take it up," she adds to Liam. She turns her attention back to me. "Chocolate chip okay?"

"More than okay." My mouth is already watering.

"Good." She turns to Liam. "One question and then I will say no more. Are you keeping safe?"

"Safer than when I was in combat."

She snorts. "I think that answer should earn me another question, but I'll give you a pass because I love you. You tell Mr. Hunter to make sure you watch your back."

"Yes, ma'am."

She nods, as if that's the end of that, then focuses on me. "Now you tell me about yourself while I make the tray."

"Can I help?"

She shoos me away with a "sit, sit," and I climb onto one of the stools by the island while Liam comes to stand beside me, his hand on my shoulder.

"Xena's the personal assistant to a pop star," Liam says. "Ever heard of Ellie Love?"

I'm certain the answer will be no, so I'm surprised when she says, "Of course. *Take Time For Me* is a lovely ballad. I confess the faster numbers just aren't my style."

"We were surprised it did so well, but thrilled. It was kind of a breakout for her. Put her on the serious performer map."

She moves about the kitchen as I talk, then pulls a tray out of a rack beneath a cupboard. The cookies are already cooling, and I look around the kitchen as she moves the cookies onto a plate.

The room is spotless and comfortable. It's huge, but still smaller than I would expect for a house this size, and I wonder if some of the connecting rooms are additional prep or staging areas for the inevitable fancy soirees that must have taken place in this house over the years.

On the whole, though, it's a pretty typical kitchen with one prominent exception. One interior wall is covered by shelving that holds cookbooks, spices, a few small appliances, and some dishes. But one section of the shelving is completely missing, replaced instead by an odd cubbyhole.

I'm so curious that I walk over to take a closer look, only to realize that the space isn't "cubby" at all. It's quite large, really. If I were better at yoga, I could fit quite comfortably in what seems to be a large box stuck inside a wall. As it is, I could still fit, I'd just be squeezed a bit. When I notice the gate-style door that is folded into one side, I turn to Helen. "What on earth is this?"

"A dumbwaiter. Haven't you seen one before?"

I have a vague memory of a dumbwaiter featuring in one of my favorite books as a kid, *Harriet the Spy*. "An elevator for stuff, right? That lets you send things upstairs without having to carry them yourself." I think about the door. "Like a freight elevator for small things."

"That's it exactly."

"There are several in the house," Liam adds. "We used to play in them. Great for hide-and-go-seek. Whoever's It checks out a room, after they leave you use the dumbwaiter to go hide in that room." He grins. "Thank goodness I wasn't claustrophobic."

I laugh, picturing his large frame crammed into a box.

"They are very handy," Helen says, "though we don't use them anymore. I don't think I've used that one since, oh … since Mr. Eli was in the master bedroom."

"Dallas's father?"

"That's right. He and Ms. Lisa live in the city now, and Dallas and Jane have the master. That's time, always moving forward."

"That's my mom," Liam says with affection. "Always saying profound things."

"Don't you tease your mother, you hear me?"

"Never. I mean every word I say."

He comes over to kiss her cheek, and she gives him a friendly swat with a hot pad.

Helen goes to the windowsill and takes a fresh daisy from a vase full of wildflowers. She trims the stem, opens a cabinet to retrieve a small glass bud vase, then adds it to the tray. "Now, what was I going to ask you? Oh, yes." Her attention is on me. "How did you get a job like that? An assistant to a singer, I mean. Do you need special training? How did you meet her?"

I glance to Liam out of reflex, and he must see panic in my eyes, because he starts to answer. I don't know what he intends to say, but I'm sure it's not either version of the real truth. Not the *she escaped from the life of a sex slave* truth or the *she was a runaway working as a streetwalker* version of the truth.

But I suddenly realize that I don't want to lie to this woman. And I don't think she will judge me harshly for it.

"Ellie rescued me," I blurt before Liam can speak. I see surprise on his face at first, but then I think it's pride.

"Did she? Well, good for her. And for you. What did she rescue you from?"

"Hell," I say simply. And then I tell her my story. All of it. She doesn't move until I'm finished, just watches me with those kind eyes, and once again, I desperately miss my mother.

When I'm finished, she nods and says to Liam. "You take this tray up to Dallas and Jane. I'll send Xena along in a moment."

"Mom..."

"It's alright," I say, and though he studies me for a moment, he doesn't argue.

"Okay," he says, then winks at me. "Don't let her pry out all your secrets."

"I think I just spilled all the secrets I have."

He brushes a kiss on my cheek before going to pick up the tray. "I'll see you upstairs in a few."

As soon as he's gone, Helen tilts her head,

studying me. "Now, why on earth would you tell me all of that?"

It's not the question I expected. I anticipated sympathy. A maternal pat on the back. And I stammer a bit as I say, "I don't know."

That gentle smile is back. "Oh, I think you do."

She's right, of course, and it's all about Liam. I wanted her to know the real truth because I wanted her to see the real me. The woman who's fallen in love with her son. Because no matter what happens between me and Liam, I want his mother to like me. To know me.

She sits on the stool next to me, her back straight and her hands on her polyester-covered knees. "Folks say you can look at someone's palm and tell about their life. Or read their future in tea leaves. Now, I don't know if that's true, but I do know that there's one surefire way to see a person's heart and future. Do you know what that is?"

"No, ma'am."

"You look at how much they've overcome and the people they keep close in their lives. What they've overcome shows their strength. And that strength is what paves their path. And what lights the path? That's the people they surround themselves with."

I blink, my eyes damp.

"You've overcome a lot, my girl. And you've got good people beside you. That singer. My boy." She reaches over and pats my hand. "I've lived in this house a long time, and I've seen a lot of horrible things. Great things, too. All that shit life throws at you. You know what to make of it?"

"Fertilizer?" I ask, and she bursts out laughing.

"Actually, yes. Not very original, I'll admit. But true." She's quiet for a moment, and I have the feeling she's searching for something in my face. "You love my boy."

My back straightens, the result of shock-induced good posture.

I start to answer, but she puts a finger over her lips. "You don't need to tell me," she says. "I have eyes, don't I?"

"I guess you do," I say.

"He loves you, too," she adds, tapping a finger under an eye.

"He hasn't said it." The words escape before I can stop them, and I hate how insecure and needy I must sound to this woman.

"Does he have to?"

I start to reply, then close my mouth, unsure what to say.

"Love's a rare thing, my girl. And believe it or not, saying it aloud doesn't make it any more true. The words are just reassurance. And I think you already know he loves you."

"I think he's afraid that love isn't enough," I

admit, wondering how much she knows about Dion and Franklin.

"Well, he had a hard time of it. But he's over-come it, hasn't he? He's got a well-paved, well-lit path. All he has to do is walk it."

With me, I think. I want him to walk it with me after he slays my demons, but I'm terribly afraid that he won't follow that path.

"And what about you," she asks. "Do you think love is enough?"

"Honestly? I don't know." If Liam loves me but leaves, then isn't it by definition not enough? And don't I already know that love is hardly a miracle cure?

"Don't you?"

A sharp stab of irritation gets me in the gut. "Well, I know that love can't save anybody," I snap, then immediately feel contrite. "I'm sorry. But love isn't a magic pill. My father loved me like every-thing, and it didn't save me."

"Didn't it? Maybe without that love you wouldn't have had the gumption to survive after you escaped. You might be like the real Susan Morgan now—dead in some unmarked grave— instead of a girl who fought her way free."

The damn tears are back. "I love a lot of quali-ties in your son," I say, sniffling a little. "Now, I think I know where he gets them."

CHAPTER TWENTY-FIVE

L iam set the tray down on one of the accent
tables in the great room as Dallas came
down the stairs.

"How's she doing?"

"Frustrated that she's stuck in bed," Dallas said.
"Also happy to stay there if that's best for the baby,
and eager to see you and meet Xena." He nodded at
the tray of cookies and milk. "I can take that up,
why don't you wait for Xena, then bring her
upstairs with you."

"Sounds good."

Dallas took a step toward the table, then hesitated before picking up the tray. "I like her, by the
way. A girl who's been through that much shit
should be pretty fucked up. But she doesn't seem
fucked up at all."

"She's not."

Dallas watched Liam's face, as if his friend was seeing more than Liam's simple denial was meant to show. "So you're heading to your apartment tomorrow?"

"That's the plan."

"Why don't we have breakfast together before you go. The four of us. I'll cook. And Jane can play hostess from her throne."

"I'm game," Liam said. "Although my mother might have something to say about it. She's very proprietary about her kitchen."

"Tomorrow's the farmers market. She's out by six and doesn't usually get back until at least eleven-thirty."

"Right. I forget. Well, I guess that's one perk of bed rest. You'll be doing the cooking, and not Jane."

Liam watched as Dallas stifled a chuckle. "Now you officially owe me one. Because I imagine you don't want me to tell Jane about that remark."

"I owe you for more than that," Liam admitted. "I owe you for pulling together this team. I couldn't bring anyone from the SSA—if any of Noyce's men were paying attention, they'd know we were here for more than research."

"Happy to help."

"How many have you lined up, and how many do I know?"

"Several, actually. I pulled from our support crew for Deliverance. I set up a video call for today, too. We'll head down to the basement when it's time."

Liam nodded. The basement used to be Deliverance's headquarters. Now it was home base for those times that Dallas—as he'd said—kept his hand in it.

"And, of course, I'm on deck, too."

"No," Liam said. "You're not."

Dallas's brows rose.

"I mean it." Liam was prepared to double-down on this. "These people are dangerous. And you're about to become a father. If you insist on coming with your team, then I just won't use your team."

"That would be a damn foolish decision. One that might get you killed."

"Maybe, but I'm not putting you in the hot zone. Not when Jane needs you. Not when your baby needs a father."

"Christ, Liam, you know—"

"I don't know anything except that's the way it is. So don't argue with me. This isn't Deliverance, Dallas. You don't have the last word."

"Fuck." Dallas ran his fingers through his hair. "Fine. You win."

"I like the sound of that," Liam admitted. "You want to take that up? I'll wait for Xena, like you said."

"Fine. Fine."

Liam laughed. "You're a terrible loser."

"Fuck you."

"Exhibit A, Your Honor."

"I was going to run something by you, but now I'll just leave you out in the cold. Don't blame me if you lose millions on the deal." Dallas let the words hang, his mouth clearly fighting a grin.

With anyone else—except Damien Stark—Liam would consider those words hyperbole. But Dallas has the Midas touch, and while Liam was doing just fine financially, if he ever wanted to start his own family—

He froze, suddenly aware of the direction of his thoughts.

"Liam? You still with me?"

"Sorry. Just remembered something. About work." He shook himself. "What did you want to run by me?"

"A real estate deal. What time are you two hitting the road tomorrow?"

"Between ten and eleven, most likely."

"Perfect. We can have breakfast at eight. I've got a meeting here at nine. This developer I've been talking to—Norman Erickson—is looking for investors in a couple of refurbishment projects up and down the eastern seaboard."

"You've checked him out?"

"Just started that ball rolling. It's still early days, but the man's had his finger in real estate for years and has a large and varied portfolio. I've got more homework, but so far he passes the sniff test."

"Tomorrow's the handshake test."

"You got it. He's catching a plane at MacArthur around noon and offered to come by the house on his way so we could talk. Since you're here and it might be a good opportunity, I thought you should join us."

"Sounds good. I'll be your wing man."

"You've certainly done that before. Speaking of, tell me what's up with you and Xena."

To anyone else, the massive shift in topic might have seemed strange. But Liam and Dallas knew each other so well, it was nothing more than a conversational river taking a bend around a rocky protrusion.

"I'm protecting her," Liam said. "I already told you the whole story."

"The SSA story. I want to know what's really going on. And don't be an ass and tell me it's nothing. Tell me what she means to you."

Everything. "Dallas, listen, you know I can't—"

"Can't?" Dallas shook his head. "I know you *won't.* And I know that it fucked you up pretty bad after Dion was killed." He dragged his fingers through his thick hair. "I've spent years not talking about it—hell, not even thinking about it—because you asked me to never bring it up. But that was before."

"Before what?"

"Before I saw the way you look at that woman."

An invisible fist tightened around Liam's heart. "Dallas, I mean it. We're not going there."

"Goddammit, Liam. You're my best friend. My oldest friend, not counting my wife. And I'm here to tell you that you have got to move on."

His body was tense, fighting the urge to lash out. "Do you really think that's possible?"

"Look at who you're talking to, for Christ's sakes. Of course I do. You know what I've been through. You know everything I risked. And you also know that part of the reason I risked it was because of you."

Liam stumbled back, shocked by his friend's words. "Because of me? How the hell was I involved?"

"Don't you remember that day on the Island?"

That would be Barclay Island, a retreat that had been in the Sykes family for generations. And Liam knew which time Dallas was referring to. A trip to the island to celebrate Dallas's great-grandfather's hundredth birthday. And one night, Liam had been pretty damn blunt in his attempt to get Dallas to see reason with regard to Jane. "I remember it all," he said. "But that's not even close to the same."

"Don't you think?"

"I'm a risk to her safety, and we both know it. What I do? It can get her killed."

"You think Jane doesn't know that about me?"

"You're out of the game," Liam reminded his friend.

"We both know that's not entirely true. And so does Jane."

"And you're willing to accept the risk. I respect that. I don't know that I am."

Dallas looked into Liam's eyes, his more serious than Liam could remember since after the kidnapping. "If you don't remember exactly what you said to me that day, I do. Shall I remind you?"

"I remember," Liam said. "I told you that Jane was a hell of a woman, and that if it was me who was in love with her, there wasn't a power on earth that could make me stay away."

He'd meant the words, too. Dallas and Jane belonged together, and nothing, not even their familial relationship, should've kept them apart, no matter what stones and arrows they might have to endure.

That's what he'd told himself, but it was more than that. Because there was danger lurking in their lives, too. Dallas was doing then exactly what Liam did now. Helping people by sticking his nose in matters that could get him killed. Or could risk the wrath of some very nasty individuals.

"Are you telling me that Xena isn't a hell of a woman?" Dallas pressed. "I think she is."

The words washed over him; he was too lost in his head. Because unlike everything tangible that Dallas and Jane had faced because they were adopted siblings—the legal barriers, the social shaming, the family's reaction—all Liam was fighting against was love and fear.

He'd always thought that he was a brave man. But maybe he was pushing back on a relationship because deep in his heart, he was truly a coward.

And he damn sure didn't like the sound of that.

***

"Oh, thank goodness," Jane said as Liam, Xena, and Dallas entered the room. "Someone other than my husband to talk to." She grinned, her slightly angled eyebrows rising with her smile as she held her hand out to Xena. "I'm Jane, which you probably already figured out. And this," she added, laying a hand on her belly—prominent even under the covers—"is Mystery."

"Tell me that name's not going to stick," Liam said.

"It started as a joke," Dallas admitted. "Now it's growing on us."

"I think it's great," Xena said. "Then again, I

chose my own name, and look what I picked out. So take my advice with a grain of salt."

"I like her," Jane said, with a smile aimed at him, followed by a wink to Xena. "Seriously, it's great to meet you. Sorry I'm not the world's most energetic hostess. Believe me when I say I want to be. And makeup and a hairbrush would have probably gone a long way, too."

"You're beautiful as always," Liam said, kissing her cheek. He meant what he said, too. Her dark brown hair hung in loose waves around her face, and her skin seemed to reflect the light.

"She glows," Dallas said, as if tracking Liam's thoughts. And sounding as proud as if he were the sunlight shooting out of her. In some ways, Liam supposed he was.

"I think you look great," Xena said. "And I love this room."

"Thanks. It was our parents, and then Dallas's, and now ours. Not much has changed. The wood paneling under the chair rail has been here since forever, but we did switch out the wallpaper above the rail. I have no idea what my mother was thinking," she added, shaking her head.

"Well, it's great now," Xena said, shifting her purse. It had her Ruger in it—easy enough to get to New York since they hadn't flown commercial—and he was glad she'd taken him seriously when he said she should keep it with her. Even in the house, it was good to maintain the habit.

"I'm so glad to be here," she continued. "Liam's told me so much about you—and I saw *The Price of Ransom*. I loved it."

Liam looked at her, surprised. He hadn't mentioned that Jane had written the book or the screenplay. She met his gaze and lifted a shoulder. "What? You didn't think I'd learn everything I could about your friends?"

Jane caught his eye, then gave one quick nod of approval. Not that Liam was surprised. As far as he was concerned, there wasn't a legitimate negative word that his friends could say about Xena. God knew he couldn't come up with one.

He was, in a word, besotted. An old-fashioned word, but it summed up his situation nicely. But why wouldn't he be? Xena Morgan was a hell of a woman, after all.

CHAPTER TWENTY-SIX

"I'm absolutely in love with Jane," I tell Liam as we get into the queen-size bed that has replaced the bunk bed in what was once his room. Liam told me earlier that this whole wing is for guests now, and while I think that's a great and practical use of the space, I can't deny that I'm sad not to have seen Liam's real childhood home.

"She's amazing," Liam tells me. "And the three of us—we latched onto each other like superglue."

"That's why what happened to them hurt you so badly, too." Not that my statement is profound. He already knows that.

I wouldn't trade the hours laughing and chatting in Dallas and Jane's bedroom for anything, but the truth is that it's been a ridiculously long day, and I'm mentally and physically exhausted. I'm wearing a tank top and sleep shorts, which made

Liam laugh since I've worn nothing in bed since that first night we were together. But this is someone else's house and it just seemed polite to wear clothes.

Now me and my excess layer of material are curled up against him, my head tucked under his arm. In deference to what he says are my strange rules of propriety he's wearing boxer shorts. But his chest is bare, and I idly trace my finger over the ridges of his abs.

"Jane knows that I love you," I whisper, not sure what prompted me to speak.

"Does she?" I can't read his tone, so I just nod.

"I didn't tell her. After you guys left for that video call, we were talking, and she just ... knew."

I stretch, then tell him about my time with Jane. We'd been talking about both the guys and about how Jane had learned about Deliverance, which Dallas had originally kept secret from her. "I guess that was sort of a pattern," she'd said. "Keeping things hidden. We didn't admit we loved each other for the longest time."

And then she'd looked at me and added, "I think he'll tell you soon. But you'll have the satisfaction of always knowing you said it first."

"How did you know I said it?" I'd asked her. "Did he tell you?"

She'd shrugged, one hand idly rubbing her belly. "I guess you told me. It's all over your face.

You don't try to hide it at all. Which makes me think he must know, too, or you'd be trying to hide it from him."

"He knows," I'd told her. "But he hasn't said it back. Not out loud, anyway."

Jane had grinned. "Yeah, well, there's saying it and then there's *saying* it. Sounds to me like he's said it."

"Maybe," I'd admitted. "But I don't think love is the problem."

She'd nodded slowly, and even in such a short time I'd come to know her well enough that in that moment I'd thought I understood what was going on in her head. She knew about Dion and Franklin, but she didn't know if I did. And I was ninety percent sure I was right when she said, "Everybody has their issues. Things in their past that color their present. Just give him time."

As far as I'm concerned, Jane's suggestion of time was a good one. After all, I'm certainly not walking away from him—or letting him push me away. But I also don't have a magical toolkit with which to tweak the way he thinks. And even if I did, would I really use it? I love him the way he is, stupid, obstinate relationship phobias and all.

Which means time is the only ally I have. That and his friends.

I smile, realizing suddenly that as much as I love Ella and Rye, I'd been very alone. Now, I think about Jane, who seems to genuinely care, and all of the women from girls' night. I don't think it's an illusion that they like and care about me, and I know I care about them, and I feel tears prick my eyes at the thought that I could lose this small posse that has been growing around me if I lose Liam.

Except I won't lose him. I can't lose him.

I'd survive if I lost him, sure. Because survival seems to be one of my superpowers. I've been surviving for years.

But I've changed since that concert in LA. And surviving isn't enough for me anymore.

"Hey," Liam says gently. "Are you still with me?"

"Sorry." I'd been relaying my conversation with Jane to him when my mind had gone elsewhere. "I started to space out. Anyway, before I came down, I told her how strange it was that she'd seen it on my face. That I love you," I add, looking him straight in the eye because I want him to feel how real it is, and how it's not going to fade even if he shoves me aside. His eyes are steady, never wavering, but they are also entirely unreadable.

"Strange?"

"Yeah. Just weird that she could read me so well. I've spent years hiding my emotions. Any hint of anger or hatred or anything could have gotten me killed. But Jane and Helen both read me like a book."

His mouth turns down as he makes a *hmm* noise.

"Jane said it was because I wasn't safe before. But I am now. With you, I mean. In your world. So thank you," I add, propping myself up to kiss him gently. "It's nice to know I'm not a mannequin anymore. And it's nice that I can say that I love you and not be afraid." *Of anything except you not loving me back*, I add silently.

He says nothing, but reaches for me and rolls me on top of him before pulling my face down for a kiss. It's long and slow and full of the promise of things to come, and I lose myself in his touch, my body warm and ready as his hands slide down my back to cup my ass and push me closer to him.

"Now," I whisper, then immediately yelp when the sharp trill of his cell phone makes me jump.

"Fuck. That's Ryan."

I roll over as he grapples for his phone, then puts it on the bed between us. "What have you got for me?" Liam asks, the moment he pushes the button for the speaker.

"I've got Mario and Quince conferenced in," Ryan says, sounding a bit like he's down a well. "Still nothing at Weil's apartment, and none of our sources have tagged him in the last few days. He's not using his credit cards and hasn't pulled money from an ATM. He's in the wind. And we can't confirm that he ever even heard from Rye that you and Xena are in the city."

I exhale, frustrated. The whole idea is to trap Weil when he comes after me at the apartment. Or, better yet, when he's holed up at his place.

"We'll work with it," Liam says, though I can tell he's frustrated as well. "Worst case, Xena and I will just enjoy our time in the city."

"That's worst case?" I quip, just to lighten the mood.

"Yeah, well while you're enjoying yourself, don't forget to watch your backs," Ryan says. "We're operating on no information here, and that's not how I like to run things."

"Agree," Liam says. "Anything on Noyce?"

"A bit," Quince says. "He's bloody clever, I can tell you that much. Enrique Castille's given me full access to Corbu," he explains, "and he's being very cooperative. Can't blame him. He's in custody while his underling has gone to the wind."

"Does he have any information about his location?"

"No," Quince says. "But apparently Noyce has been collecting aliases for years. Corbu says he doesn't even know all of them, and I believe him."

"Why?" I ask.

There's a pause, then Quince says, "I'm very good at what I do."

I meet Liam's eyes, and he nods. I think about

Quince, such a nice guy who's so sweet to Eliza, and try to imagine him in an interrogation room. It's not clicking for me, but I don't doubt his word.

"Have you learned any of his aliases?" Liam asks.

"Several. Emile Neely. Eric Nehu. Edgar Norton."

"Nice that he's predictable."

"Can't argue with that, but according to Corbu, he has such a stockpile, he could just disappear."

"But then I'd be safe, right? If he disappears, it would be because he gave up on me and is just going to go live his life in Fiji or something."

"Maybe," Ryan says. "But how would you know? He's not going to send you a registered letter saying *Hey, not trying to kill you anymore. Going into hiding, they'll never find me, and you'll never have to testify.*"

"Which means I spend the rest of my life looking over my shoulder."

"I want this fucker," Liam says. "I want him for what he did to all of those women, not just Xena. And I want Xena to not just feel safe, I want her to be safe."

"So do we all," Ryan assures us. "And we're working through all of his aliases, hoping one of them pops. Seagrave's got the SOC on it, too, and Quince has pulled in MI6. I've got Ollie McKee working with the FBI, and we've reached out to other agencies and private entities, too. We'll find him. It just might take some time."

I nod, though Ryan can't see me. I want it over now, but at least the road to getting there is becoming clear.

"Which name is real?" Liam asks. "Edward Noyce?"

"We don't know," Mario says. "That's the name Corbu met him as, and the name he checked out back when he let Noyce into the inner circle. According to him, Noyce made wise investments and managed to turn a decent inheritance into a fortune. But who knows if that story is true, either. I can confirm that Edward Noyce—alias or not—did earn money in the market, but that doesn't prove that it's his primary, original name. Corbu also confirmed that Noyce procured the building that Xena was kept in, and he set up the various shell companies that owned it. Considering that didn't come out while he was in custody, we know the man has solid skills at becoming invisible."

Liam rubs the back of his neck, his expression frustrated. "Bottom line, the man is a chameleon who also knows how to be a ghost."

"At least he has a pattern," I say. "That's something, right?"

"That's something," Quince agrees. "But it's not much."

After a bit more housekeeping, Liam ends the

call, his eyes hard on me. "What were you saying about safe?"

"Oh, no," I say, shaking my head. "If I'm not safe it's because of me. My past. Not because of what you do. You're the one who keeps me safe, and you know it."

"Maybe so, but we both know it will never end. Even when Noyce is behind bars—and we will catch him—you'll still be in danger. You'll be in danger because you're my Achilles' heel, and anyone who pays attention will know that."

"Liam, don't. You don't have to be alone because of what you do. Is Dallas? Quince? Ryan?"

He sits up, sighing deeply as he reaches up and rubs his temples with the thumb and middle finger of one large hand. "What I do ... it puts people at risk. And you've been at risk enough. But I'm not sure I care any more. I need you. And I will do whatever I can to protect you."

"I—" My heart is beating so loud I'm not even sure I really heard what he said. "Liam, are you saying—"

"I'm saying that maybe you and Dallas have managed to get through my thick skull. I'm saying I love you. And I'm saying that I couldn't stand it if something happened to you. So I either curl up in a ball and hide from reality, or I go all in and love you —and protect you."

My throat is thick with unshed tears.

"So I'm giving you one chance—just this one chance—to say no. Because if you say yes—if you stay—I'm not ever letting you go."

It's hard to talk, my tears are flowing so freely now, but I nod ferociously, and finally manage to find my voice. "I've never thought of myself as all that smart. And neither are you if you think you can get rid of me that easily."

"Thank God," Liam says, as he pulls me close. His lips brush over mine, soft and incredibly sweet and so full of love it makes me want to cry.

His touch is tender as he slowly peels off my tank and my shorts, then turns more demanding when I'm naked beside him. He undresses as well, then pulls me on top of him. I straddle his waist, my thighs tight against his torso as he reaches up to stroke my cheek.

"I'm sorry," he says.

"What for?"

"For ever thinking I could walk away from you."

Happiness swells inside me as I slide down his body, my sex stroking his erection. I meet his eyes, them slowly take him in, and neither of us look away as I slowly ride him.

One of his hands cups my rear, but he never steals control. The other plays with my breast, and I bite my lower lip, lost in the sweetness of his touch and the power of our connection.

"I want this to last," he says, and I can hear the strain in his voice. He's close and so am I, both of us right on the edge, but not wanting this moment to end.

I press my hands to his chest, feeling his heartbeat through my palms as I rock against him, the slow, easy motion of our lovemaking taking us both higher until, whether we want to or not, we're both forced over, crashing together as our bodies explode as one, pleasure careening through us until I have no choice but to collapse on top of him, our hearts beating as one as my body slowly recovers in his arms.

"That was incredible," I say, propping myself up enough to see his face. "You're incredible."

"I love you," he says, in a voice so full of emotion I feel tears prick my eyes. "And I'm never letting you go."

CHAPTER TWENTY-SEVEN

"So that's the proposal." The lean, fifty-something man with silver-streaked dark hair said, gesturing to the plat maps, blueprints, and colorful brochures that littered the formal dining table.

Norman Erickson had arrived less than an hour ago. And while Xena had stayed upstairs with Jane, the two deep in conversation about Jane's experience writing the *Price of Ransom* screenplay and her friendship with Lyle Tarpin, the now-A-list Hollywood star, Dallas and Liam had come down to hear Erickson's pitch.

The man was well-spoken and confident, a born salesman, and Liam imagined that many a deal had closed as a result of his personality as much as his actual projects. As for that, Liam had to agree that in the moment, the development investment that Erickson proposed sounded sweet.

Of course, con men were skilled in making anything sound sweet, and despite Erickson's affable nature, there was something about him that rubbed Liam the wrong way.

Since Liam and Xena were heading into the city in about an hour, Erickson was stealing the last few minutes of their time with Jane and Dallas. So maybe he was just disposed to be irritated with the man.

"I've completed a similar project in Dallas," Erickson was saying. "Taking the decaying infrastructure of an underutilized former industrial area and converting it into a community within a community, complete with high-end condos, a few single family homes, restaurants, theaters, day care, a variety of high-end but unique retail stores, and various other facilities such as spas, fitness centers, medical facilities. Plus plenty of greenspace, of course."

"It's definitely interesting," Dallas said, and Liam couldn't disagree.

"What kind of investors are you looking for, and how many?" Dallas asked.

"You're curious about how many slices of the pie I'm anticipating, and that depends entirely on the quality of the investors. With you involved, perhaps everyone takes a bigger slice. And if that's a factor that plays into your decision, I'm open to talk. Early stages, as I said."

"Are you already negotiating with specific retailers? And who's your architect?" Liam asked, only to say, "Sorry, I need to take this," when his ringtone signaled a call from Winston.

He stepped to the far side of the massive room, his back to Dallas and Erickson as he said, "What have you got for me?"

"Nothing good. Rye's admitted that he told Weil about Ella's cabin—that's how they found you in the mountains. And about your visit to Ellie Love's house the day you almost got run off the road."

"How? You swept for electronics."

"My fault," Winston said. "He had a burner phone, and I fucking missed it."

"Well, you ultimately found it."

"No," Winston said. "I had a come to Jesus with both of them this morning—Christ, they're early risers—and apparently Ellie had mentioned to him how terrified she was for the two of you, and he couldn't live with his conscience. I was right about one thing—he's head over heels for that girl. That's why he did it."

"They threatened her if he didn't help," Liam said, keeping his voice low.

"Got it in one."

"Fucking hell."

"His heart may have been in the right place, but his actions weren't. He should have come to us, not played their game. I'm not sure if Ella's going to forgive him for that."

"Right now, I don't have a lot of sympathy for the man."

"It gets worse," Winston said. "Yesterday, Ellie told Rye how worried she was about the sting at your apartment, and said she was glad they were going to Dallas's first. So at least you two would have a breather before shit hit the fan."

Shit.

With a sudden sense of trepidation, Liam glanced up and watched as the usually clear security disk turn blood red. "Sorry, buddy," he said. "It's too late for that."

———

Dallas was glancing at his phone when Liam casually approached. He nodded, just the hint of movement that let Liam know that Dallas was aware of the threat as well.

The corner indicator turned solid red—emergency services had been called—and then shut off completely.

"Mr. Erickson, if you could wait here, I just received a text from the property caretaker. Apparently we have a small fire in one of the detached houses."

"Oh! I'm so sorry to hear that. I—well, of course I can wait."

"Liam, would you mind giving me a hand?"

"Not a problem."

They left the dining area, shutting the double doors behind them. "Noyce or Weil?" Liam asked as soon as he was certain Erickson wouldn't over-hear them.

"Can't get a solid visual," Dallas said. "But the breach is in the guest wing. Someone broke a window and ninja'd their way in."

He passed Liam his phone, which displayed the security system's video feed. The intruder wore a black skin suit along with a hood, but the place-ment of his head made it impossible to see his face.

They hurried past the kitchen and into the wing where Liam had grown up—and where Liam knew there were only three routes to the rest of the house. A twisting passage that passed near the kitchen—their current location. The solarium walkway that led along the length of the house and terminated at the morning room. And the stairwell in the middle of the hall that led to the second floor and was slightly closer to their position than the intruder's entrance point.

"I remotely locked the stair door," Dallas said as they rounded the penultimate corner. "With luck, we'll get there before he breaks through. You armed?"

"These days, always."

"Good."

"You?"

Dallas shot him a wry look. "At home, not usually. With you two in the house, I decided to carry."

"Smart man."

They were close to the final turn, and Dallas held up a hand indicating silence, and they moved the rest of the distance more slowly, taking care not to let any sound give them away. Liam said a silent prayer that the perp was still there. From this position, once on the second floor, he was too damn close to Xena and Jane, and he hoped like hell that Jane had seen the alarm. Dallas would have locked them in remotely, but Liam wouldn't feel safe until he had Xena in his arms and saw with his own eyes that Jane and the baby were fine.

Slowly, they approached the corner, and when Liam sidled in front of Dallas, his friend let him, presumably understanding that Liam considered this his fight.

The bastard was there, and when he lifted his head, Liam saw it was Square Jaw, aka Weil. In one motion, Liam lifted his weapon, fired a warning shot, and told the fucker to drop his gun. He'd have preferred to put the bullet right between the bastard's eyes, but they needed him if they were going to have any chance of finding Noyce.

Weil, however, wasn't cooperating, and as Dallas approached on Liam's left, Weil lifted his gun, the sight on Dallas. A cold blast of fear and fury sliced through Liam, and he threw himself onto Dallas, knocking him out of the way a split second before the gun discharged.

His ears rang from the shot, and his left shoulder stung like a bitch.

He was on the ground on top of Dallas, and only barely realized it when Dallas shoved him off, pulled out his own gun, and fired.

Weil dropped, and Liam struggled to his feet as Dallas approached cautiously, his weapon trained on the fallen man.

"Dead," he said, turning back to Liam. "Shit, man."

"Clean entry and exit," Liam said, as Dallas scowled and hurried over. "I'll be okay." He was still in shock and his ears still rang, but his upper arm was numb, and that was a blessing. His fingers worked fine, and as far as he could tell, the bullet hadn't hit any major vessels.

He used his good hand to unfasten the buttons of his shirt, then handed it to Dallas. "Tight," he said, as he fumbled for his phone and the rarely used home security app for the Sykes house. Video surveillance was always unavailable unless there was a breach, and in that case, every room became visible. And even though he could see Weil's corpse, he wanted to confirm that the girls were safe.

They weren't. And what he saw made his blood run cold.

"Norman Erickson," he said, his voice raspy. "Initials N and E." He met Dallas's eyes and saw his own dark fear reflected right back at him. "He studied me. Realized we were friends. He knew I'd eventually come here."

"He's been positioning himself with me," Dallas said. "He set me up—he set both of us up. And now he's got Jane and Xena."

Liam forced down the fear and the pain, operating only on raw fury. That's what he needed. That's what would destroy the sick fuck.

He paused as they started to race up the stairs. "Go," he said. "I have an idea."

"What—?"

"Just *go*. I'll meet you. And hurry."

Dallas didn't argue, and Liam backtracked, hoping this would work, hoping he wasn't crazy. Because it *had* to work. He couldn't lose her.

He *wouldn't* lose her.

Not now that she was finally his.

CHAPTER TWENTY-EIGHT

"I'm so happy for you," Jane says after I tell her about last night. It's not the first thing we talked about, of course. We started out gossiping about movies, and even though I work with a rising pop star and have met several celebrities, I'm still in awe of the people Jane has worked with.

But the fact is, I simply couldn't hold it in any longer, and so it all spilled out in one gooey, mushy rush of happiness.

Well, not all. I didn't tell her about the entire night. Just the conversation with Liam, his confession of love, and, most importantly, his willingness to move forward together and not shove me aside out of fear.

"Didn't I tell you?"

"You did," I say happily. "I just wish all of this were over. I feel like I'm in a fairy tale and the prince has kissed me, but the curse still hasn't lifted."

"It will," Jane says. "Liam and Dallas make a good team, and with us beside them, how can they miss. I mean—"

She stops mid-sentence, and I slide off the edge of the bed where I've been sitting, my pulse pounding. "Is it the baby? Jane? Jesus, Jane, what's going on?"

"Alarm," she says and I look up and see that the glass thingie is flashing red.

"What happened?" I ask, even as she reaches for her phone, and I remember what Liam said about an app.

I see her eyes widen, and one hand goes protectively to her belly. Above us, the alarm light goes out.

"Guest wing," Jane says. "Someone broke a window. The system alerted 911." I can tell that she's trying to stay calm, but the quiver in her voice gives her away, and I know that she's thinking what I'm thinking—Liam and Dallas.

"They have to be okay," Jane says, reading my thoughts. "Dallas locked us in."

"What?" My chest tightens with panic.

"Remote locks." She nods toward the door. "We're locked in. No one can get through from either side until it's disabled."

"Oh, God," I say, the panic rising. With Liam at

my side, I haven't had an attack in days, not even that day in the car. But now, with him locked away from me...

My throat tightens, and I fight the sensation. I can't lose control. I have to fight.

I think of Liam. His touch. His love.

I have to fight so I can live.

I draw a deep breath. "The lock," I say to Jane, whose face looks as scared as I feel. "Can you disable it? I need to go help them." I glance wildly around for my purse, which has my tiny Ruger in it, and see it on the bedside table on the far side from Jane.

"No, never mind," I say, immediately contradicting myself. It's not like either of them need my meager skill set. I'd only be in the way. But Jane is in no condition to fend for herself. All she has now is me.

I take a deep breath and tell myself that I've got this. We're safe in this room. Dallas and Liam have mad skills. And the cops are on the way. We're safe as houses, whatever the hell that means.

I take a step toward my purse, then freeze when a sharp crack just about shatters my eardrums. Jane's scream mingles with my own, and when I automatically look in her direction, I see that whoever is outside has shot the door lock. The doorjamb is shattered, too, and before I can even catch my breath, the door is kicked open and I find myself face to face with Edward Noyce, the man from my past and my nightmares.

And I'm staring straight down the barrel of his gun, cold fear icing my veins.

To my right, I see Jane slowly inching toward my purse. I hadn't told her I have a gun, but considering I was searching for my bag before my announcement that I had to go out and help the men, I'm guessing she assumes I have something more useful than lipstick in there.

"I wouldn't do that, Mommy. Not unless you and the little one want to be the next to die."

"You'll never get out of here alive," Jane says.

"She's right." That hard, cold voice belongs to Dallas, and as he speaks he moves into view behind Noyce, his gun aimed at the back of the bastard's head.

"I wouldn't be too sure of that. I'm a slippery motherfucker. But even if I die, at least I'll have the satisfaction of taking her down with me."

I'm freezing cold. I've known fear, but this is different. Before, I'd half-wanted to die, believing it was the only way out of the nightmare that was my life. No, I had no life back then. Just an existence. And while I feared the pain, death would have been a relief.

Now, though...

Now, I have Liam, and the terror that this man can take that from me—from us—runs through me like ice. I can't think. I can't move. I can only pray for a miracle that I know won't come. After all, how many times had I made that plea in my past, only to wake up disappointed.

Now, though, another horrible thought comes to me. *Where's Liam?*

I try to swallow my fear. I force myself not to scream out the question to Dallas. He has to be okay.

He has to.

"We can work something out," Dallas is saying. "Testify against Corbu, and we can make a deal."

"And deny myself the pleasure of watching this bitch die?"

There is a dresser on the wall to his left with a mirror, and although he and Dallas can't see it, I can. And what I see brings both hope and dread. Because what I see is a panel of wood sliding slowly to the side, right across the room from Noyce.

Liam. It has to be Liam.

"Dallas is right," I say, trying to keep him engaged. Trying to buy a few minutes of life—a few minutes that might end up buying me a long and happy life with the man I love. "Testify and cut a deal and you can get everything erased. Do you think I care about pressing charges? I don't."

"She just wants her life back," Jane says, and I'm not sure if she's seen the moving panel, too, or if she's just trying to keep him talking.

"And what do I care about you?" Noyce asks, lifting his gun as the panel moves enough to reveal the grate of the dumbwaiter.

I don't know what kind of gun he has, but I do know it's a revolver. And I do know he's just pulled back the hammer.

More than that, I know that I am directly between the gun and the dumbwaiter, and even though I'm terrified that by moving I'll reveal Liam before he's ready, the only thing I can think of to do is get the hell out of the way. And I do that by screaming, "Now!" and diving to the floor and rolling away just a split second before Noyce fires, his bullet boring into the opposite wall. Liam fires, too, his bullet passing through the dumbwaiter's grate to angle up and catch Noyce right between the eyes.

In almost the same instant, another shot rings out, and the force of the bullet from Dallas's gun knocks Noyce forward. He falls facedown onto the exceptionally nice carpet just as the sound of approaching sirens fill the room.

I ignore him, rushing across the room to Liam who is unfolding himself from the dumbwaiter. "Tight fit," he grumbles as he stands, then pulls me close to him, holding me so tight I can barely breathe.

On the bed, Dallas holds Jane, who sobs quietly

in his arms, even more worked up than I am; thanks, I'm sure, to hormones.

For a moment, Liam and I just cling to each other. Then he puts me at arms-length, inspecting me for injuries. "I'm fine. I'm fine," I assure him, then freeze when I see his arm. "Oh my God."

"I'm fine, too," he says. "They'll stitch it up. No big deal. You're safe," he says. "It's over."

"Over? What about Weil?"

"Dead," he tells me, and that's when my knees really do collapse. Liam drops down beside me, pulling me close. I let him hold me, trying to adjust to this new reality. "I'm safe," I say, enjoying the taste of the words on my tongue. I look up at him, happier than I can ever remember being. "I told you I was safe with you."

"So you did," he says, then grins. "Looks like we've won. And our prize is each other."

"Tell me you love me," I say, just because I want to hear it.

"I love you. And I will happily spend the rest of my life proving it to you."

I grin, then squeeze his hand as the cops and EMT guys rush into the room. "In that case, let's get you stitched up so that you can take me home and start making your case."

"Um, guys," Jane says, as Dallas beams beside her. "I think that Liam may not be the only one who needs to go to the hospital."

"Everybody, if I could have your attention, please." Liam stands on the edge of the hot tub in Damien Stark's back patio, his position giving him at least a foot of height over everyone else. It's a gorgeous space, with an infinity pool that looks out over his Malibu property and the Pacific ocean.

'Everyone' includes most of the staff at Stark Security, plus significant others and friends. Damien and Nikki are here, of course, along with Jackson and Sylvia, Cass, Emma, and several of the guys who used to work with Dallas at Deliverance.

And, most important, Dallas, Jane, and their three-month-old daughter, who is the star of this particular party.

"It is my very great pleasure to introduce to you Lisa Mystery Sykes. A toast," he says, then lifts his glass of champagne. Everyone else does the same, and we all sip our fizzy drink, mine a new raspberry and lime sparkling water.

I wait for Liam to come to my side, then twine my fingers with his. "Three months," he says. "It's our anniversary, too. Of being together, and of you being free."

I tilt my head up for his kiss. "We'll have to celebrate."

"Definitely." His brow furrows as if in thought. "But how best to do that..."

I flash what I hope is a wicked grin, making him laugh.

Eliza and Quince join us, waiting in what has become a cluster more than a line of people who want to see the baby. "So when are you two joining that club?" Liam asks Quince. It's become a running joke between them, and Eliza and I exchange amused glances.

"Probably about the time you finally pop the question to that one," Quince says, nodding toward me.

"Oh, soon then," Liam says, and I almost choke on my water.

Quince and Eliza exchange glances, too, but Liam only smiles, as if it was the most ordinary comment in the world. "I didn't say tomorrow," he whispers to me. "But soon is very much on my radar. If that's too fast for you, tell me now."

"No," I say, my heart tripping. "No, soon is just fine."

"Did you see Emma?" Eliza asks, her voice almost as giddy as I'm now feeling. "She was talking earlier to Damien and Ryan."

It took a few weeks after the drama in Southampton, but I finally met Damien Stark, and though he used to intimidate me—gorgeous, rich, very self-possessed—I finally realized he is simply a great guy in really awesome packaging.

"What were they talking about?" I ask.

"Emma is now officially with the SSA."

"I know," I say. "Isn't it great?"

Her face crumples. "You knew? But you didn't know," she says to Quince, her voice almost an accusation.

"Sorry to disappoint you, love, but I only catch the bad guys. As our office manager, Xena does the paperwork. And that would include setting up payroll."

"Well, hell," Eliza says, eyeing me. "Guess I'll start getting my gossip from you."

"Antonio is here," Quince tells Liam.

"He was in Deliverance with you, right?" I ask as we inch slightly forward.

Liam nods. "Great guy. I haven't seen much of him in the last couple of years."

"Neither have I," Quince says.

"Maybe he's joining Stark Security," Eliza says, looking at me.

I laugh. "I have no knowledge. Swear."

"I doubt it," Quince says. "He seemed relieved when we disbanded. I got the impression he had things of his own to work out."

From the look on Liam's face, I think he agrees, but I don't have time to ask because we've arrived at the baby. Dallas looks about to burst with pride as he holds his daughter and Jane looks exhausted but happy as she gives me a hug.

"I looked for you earlier," I tell her.

"I snuck away for a bit to change and feed her."

"I'm glad you kept Mystery," I tell her, my voice low.

"You inspired us," she says, and we both laugh.

"How's mommyhood?"

"Tiring," she says. "And absolutely freaking amazing."

"I'm so glad."

I feel a hand on my shoulder, then hear a soft whisper at my ear. "Someday."

I turn back, but Liam looks so innocent I can almost convince myself it was my imagination. I hope it wasn't. I want a family; I want it with Liam. And I've even started researching getting my tubal ligation reversed, even though I know I'm getting a little ahead of myself.

Behind us, Sylvia and Jackson come up to see

the newest addition to the Sykes family, so Liam and I step aside after Jane promises to find me later to catch up. We're leaning against a stone wall, just holding hands and looking at the view, when Liam says, "There's Antonio."

He's clean-shaven in his mid-thirties with dark hair, warm brown skin, and a friendly, open face.

Liam starts to take a step toward him, but then pauses when Damien approaches, his hand outstretched. We watch as the two men shake. We're in the open, not intentionally eavesdropping, but I still feel like this is a private moment. At the same time, leaving would just call attention to ourselves.

Besides, Liam wants to talk to his friend, and lingering is the traditionally accepted cocktail party method of catching someone's attention.

All of which is to say that we can hear perfectly when Antonio says, "Thanks so much for inviting me. It's great to have the chance to see Dallas and Jane and the baby. And your house. It's exceptional."

"Thanks. Is that the only reason you accepted my invitation?"

Antonio grins. "I think you know it's not."

"What can I do for you?" Damien's hands are in the pockets of his khaki slacks, and the sun makes his raven-colored hair gleam.

"Do you remember what you said in Paris?"

"After you came to my wife's rescue? I'm not inclined to forget things like that. I said that if you ever need help, Stark Security is there for you. Anytime. Anything."

"Well," Antonio says, "it turns out I do need some help. Specifically, I need a woman."

I hoped you enjoyed Liam and Xena's story! And I hope you're excited to meet **ANTONIO** in *Wrecked With You!*

Be sure to subscribe to my newsletter or **Text JKenner to 21000** to subscribe to JK's text alerts and be among the first to know about the *Wrecked With You* preorder and on-sale date! Plus, you'll get all the news about new books, sales, free content, and other fun stuff!

The Stark Security books are set in the world of Stark International, a world that first came to life for me in *Release Me*, Damien Stark and Nikki Fairchild's story. But several of the characters in *Ruined With You* have their own stories, too.

. . .

You may have already met Quince and Eliza in *Shattered With You* or Denny and Mason in *Broken With You*.

But did you know that you can find Jamie and Ryan's story in *Tame Me*?

And as for Dallas and Jane, their trilogy begins with *Dirtiest Secret*, and I'm including the first chapter to give you a taste because I love this book so much and want everyone to read it! Just keep turning pages! (but be sure to subscribe to the newsletter first so you don't forget!)

Happy reading!

JK

THE KING OF FUCK

Even by Southampton standards, the party at the nine-thousand-square-foot mansion on Meadow Lane reeked of extravagance.

Grammy Award–winning artists performed on an outdoor stage that had been set up on the lush lawn that flowed from the main house to the tennis courts. Celebrities hobnobbed with models who flirted with Wall Street tycoons who discussed stock prices with tech gurus and old-money academics, all while sampling fine scotch and the season's chicest gin. Colored lights illuminated the grotto-style pool, upon which nude models floated lazily on air mattresses, their bodies used by artisan sushi chefs as presentation platters for epicurean delights.

Each female guest received a Hermès Birkin bag and each male received a limited edition Hublot watch, and the exclamations of delight—from both the men and the women—rivaled the boom of the fireworks that exploded over Shinnecock Bay at precisely ten P.M., perfectly timed to distract the guests from the bustle of the staff switching out the dinner buffet for the spread of desserts, coffee, and liqueurs.

No expense had been spared, no desire or craving or indulgence overlooked. Nothing had been left to chance, and every person in attendance agreed that the party was the Must Attend event of the season, if not of the year. Hell, if not of the decade.

Everyone who was anyone was there, under the stars on the four acre lot on Billionaires' Row.

Everyone, that is, except the billionaire who was actually hosting the party. And speculation as to where he was, what he was doing, and who he was doing it with ripped through the well-liquored and gossip-hungry crowd like wildfire in a windstorm.

"No idea where he could have disappeared off to, but I'd bet good money he's not pining away in solitude," said a reed-thin man with salt-and-pepper hair and an expression that suggested disapproval but was most likely envy.

"I swear I came five times," a perky blonde announced to her best friend in the kind of stage whisper designed to attract attention. "The man's a master in bed."

"He's got a shrewd head for business, that one," said a Wall Street trader, "but no sense of propriety where his cock is concerned."

"Oh, honey, no. He's not relationship material." A brunette celebrating a recently inked modeling contract shivered as if reliving a moment of ecstasy. "He's like fine chocolate. Meant to be savored in very limited quantities. But so damn good when you have it."

"More power to him if he can grab that much pussy." A hipster with beard stubble and a man-bun wiped his wire-rimmed glasses clean with his shirttail. "But why the fuck does he have to be so blatant about it?"

"All of my friends have had him." The petite redhead who pulled in a six figure wife bonus smiled slowly, and the flash of her green eyes suggested that she was the cat and he was the delicious cream. "But I'm the only one of us to enjoy a second helping."

"All your friends?"

"How much pussy?"

"At least half the women here tonight. Maybe more."

"Man, don't even ask that. Just trust me. Dallas Sykes is the King of Fuck. You and me? Mere mortals like us can't even compare."

Three floors above the partygoers, in a room with a window overlooking the Atlantic Ocean, Dallas Sykes sucked hard on the clit of the lithe blonde who sat on his face and writhed with pre-orgasmic pleasure. The blonde's cries of "yes, yes!" mingled with the throaty moans of delight coming from the curvaceous redhead who straddled his waist while he finger-fucked her hard and deep.

They'd surrendered to him, these women, and the knowledge that they were his tonight—for tenderness, for torment—cut through him. A wicked aphrodisiac with an edge as sharp as steel, and at least as savage.

He was drunk—on sex, on scotch, on submission. And right then, all he wanted was to get lost in pleasure. To let all the rest of the shit just melt away.

"Please." The redhead's muscles clenched tight around his fingers, and a tremor ran through his body, his need for release now so potent that it crossed the line into pain. "I'm so close, Dallas. I want you inside me. Now. Oh, god, please. Now."

He could barely understand her words, lost as they were in the wet sounds of his mouth on the blonde's sweet pussy. But he heard enough, and in one wild, rough movement, he rolled the girl above him to the side, so that she stretched and trembled on the bed, her nipples hard and her pussy slick and open and inviting.

Dallas felt his body tighten with need. With desire. But only for release. He didn't want either of these women. Not really. Their company, yes. The escape they offered, sure. But them?

Neither was the woman he craved. Neither was the girl who had both saved and destroyed him. The woman he wanted.

The woman he could never have.

And so instead he sought pleasure and passion in the violent rapture of hard, hot sex.

"Sit back," he said to the blonde as he pushed away his dark thoughts and regrets. He reached for the crystal highball glass and downed the last of the Glenmorangie, relishing the way it burned his throat and buzzed his head. "Back against the head-board. Legs spread wide."

She nodded, moving eagerly to obey as he urged the redhead off his waist. "Fuck me," the redhead begged. Her green eyes flashed, her expression pleading. Her lips were swollen, her skin flushed. She smelled of sex, and the scent—so familiar, so dangerous, so goddamned compelling—made him even harder. "I want you to fuck me." Her words were a pout—a plea—and Dallas almost smiled in response.

Almost, but not quite.

Instead he lifted a brow. "Want? Baby, this isn't about what you want. This is about what you need."

"Then I need you to fuck me."

His lips twitched. He liked a woman who knew her own mind, that was for damn sure. And the redhead truly amused him. He'd plucked her from the crowd downstairs because he'd liked the way she'd filled out the flirty black dress that was now crumpled in a heap on his bedroom floor. That, and the fact he happened to know that she had a cousin who worked for a government official in Bogotá, and that connection might prove handy one day.

As for the blonde, Dallas had no particular agenda with her. But he appreciated her limber little body and quiet obedience. Right now, she was sitting exactly as he'd told her, her legs wide apart and wonderfully vulnerable. She wasn't moving a muscle, but the beat of her pulse in her throat telegraphed her excitement at least as much as her tight nipples and hot, wet pussy.

He met the redhead's flashing green eyes, then nodded toward the blonde. "You want to get fucked. I want to watch. And I promise you, she wants to do whatever I say. Sounds like a perfect recipe, don't you think?"

The redhead dragged her polished white teeth over her lower lip. "I've never—"

"But you will. Tonight." He met her eyes. "For me."

She licked her lips as he slid off the bed and stood. She was still sitting, her knees pressed into the mattress as she sat back on her heels. He leaned forward, then took her in a long, slow kiss. She tasted of strawberries and innocence. He wanted to devour the first; he wanted to erase the second. "Hook your legs around her waist and kiss her deep. Suck her tits. Touch her however you want to. But she's going to fuck you with her fingers while you and I both imagine it's my cock. And, baby? You're going to come harder for me than you've ever come for anyone."

"And you?"

He could hear the tremor of excitement in her voice and knew that he had her. "I'll be right here," he said as he took her hand and urged her toward the blonde, who was flushed pink with anticipation. He moved behind the redhead, cupping her breasts as she put her legs around the blonde's waist, then he squeezed her nipples hard as the blonde's fingers slid into her core.

Pressed against her back, he could feel every tremor of pleasure, every quickening in her pulse. And as she started to shake with a series of little convulsions, he slid his hand between her legs from behind, dipping his fingers into her wet pussy. As he did, his hand brushed up against the blonde's, whose sensual moan shot straight to his cock.

Next, he slid his now-slick finger up to tease the redhead's ass as she bucked against him, her body clearly on fire from this dual assault. "Dallas," she moaned as her body shook with release. "Oh, god, Dallas, this is so fucked up."

"That's the way I like it, baby," he said. "That's the only way I play."

It was true. He liked his sex dirty. Wild. He wanted to be reminded of who he was. What he'd become.

The King of Fuck. He'd heard what they all called him, and he had to appreciate how apt—and ironic—the moniker was. Because god knew he was fucked up. His whole goddamn life was an act. A facade.

He was damaged goods. As broken as a man could be. But he'd turned that shit around. Claimed it. Made it his own.

Maybe he would never again have the woman he craved in his arms, but if that was his reality, he was going to damn sure make the most of it.

With his free hand he reached down to stroke

his cock. The sensation of his sex-slicked palm moving rhythmically over the steel of his erection mingled with the wild, almost feral sounds of the two women. He closed his eyes, imagining another place. Another woman.

He thought of her. He thought of Jane.

But not like this. Not fucked up. Not like a goddamn evening's entertainment, as fungible as a night at the movies and at least as unimportant.

Except everything was fucked up. Him, most of all.

Goddammit. He needed to shut it down. These thoughts. These wishes.

All these damn regrets.

The sharp trill of his cellphone startled him from his thoughts, and he slid back away from the redhead who cried out in protest.

"Sorry, baby." His voice was tense, his chest tight. "That's the one ringtone I always answer." He grabbed his phone off the bedside table, lightly brushing both women's skin before turning his back to them and taking the call.

"Tell me," he demanded, expecting the worst. His best friend, Liam Foster, wasn't due to report in until the next morning. If he was calling now, it meant something had happened.

"It's all good, man," Liam said, his voice as close to excited as his military training would allow.

"The child?" Dallas had sent his team to

Shanghai to recover the eight-year-old son of a Chinese diplomat who'd been kidnapped ten days prior.

"Fine," Liam assured him. "Dehydrated. Malnourished. Scared. But he's back with his family, and physically, he should make a full recovery."

Physically, Dallas thought, the word sounding vile in his head. Because that wasn't all of it, was it? Not even close.

He shoved the thoughts aside, forcing himself to focus. "Then why are you—"

"Because the German asshole who grabbed him tried to trade freedom for intel. He knows, Dallas. This dickwad Mueller knows who the sixth kidnapper was."

The words were simple. The impact on Dallas wasn't. His blood turned to fire. The room turned hot and red. He wanted to beat the shit out of the sixth man. He wanted to curl up into a ball and cry.

He wanted to finally know the truth.

There had been two in charge of the six fucks who had snatched them—and surely this sixth man could identify his employers. First, there'd been the main guy who sat back, keeping his hands clean, but who was dirtier than all of them. That man lived in Dallas's memory only as hints and impressions. He'd been smart. He'd kept his distance. But he'd been the puppeteer, the one who'd hired the six and pulled all the strings.

Dallas and Jane had come to think of him as the Jailer, and he'd spoken directly to Dallas only twice. He'd told Dallas that he deserved it all—every moment of agony, every pang of fear, every prick of humiliation.

And then there was the Woman. She was supposed to feed and tend to Dallas and Jane, but instead she brought pain and fear along with a twisted darkness and a bone-deep shame that hadn't faded even after Dallas was free of the confinement of those mildewed walls.

But he wasn't fifteen anymore. He wasn't locked in the dark, tortured and hungry and helpless.

He might be damaged goods, but he had money and power and he knew how to wield both like a goddamn medieval mace.

"We're getting close to ending this thing," Liam said. "We use this douchebag's intel to grab the sixth. We interrogate him. Get him to tell us who hired him. It's the last puzzle piece, Dallas. We get that, and you can finally say that it's over."

Dallas closed his eyes and drew in a breath, soaking in the words. Liam was wrong, of course. It would never really be over. But he couldn't deny the anticipation that was building in him. The fantasy that he really could end this.

For himself.

For his sanity.

But most of all, for Jane.

Grab your copy of *Dirtiest Secret* now!

Play My Game

Seduce Me

Unwrap Me

Deepest Kiss

Entice Me

Hold Me

Please Me

Indulge Me

The Steele Books/Stark International:

He was the only man who made her feel alive.

Say My Name

On My Knees

Under My Skin

Take My Dare (includes short story Steal My Heart)

Stark International Novellas:

Meet Jamie & Ryan-so hot it sizzles.

Tame Me

Tempt Me

S.I.N. Trilogy:

It was wrong for them to be together...

...but harder to stay apart.

Dirtiest Secret

Hottest Mess

Sweetest Taboo

Stand alone novels:

Most Wanted:

Three powerful, dangerous men.

Three sensual, seductive women.

Wanted

Heated

Ignited

Wicked Nights (Stark World):

Sometimes it feels so damn good to be bad.

Wicked Grind

Wicked Dirty

Wicked Torture

Stark Security:

Charismatic. Dangerous. Sexy as hell.

Meet the elite team of Stark Security.

Shattered With You

Shadows Of You (prequel/short story)

Broken With You

Ruined With You

Blackwell-Lyon:

Heat, humor & a hint of danger

Lovely Little Liar

Pretty Little Player

Sexy Little Sinner

Tempting Little Tease

Man of the Month

Who's your man of the month ...?

Down On Me

Hold On Tight

Need You Now

Start Me Up

Get It On

In Your Eyes

Turn Me On

Shake It Up

All Night Long

In Too Deep

Light My Fire

Walk The Line

Man of the Month Box Sets

Winter Heat (books 1-3)

Spring Fling (books 4-6)

Summer Love (books 7-9)

Fall Fantasy (books 10-12)

*Bar Bites: A Man of the Month Cookbook

(by J. Kenner & Suzanne M. Johnson)

Extraordinarily Yours

Sexy paranormal rom-coms!

So (Very!) Much More than the Girl Next Door

The Charmed Affair of an Invisible Bodyguard

The "Super" Secret Life of an Accidental Daddy

Never Trust a Rogue on a Magical Mission

Mayhem, Matchmakers, and a Bit of Bewitching
(novella)

How a Sexy Hero and a Marvelous Makeover (Sorta!)
Saved the World (novella)

The Seductive Charm of a Sexy Shifter (prequel)

The Extraordinarily Yours Collection #1

The Redemption Chronicles

A sexy apocalyptic urban fantasy trilogy!

Born in Darkness

Lost in Shadows

Surrender to Dawn

The Redemption Chronicles Collection (All 3 books!)

Demon Hunting Soccer Mom

Like Buffy ... grown up!

Carpe Demon

California Demon

Demons Are Forever

Deja Demon

The Demon You Know (short story)

Demon Ex Machina

Pax Demonica

Day of the Demon

The Trouble With Demons (Books 1-5 Box Set)

ABOUT THE AUTHOR

J. Kenner (aka Julie Kenner) is the *New York Times*, *USA Today, Publishers Weekly, Wall Street Journal* and #1 International bestselling author of over one hundred novels, novellas and short stories in a variety of genres.

JK has been praised by *Publishers Weekly* as an author with a "flair for dialogue and eccentric characterizations" and by *RT Bookclub* for having "cornered the market on sinfully attractive, dominant antiheroes and the women who swoon for them." A five-time finalist for Romance Writers of America's prestigious RITA award, JK took home the first RITA trophy awarded in the category of erotic romance in 2014 for her novel, *Claim Me* (book 2 of her Stark Trilogy) and the RITA trophy for *Wicked Dirty* in the same category in 2017.

In her previous career as an attorney, JK worked as a lawyer in Southern California and Texas. She currently lives in Central Texas, with her husband, two daughters, and two rather spastic cats.

Visit her website at www.juliekenner.com to learn more and to connect with JK through social media!

Made in the USA
San Bernardino, CA
01 April 2020